# SALVATION

By

D.A. Schneider

ISBN: 9798986309903

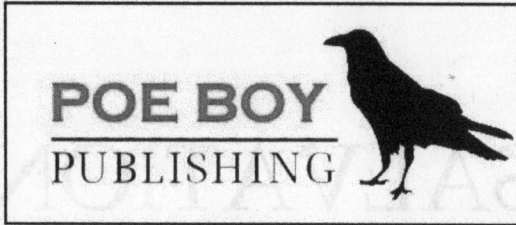

**POE BOY**
PUBLISHING

For Becky, DJ, and William

# 1

## Judas

In the first place, the bar was a shit hole.

Judas moved through the swirling cigarette smoke and past a raised platform where a stripper, who appeared to be seven months pregnant, gyrated to the music from the band on stage. He took a seat at the bar, ordered a beer, then turned to watch the band as it stepped into a new song that he recognized. *Sultans of Swing* by Dire Straits. When the blond-haired kid with the beat-up, left-handed guitar ripped into the solo, it was with a skill few others on the planet could match. A fluid wail that reverberated through the shit hole like a chorus of angels, echoing through the heavens and spilling onto the mesmerized expressions of the hillbillies who peppered the tables around the stage.

*Sad*, Judas thought, *such ability and it goes to waste in shit holes like this.*

Judas felt lost to it though. The kid knew his shit and had every foot in the place tapping. The females twirled and shook on the dance floor in front of the stage. They wanted the kid. Ached to touch him. There wasn't a dry vagina in the house.

And the men? Hell, every last one of them wanted to *be* him. To manipulate the crowd the way he did. To make love to the instrument and pull the lady of his choice backstage after the show to fuck her rotten.

*Sultans of Swing* gave way to a blues tune that Judas was unfamiliar with, but the guitarist made it his own as he did with the last song. The guitar solo alone lasted a full five minutes and by the end of it, Judas felt an almost exhausting calm rush over him, similar to what he would feel after throwing a load onto the stomach or ass of one of the random rabble he picks up from bars like this one all over the country. A breathless quiet that comes with the mutual orgasm of two people following a thorough, passionate round of sex.

The music is the most enjoyable part of his job. Despite the loud, raucous tunes that the bands create together, it truly is the calm before the storm. Soon, the music would stop, and the *real* chaos would begin.

By the time the set was over, Judas was eight beers in. This only created a slight buzz at the back of his head. After all the years of drinking, drugs, and deviant behavior, he was no lightweight. Not by a long shot. But there was a sickening excitement festering in him that he would soon release, and it seemed to aid the beer in his intoxication.

The band ste320

4pped off stage and Judas watched the guitar player closely as he slug the axe over his back and walked over to the bar.

"Can I buy you a drink?" Judas asked.

The kid pushed his long, blonde hair away from his face and studied Judas a moment. "I'm really not into dudes, if that's your angle. No judgement, though."

Judas couldn't help but laugh. "No, I'm a big fan of the lady parts myself. I just have great respect for your skill with that instrument on your back. I'd like to show you my appreciation with a beer."

"I'm not one to pass on a free drink."

Judas motioned to the bartender and ordered two more. "Last call was a few minutes ago," the bartender said. "Don't let anyone else know I gave you these." He handed off the beers and chuckled as he walked away.

The bar thinned out, but it was still a little too crowded for the business that needed to be conducted. Judas had to kill some time with small talk, so he asked the question he already knew the answer to. "How is it that a guy with your talent isn't signed to a recording contract?"

"That's a long story," the kid who wasn't really a kid said. "Let's just say my sound doesn't translate well in a recording studio."

"I find that hard to believe."

"And yet, it is the case."

"What if I told you I could give you a contract? A damn good one too."

"I'd have to say, thanks, but no thanks. It'd be a waste of your time and mine."

Judas glanced around the shit hole. Almost time. Only the two of them, the bartender, and a waitress left, once the drunken asshole near the door stumbled all the way out. "So, you'd rather keep hiding your gifts away in the crappiest bars Atlanta has to offer."

"I'd rather *not*, but I have no other choice. My fate, as sad as it is, will be played out in venues just like this one."

"Just imagine the women though. Beautiful, sultry little groupies throwing themselves at you. You'd get more quality tang than you'd know what to do with."

The guitarist shrugged. "I do just fine around here."

"What, with these dull-eyed, witless in-breeders? I mean nothing against the finer areas of Georgia, but this is not one of those areas."

The guitar player shrugged. "It is what it is."

"That's a shame. We could have done great things together."

The kid gave Judas a slight, sad smile. "I'm sorry I have to decline. Thanks for the beer though, Mister...?"

"The name's Judas."

The guitarist chuckled. "Kind of like in the Bible?"

"No," Judas said and reached into his jacket. "Exactly like in the Bible."

The kid's smile faded. He stood abruptly, knocking the barstool over in the process. Judas raised the heavy semi-automatic .45 caliber handgun and leveled it at the kid's head. "It's nothing personal, friend," Judas said.

The kid who wasn't a kid nodded. "I know."

The gun spoke with a thunderous crash. The kid's head jerked back as the gold slug was buried in his brain. Then his body crumpled to the sticky floor. Judas was vaguely aware of the waitress' screams and the bartender's lunge under the bar for the shotgun hidden there. Judas deftly pulled a second gun from his belt (this one a 9mm loaded with lead rounds) and shot the two of them dead. Small, clean holes in each forehead. An awful mess where the slug exited. He re-holstered both guns and stood over the guitar player. Something happened in that moment Judas couldn't see with his naked eye, but he knew the act was complete when the angel's guitar took on a new, luminescent appearance. A shine that could only be seen by Judas and those like him.

With a greedy gleam in his eyes, Judas reached down, pulled the guitar from the kid's back and slung it over his own. Whistling *Sultans of Swing*, he fished a bottle of rum from behind the bar and walked out into the humid night.

## 2

## Garvey

The humidity was the first thing that hit them as they rode into Tampa. Even with the rush of air against them, the heat was incredible, and the hot twin engines that rumbled beneath them didn't help matters.

John Garvey led the pack on his Harley Davidson Fatboy. Behind him was Buck on his Panhead and Huff on his own Fatboy. Buck gave Garvey a signal he knew all too well. The fat man had a caffeine addiction and his travel coffee mug had been dry all morning. This was only about the hundredth time he'd given the little signal and Garvey figured he'd finally give in, seeing as they had arrived early.

The three of them pulled into a gas station and killed the engines on their bikes. The heat weighed down on them like a wet blanket.

"Hot as a motherfucker down here," Buck observed. "Lucky you two ain't got this extra weight to carry around."

"No," Garvey answered. "Pretty damned tempted to shave this beard though."

"Fuck that," Huff said. Though the black man had a striking resemblance to Shemar Moore, which always allowed him a line of women ready to jump his bones at any given second of the day, he had never been able to grow decent facial hair and had often confessed his envy for Garvey's thick, chest-length beard. "We'd have to set up a fucking memorial service the day you shave that motherfucker."

The three of them laughed. Buck went inside to fill his mug, and Garvey looked around the lot. He was uneasy, but then he always was when he left Indiana, being well aware of the consequences.

"So, what's the plan?" Huff asked. "We cutting from these guys?"

Garvey scratched his beard, deep in thought. "Not yet," he finally replied. "I think they may suspect we've found a new supplier, that's why I decided to come along this time. Try and gauge the situation. But I think we can string them along for a couple more shipments. Then we double our supply *and* our profits."

"Nice. How do we break from them when the time comes?"

"That's the tough part. These guys aren't the type to let people just walk away from a deal. Things will get ugly. You going to be ready for that?"

"Shit, I'm always ready."

"Good."

Buck stepped out of the gas station with his coffee mug in one hand and a flip phone in the other. A burner used for the type of illegal operations they were often running. "That was Izzy and Newt. They got the truck and are sitting in front of the bar now."

Right," Garvey replied. He nudged the kickstand of his hog back. "We better head out."

The three of them started their bikes and made their way west toward The Gulf. They hit Gulf Boulevard near Indian Rocks and followed it north to Clearwater Beach. The bar was nothing but a little open-air shack that sat across from the beach in a prime location for tourists, though there was little to no traffic in the area this early in the morning and the bar was still hours away from opening.

Izzy and Newt were there, sitting in the cab of the old Ryder moving van they'd lifted from who knows where. When it came to procuring untraceable vehicles, the brothers were the best you could get. Garvey never questioned their methods. He waved them around back and then pulled in behind the truck with Buck and Huff at his flanks. As soon as the engines were cut on the bikes, a heavy metal door popped open at the back of the bar and a man in a Hawaiian shirt motioned for them to step inside.

Garvey hitched his shoulders to readjust the guitar strapped to his back, a sheen of sweat formed beneath it already. "Stay alert," he said to the others as Izzy and Newt join them.

Garvey stepped into the bar first. As his eyes adjusted, he ran a hand over the butt of the pistol that was tucked into the waistband of his jeans. Suddenly, Enzo stepped out of the kitchen area with Bruce at his side. Enzo was the supplier, Bruce the owner of the bar and Enzo's childhood friend. Garvey could only assume Hawaiian shirt was hired muscle. He was tall and fat but looked to be strong nonetheless. Another man, this one all muscles in a wife-beater, leaned against the bar. Tension was already thick in the room.

"Garvey," Enzo said. "What brings you out of Indiana?"

"Well, I was concerned about our relationship," said Garvey. He eased past Enzo to scan the room, then turned back. "Buck tells me you seem a little jumpy. My being here is an act of good faith. Just wanted to prove to you how much our partnership means to me and my club."

Enzo smiled, nodding his head with something resembling disbelief, his long, black hair fell over his forehead. "See, what I'm hearing is, you got yourself another supplier and you're looking to cut ties with us. And that doesn't sit very well with me. See, you and I have a deal that goes way back. If you don't honor that deal, things could get messy for you and your boys."

Garvey shrugged and ignored the threat. "You heard wrong."

"Really?"

"Really. We *do* have a new supplier, that much is true, but they aren't supplying us with drugs. We're moving into guns."

Enzo studied him a moment, trying to decipher whether he was telling the truth or not. Luckily, Garvey was a great liar, he certainly had a lot of practice at it over his many years.

"OK," Enzo finally said, a relieved smile spreading over his face. "You've put my mind at ease."

Garvey smiled back and the two men shook hands. "I'm glad we could clear this up."

"As am I, my friend. Shall we get to business?"

"Of course."

"The shit's in the back, ready to load up. I got samples for you, as requested."

Garvey followed him to a table against the wall where there were small bags of heroin, cocaine, and marijuana. He dipped a finger in the coke and rubbed it over his gums. The shit was as good as it had ever been, but the new supplier's shit was even better at a lower price. Still, it would be profitable to keep Enzo producing for as long as possible.

"You know, Garvey," Enzo said from behind him. "I always wanted to ask you, what's the deal with this guitar? Why do you always have it strapped on your back?"

Garvey paused, glancing at the supplier over his shoulder. "Sentimental value."

"Is that right? What, was it your dad's or something?"

There was a tone to the man's voice that Garvey didn't like. As if he were a bully in a schoolyard and Garvey, with his guitar, was a nerd ripe for picking at. "Something like that."

"Looks valuable," Enzo went on. He read the name on the head. "Martin acoustic."

"No, just valuable to me," Garvey replied.

"I never seen you play it." Enzo looked to Buck and Huff. "You guys ever see him play it?"

The two said nothing. They knew the guitar was a sensitive subject for their president, even if they didn't know why.

"I play," Garvey said, "just not as much as I used to."

"Huh," Enzo said. Garvey hoped he'd let the topic go and he went back to examining the drugs. Then Enzo spoke again. "You mind if I check it out?"

"Yeah," Garvey said. "I do mind. No one touches the guitar."

"C'mon, quit being a little shit. I play pretty well myself."

"Drop it, Enzo."

"Fuck that!" With that, Enzo reached out and grabbed the neck.

"Oh shit," Buck mumbled.

Garvey's speed was uncanny and the gun was out of his waistband and in the supplier's face before anyone in the room could register what was going on.

"What the fu-" was all Enzo was able to say as he was shot in the face. Before his body hit the floor, Buck and Huff had pulled their own pistols and dropped the two goons on the other side of the room. Bruce stood whimpering, a wet stain spreading across the front of his pants.

"Change of plans," Garvey said. He grabbed the sample bags and walked toward the back door. "Load the truck."

Buck looked back to Bruce and shrugged. "The man doesn't like people touching his guitar." Then he shot Bruce in the head.

The truck was loaded and Garvey led the way out of town. By the time the bikers, with their truckload of drugs, hit the Florida/Georgia line, pandemonium erupted in the state they'd left behind.

# 3
## Marion

The iPhone on the nightstand rang and vibrated, pulling Marion out of a deep sleep. With a groan borne from the purest sense of annoyance (for Marion valued sleep and her bed over most anything else in life), she got up on one elbow, put on her glasses, and looked at the name on the phone. Director Fuller.

"This is Agent Oliver," she answered. Then she looked at the man next to her, who smiled at the sound of her voice even though his eyes were still closed. "I mean, Agent Kern."

"Don't worry, you'll get used to it," came Fuller's voice over the phone. "How was the honeymoon?"

"Wonderful," she replied, "but far too short."

"Well, I got something strange for you on your first day back. Shooting at a bar on the lower east side of Atlanta. One of the victims has some details that defy human explanation."

"Meaning?"

"The locals will fill you in when you get to the scene. I'll text the address."

"Right. On my way."

"Welcome back, Agent."

"Thank you, sir."

Marion ended the call and James wrapped an arm around her waist and pulled her close. She went to him willingly and nuzzled against his firm body.

"Call in sick," he said. "We can stay in bed all day."

Marion laughed. "I just talked to my boss, he knows I'm not sick.
"Still."

She rolled over to face him and kissed his lips. "We can have a quickie before I go. Best I can do."

James smiled. "I'll take it."

The quickie wasn't so quick, and Marion found herself in a rush to get to the crime scene before the local CSI team left. As she made her way into the bar, she flashed her credentials to each of the officers and got the same disgusted look from the both of them (as usual she was unsure if it was the fact that she was FBI, a woman, or a black woman that rubbed them the wrong way) then ducked under the yellow crime scene tape and surveyed the room.

The body of a waitress lay lifeless among the chairs and tables and the body of a blond-haired kid was on the floor near the bar. Agent Eric Mann, Marion's partner for the last two years, met her by the kid.

"What took you?" he asked.

"Traffic was bad," she lied.

"It's Atlanta, it's always bad."

"What do we have?"

"Three bodies, the bartender is behind the bar, owner of the bar came in at 8 am to work on the books and get ready for opening at 11, found the bodies and dialed 911 right away. We found three shell casings. Two 9mm, one .45 cal."

"Two shooters?"

"Doesn't appear so. As far as the CSI team can tell, the shooter used two different guns from right here in front of the bar. He shot the young kid point blank with the .45, hit the other two with the 9."

"What brings us here?"

"The kid. He has black blood."

"What?" Marion pulled on a pair of medical gloves, then bent to study the kid and found the blood around his wound was indeed black. Carefully, she turned his head to examine the back to find nothing there at all. "No exit wound from a .45?"

"No, the slug is still in there."

"That's odd."

"Very. But there's more. Here's the shell casing that was found. Notice anything off about it?"

Marion studied the shell in the evidence bag and found the barely discernible gold flakes around the edge right away. "What's up with that?"

"Not sure. We'll have to wait for an autopsy to get more answers on that."

"Have you questioned the owner yet?"

"No, figured I'd wait till you got here."

"Alright, let's do it."

Agent Mann led the way through the bar to the small office in the back where an officer stood with the owner, a small, balding man with a protruding beer gut. "Mr. Wilson, I'm Agent Mann and this is my partner, Agent Oliver."

"Agent Kern now," Marion corrected.

"Right. Agent Kern. We would like to ask you a few questions."

"I already told the detectives everything, don't you people compare notes?" Mr. Wilson said, clearly annoyed and dismayed by the murders of his employees.

"Our investigation will differ from theirs," Marion explained. "We're part of a special unit that studies strange crimes. We're called in if anything out of the ordinary appears on a crime scene."

"What, like The X-Files?"

Marion always hated this comparison because what they did rarely uncovered supernatural beings or extraterrestrials but often found it was easier to just play along. "Yes, something like that. What can you tell us about the victims? Did they have any enemies that you knew of?"

"None," the owner said. "We're too small to employ a security team, so Greg Dunn, the bartender, acted as a bouncer as well. He'd have to throw out drunks here and there, but the same guys were usually back the next night. I can't recall anything too serious."

"And the waitress?" Marion asked as Mann scribbled notes in his pad.

"Oh, everyone loved Beth. She was the best looking one of the bunch. Everybody would ask her what she was doing in a dive like this."

"What about the kid?"

"Kid has been playing on stage for me for the last six months or so. Name's Rich Killion. He was a quiet kid, kept to himself mostly, but I don't think he had any enemies. Hell of a guitar player though, I never saw anyone better. He actually brought in a lot of business, especially on the weekends. He became kind of a local legend. Funny thing is, he always carried his guitar on him. Never went anywhere without it strapped across his back, but I didn't see it out there."

"So, the guitar is missing?"

"Yeah."

"Anything else taken?"

"No, not as far as I can tell. Registers weren't tampered with. I got a safe right here that wasn't touched. Nothing in the bar is out of place but I haven't had a chance to do inventory. Just the guitar."

"What did the guitar look like?"

"Fender Stratocaster, left-handed, orange and white like a cream sickle. Looked a little beat up, but not too bad."

"And where were you last night?"

"I took the night off for my anniversary. The wife and I stopped in around eight last night, just to check in, see how things were going. Wednesdays are typically pretty slow though and we only stayed a few minutes before we went out for dinner."

"Thank you for your time, Mr. Wilson," Marion finished. "Here's my card, if anything else should occur to you, please don't hesitate to call."

"Sure, sure."

Marion left the office with Mann in tow.

"Have the locals checked Wilson's alibi?" she asked her partner.

"Yeah, it checks out. Even the wait staff at the restaurant remembers him because he threw a fit over wine prices."

"Alright, have the lead detectives take statements from the other employees, get everything we can find on all victims, particularly the guitar player. I have a feeling he was the target. The other two were just in the wrong place at the wrong time."

"Ain't that a bitch?"

"Yeah, it is. Any security footage?"

"No. Only camera in the place points straight down at the register."

"That's unfortunate. Let me know if anything else turns up."

Marion left the bar and got behind the wheel of her SUV. She exhaled through her nose, thankful that the scene wasn't more gruesome. She had definitely seen worse and those had a tendency to stick with you. The fact that it was so clean pointed to a professional hit. The shooter had gone in there on a mission. A specific target in mind, most likely the guitarist. Pulling her iPhone from her pocket, she brought up the web browser and searched gold bullets. Everyone knew what silver bullets were meant for, thanks to an endless number of werewolf movies and books, but gold was a new one on her.

She didn't find much. A couple of gun fanatics debating over the pros and cons of gold bullets over lead. A few websites which sold gold bullets. Nothing on what specific uses a gold bullet would have, supernatural or otherwise. In her early years with the department, she wouldn't have considered anything supernatural. The Daylight Savings case in Indianapolis had changed all that. Or as Agent Mann referred to it; Daylight Slaying Time. He often asked her about the case, but it wasn't one she cared to re-live. It was by far the bloodiest case she'd ever worked. As well as the strangest. It also happened to be highly classified.

It was on that case that she first met Adrian Dillard, an expert in the strange and unusual. She had a funny feeling she would need his help again.

# 4
## Judas

Judas had come to the conclusion that he hated Georgia. To say it was hot as Hell would be an overstatement, but it was still pretty fucking hot. The air conditioner in the old Dodge had crapped out before he'd even made it to Atlanta. It was time to trade up. Luckily, he knew just the place. On the west side of town, there was a used car lot that had seen a surge in business lately. Judas knew why and there was a good chance he'd be able to come away with a fairly new car while giving up next to nothing.

The sun beat down through the windshield of the old car and Judas was sweating profusely in his three-piece suit. He dared not take it off, however. That would mean taking his guns off as well and with the work he'd been doing, protecting himself could be a necessity at any given moment. He'd just have to suffer and keep his pistols safely tucked inside his suit coat. However, if he would have to suffer, he would do so in a car with air conditioning.

Judas emerged from the Dodge and walked toward the entrance of the dealership, sweat running down his back in rivulets. The salesman came out and assailed him with his rehearsed verbal diarrhea right away.

"Good afternoon. How are ya today?" The man was short and chubby with a headful of thick, black curls and glasses like the bottom of Coke bottles. "Can I help you find anything in particular?"

Judas looked around the lot, then at the sales floor, where it was no doubt much cooler than where they stood in the lot. "Why don't we talk inside?"

"Inside? Sure, sure. C'mon in. Hotter than the Devil's asshole out here."

The salesman held the door open and Judas stepped inside where cool air blew down from a vent just through the doorway. He stood under the vent and closed his eyes, relishing the temperature change. After a moment, he was aware of the salesman speaking.

"Sir? Sir? Are you alright? Can I get you anything? A bottled water perhaps?"

Judas snapped out of his trance. "Yes, water would be wonderful."

The little man scurried away, and Judas strolled across the showroom floor, looking inside the cars and trucks parked there and enjoying the blessedly cool room. All around him other salespeople went about their con game, trying desperately to get suckers into overpriced pieces of machinery that one finance company or another would bleed them dry for with interest rates that were ridiculous and perfectly legal. It was highway-robbery. Legalized extortion. Pure devilry.

The chubby salesman returned to him with bottled water in hand. Judas drained it, all the while studying the little man and thinking about what an amazing coincidence it was that this particular salesman had jumped to help him. The very man he was looking for.

"It's a scorcher out there, huh?" the salesman said. When Judas didn't answer the man continued. "My name is Dave, by the way. I'm here to help get you in the new car you deserve." He held his hand out to shake, but Judas ignored it, not willing to make skin-on-skin contact with his kind.

"Is there somewhere we can talk in private?" Judas asked.

"Sure, step into my office."

Judas followed Dave into an office along the back wall. As he rounded his desk, Dave kept his act going. "You know; we have a great selection of previously owned vehicles as well. Whatever you're in the market for."

Judas closed the door behind him and then shut the blinds after making sure they weren't observed. When he turned, he found Dave the salesman staring at him with an expression that was close to fear. Judas sat down and began to speak. "I'm looking for a car with outstanding gas mileage, preferably something reliable, maybe an import. Most important of all; I *need* air conditioning."

"Great, no problem," Dave replied. "We have a hundred cars on this lot that fit that description. Why all the secrecy?"

"Well, I'm afraid I have no money to put down."

"That shouldn't be an issue. We can use your trade as the down payment as long as you have decent credit."

"That's the thing. I have no credit at all. I don't even have an identity."

Dave let out a nervous laugh. "What did you say your name was?"

"My name is Judas and I know who *you* are. Who you *really* are?" Dave sat back in his chair and studied Judas, all the good- humored small talk forgotten. The line of bullshit dropped from his thoughts.

"How are you here?" asked Dave. "What's this look you got going? Was shockingly handsome, middle eastern man *your* choice? And a perfect British accent to go with it. Jesus, you must be pulling down all kinds of pussy, am I right?"

"Look, I'm here on a mission. One that could clear my name and get me out for good. And please, don't say the J word around me."

"Oh shit! Right, sorry. I didn't even think about it. Look, I'm happy for you, really, but I don't see what you want from me."

"I need a new car. You're going to give me one."

Dave laughed. "How do you expect me to do that. No identity. No money. Can you even make payments?"

Judas smiled. "I have no intentions of making payments of any kind. What I have to offer you in trade is far more valuable than anything of earthly possession."

Dave's smile faded. "What might that be?"

"I have a very special guitar in the trunk of that Dodge," Judas said with a smile.

Dave stood so suddenly, his chair tipped over and clattered against the wall. "Shit!" Once he righted the chair, he looked back to Judas with a mad fire in his eyes. "Wait, you mean…are you saying you have…?"

"That *is* what I'm saying. Get me a car and it's all yours."

"All mine? Are you serious?"

"Can you make it happen?"

Dave ran a shaking hand through his curly hair, pondering the possibilities. "Give me an hour."

"I'll be waiting in the showroom."

"Right. Hey, there's complimentary coffee out there. Help yourself."

"Thanks, Dave."

Judas left the office and rounded the corner to a waiting area that held a couch and a few chairs around a television which was airing a Braves game. He made himself a coffee with plenty of cream and sat to watch the game. He felt sorry for the players on the screen, out in that heat with sweat dripping down their faces. How awful they must feel. *Better them than me,* he thought.

The showroom was so cool that he began to feel a bit chilled. He relished it. Once he finished his coffee, he made another and a third after that. He continued to delight in all of the little things modern life had to offer, which modern man took advantage of.

An hour later, Dave sat down next to him with a smile on his face. "I got a car for you, but I want to see the guitar before we close the deal."

Judas nodded. It was a reasonable request. He led the way out through the wide doors and back into the blistering heat. Walking quickly, he moved to the back of the dodge and popped the trunk. The guitar was there with a soft glow that was still evident even in the bright sunlight.

"It's beautiful," Dave said, practically salivating.

Judas closed the trunk. "How'd you work it out?"

"It's taken care of. Don't worry about it."

"I need to know. I can't have any more trouble breathing down my neck than I already have."

"Alright. I used someone else's identity. Guy that just died. It'll be two months before anyone figures it out and even then, it won't come down on you or me. I sold it using one of the other salesmen's logins and the Dodge as a trade."

"So, they get fired if it comes back, and you won't. Very deceitful."

"Hey, it's what we do."

"You mean car salesmen or…?"

"Both. So, do we have a deal?" he dangled the keys in front of Judas.

Judas popped the trunk again and carefully pulled out the guitar. They made the trade at the same time.

"I will cherish it," Dave said, cradling the instrument like a woman.

"Which car?" Judas asked.

"Huh? Oh, the black Toyota, parked by the door. Only a couple of years old, twenty-seven thousand miles on the fucking thing."

"A/C works?"

"Oh yeah."

"You really came through for me Dave." Judas handed over the keys to the Dodge.

"Totally worth it, pal. You enjoy that ride. And good luck with your mission."

Judas nodded and said nothing more. He sat inside his new car and started it. Then he cranked the air up as high as it would go and pulled out of the lot, ready to leave Atlanta behind for good.

# 5
## Garvey

By the time John Garvey and his men crossed back into Indiana, they found their home state was nearly as hot and humid as Florida and Georgia had been, even well after nightfall as it was. Once they hit Indianapolis, Garvey split from the crew on 465, heading north to West 10th street while the others exited onto West Washington. He would meet up with them in the morning but first, he needed to see Gwen. There was a lot of stress weighing on him and he needed her presence.

Off 10th and Girl School, there was an old housing edition across from a high school. Garvey steered his bike down the streets that were canopied by old tree branches which stood still and silent in the heat of the summer night. In the fall the trees created a brilliant tunnel of colorful leaves that Gwen found positively charming. It was the reason Garvey had bought her a house in the little neighborhood.

The house was a brick-covered ranch that sat back against a row of trees separating the yard from a small creek. Garvey still had fond memories of playing with their two children in the creek, catching crawdads and building dams while his guitar leaned against a nearby tree. Both Seth and Elizabeth were grown now and leading their own lives.

Garvey pulled into the cracked driveway and killed the engine on his bike. As he dropped the kickstand down, the screen door opened and she was there, staring at him with her blue eyes and beaming, beautiful smile. She met him halfway down the sidewalk and he took her in his arms, kissing her deeply and savoring her familiar form pressed against him.

"How was your trip?" she asked after they were inside.

"Not great," he answered honestly. "The meeting didn't go as planned."

"And you've come by for a little something to take your mind off things for a while."

Garvey didn't answer. Instead, he took up her hand and led her to the bedroom where they made love in the dim light supplied by the full moon shining through the window. In the aftermath, they lay quietly studying each other. He ran a hand over her cheek and through her hair. She smiled at him and spoke in a voice close to a whisper. "What are you thinking?"

"About how much I've missed you. How much I love you."

Gwen sighed. "Even with the crow's feet around my eyes and the wrinkles starting around my lips?"

"You're just as beautiful as you always were."

"John, I'm forty-one and you look like you're twenty-five. What are people going to think when I'm in my sixties and you *still* look twenty-five?"

"I don't give a fuck what people think. Besides, in a couple of years, we'll have enough to retire and move to that secluded cabin by a lake we've always wanted."

Gwen ran a hand through his thick beard, then over his long hair. "I can't wait for that. I love to be around water."

"I know you do."

"I wish I could have gone to Clearwater with you."

"Well, things got violent. I knew that was a possibility going in and there was no way I'd have put you in that situation."

"I know."

"Plus, you know I can't stay in another state long. I think I was there too long anyway."

She moved to straddle him, placing her hands on his tattooed, muscular chest and leaned in for a long kiss, her auburn hair spilled around his face. He was hard again and she moved her hips so that he slid back inside her. After a deep moan she said, "Try not to think about it."

And Garvey did exactly what she said. He closed his eyes and enjoyed the wetness of her, moving his hands up her stomach to caress her breasts and squeeze her erect nipples between his fingers. They continued their reunion until the early morning hours while the Martin acoustic leaned against the headboard.

Garvey blinked against the harsh morning light. Rolling over, he reached for Gwen, yearning to pull her naked body against his, only her side of the bed was empty, and he was suddenly aware of the smell of bacon permeating the bedroom. He got out of bed and stepped into the bathroom, relieved himself, then splashed water on his face. The man that looked back at him in the mirror was still young and handsome, with long, dirty blond hair and a thick, dark beard, though inside he felt old and tired. After he was dressed, he strapped the guitar across his back and left the bedroom for the kitchen.

Gwen was at the stove wearing only skimpy panties and a tank top, cracking eggs into a pan. Garvey stepped silently behind her and ran his fingers up her bare back. She jumped and squealed, turning to slap at him playfully. "You motherfucker! You scared the shit out of me."

He bent to wrap his arms around her and kissed her neck savagely. She giggled and turned to kiss his lips. "Busy day today?" she asked.

"Just have a bike to finish up at the shop," he replied. "Shouldn't take more than a few hours."

"Dinner tonight?"

"Absolutely, anywhere you want."

"I'll have to think about that. I promise you this, though; we are not going to Taco Hut again."

"Fine. I'll get it for lunch."

"Fine. You do that." She gave him another kiss, then said, "Sit. Eat. I got your coffee ready."

Garvey took a seat at the table and pulled the Colts coffee mug toward him. Seconds later, Gwen sat a plate of steaming food under his nose."

"Why are you so good to me?" he asked.

"Because I love you. And you're good to me."

"Well, that's because I love you too. And because you're amazing in the sack."

"In that area we are doubly blessed." Gwen sat across from him with her own cup of coffee and a plate with only two pieces of sausage and buttered toast. "Have you heard from Seth lately?" she asked.

"Texted him yesterday. He's supposed to meet me at the shop to help out a little."

"Do you think he will?"

Garvey shrugged. "Hard to say. You know how he is."

"If he does, tell him to come see his mother. I worry about him."

"You *are* a worrier. Seth is fine. Elizabeth is fine. But I will be sure to tell him."

"I don't worry about Elizabeth as much. She's got a good head on her shoulders. Seth, on the other hand."

"I know. It's a wonder we aren't grandparents by now."

"I wish he'd find a nice girl and settle down instead of banging all these skanks that hang around the bar."

"He will. He's still young, dumb, and full of cum. It'll happen eventually."

"I know. I know."

Garvey cleaned his plate and placed it in the sink. "I got to go. See you tonight."

"I can't wait. I love you."

"Love you too."

After a kiss, Garvey left the house, scanning the street as he mounted his bike. The V-Twin engine rumbled to life, breaking through the silence of the sleepy streets. Twenty minutes later, he was pulling into the small parking lot of the shop he co-owned with Buck. The fat man appeared from an open bay door and greeted him with a wave. Garvey parked the bike in a space to the right of the garage and killed the engine.

"What do ya say, brother," Buck called. The two shared a brief bro hug and walked together back toward the office of the shop. "How was your night?"

"I was with the soul mate," Garvey replied with a shrug.

"Alright, 'nuff said."

"How about you?"

"Fantastic. Picked up some hot little number at Sticks n' Stones and took her home. Threw a big load of ball batter all over her big naturals, then slept like a baby."

"Nice," Garvey said patting his friend's shoulder. Way too much information as usual, Buck, but good for you."

"Seth coming in today?"

"That's what he says."

"Well, we can use the help. Barnes was in an accident last night. He's laid up in the hospital."

"Holy shit!" Garvey exclaimed, turning to look at Buck. "Don't you think you should have led with that?"

"Aw he's fine," Buck said with a wave. "Just a few bruises. Barnes getting hurt ain't nothing new. Me getting laid, on the other hand, *that's* news."

Garvey laughed as they entered the air-conditioned office. "The brothers get the truck stashed alright?"

"Yeah, it's all under control. We're gonna distribute to the dealers on Wednesday, like usual. It's all moving like a well-oiled machine."

"Good. That's the way I like it."

Garvey moved through the office and out into the garage. Here he had his own bay with his own tools, and it was a space he could remove the guitar from his back, relax, and get his hands dirty doing what he really loved, restoring classic motorcycles. He was working for nearly an hour in the stifling summer heat when Seth came strolling in wearing a ripped and stained tank top. The sunglasses over his eyes, even in the dim light of the garage, was evidence that he'd had another wild night.

"Hey, Dad," he said, bending to retrieve a bottle of water from the minifridge in the corner. "Did you have a good trip?"

"Wasn't bad. Wasn't good either. You look like you had a rough night."

"Nah, great night," Seth said with a smile. "It just resulted in a rough morning."

Garvey smiled. "Glad to see you're embracing twenty-one."

"Yeah, like my age ever stopped me from partying."

"True. Hand me that socket wrench."

Seth passed the tool to his father and took a seat on the stool near the workbench. Garvey stared at him for a moment. The kid was in desperate need of a haircut. Or at least a brush. His bright red locks seemed to veer off in every direction. Plus, his beard was straggly and uneven, thin in spots. He topped this off with a pair of grease-stained jeans that barely hung from his slender hips. Tall and lanky, rough and unkempt, still it all worked for him and he never had trouble with the ladies.

"You go see Mom?" he asked.

"Yeah, I stayed with her last night."

"How is she?"

"Fine. You need to go by and see for yourself. She worries about you."

"Yeah, I will. After I leave here."

"Well, we're shorthanded today, we could use your help. There's a break job in bay four."

"I'll jump right on it."

"Thanks, big dog."

Seth pushed his long, red hair away from his face and smiled.

"You haven't called me that in a while."

"Well, we haven't talked this much in a while," Garvey said, returning the smile.

"Listen, Dad, I appreciate you letting me do some work around here, but I was hoping to get into the other side of the business. Make some better bank."

Garvey's smile faded. "You know I don't want you involved in that. It's too dangerous."

"I know, but I'm not a kid anymore. I can handle myself, you know that. Besides, if you're still planning on retiring in the next few years, you're going to need somebody to take over your end of the business. Buck can't handle it alone."

Garvey stared at his son for a while, knowing he had a valid point. "Tell you what; you've shown me over the past couple of months that you're finally maturing. You keep going and I'll consider it."

The younger Garvey nodded. "That's fair."

"Just remember; it takes more than maturity to run this operation. It takes intelligence and courage. Sometimes you have to be cunning, sometimes you have to be clever. Sometimes you have to do bad things to people. Things you'll carry with you for the rest of your life. Are you prepared for all that?"

"No," Seth answered honestly. "But I think I can get there."

"Alright," Garvey said, after some thought. "First step, we get you into the club."

"Seriously?"

"Well, I have to run it by the other guys, and your mother of course..."

"Of course."

"...but I think we can start you out as a pledge. There will be no special treatment, though. You have to start at the bottom like everybody else."

"I understand."

"Alright, are you ready to be a Red Titan?"

Garvey rarely said the name of the club aloud and it sounded funny to his own ears. He'd never liked the name, arguing that it sounded like the name of a small college football team rather than a motorcycle club. But Seth only smiled with nervous excitement.

"Yeah, I'm ready."

"Alright. For now, let's get some work done."

"Sure, Pop."

With that, Garvey's son (who by all appearances looked more like his younger brother) went to work on the brakes of an old Ford truck. Garvey returned his attention to the hog in his bay and smiled. Having his son nearby would be a good thing. This way he could keep an eye on him. Keep him out of trouble. Little did he know, trouble would come to them.

# 6
## Marion

Marion tried the number again and, again, it rang through to the voicemail. So again, she left a message.

With a sigh, she sat back in her chair and stared over the crime scene photos that were spread over the desk. The autopsy was taking far longer than usual, and she couldn't reach her expert to answer the plethora of questions on her mind. In the meantime, she'd gone over and over the statements from the other employees at the bar and examined and re-examined every photo and detail of the case. After speaking with the families of the other victims it had become apparent that they were indeed in the wrong place at the wrong time. The guitarist, however, had no family to reach. In fact, his entire identity seemed to be fabricated. His fingers had no prints. There was no dental record to match his near perfect teeth. The man was a ghost. Agent Mann's theory suggested the guitarist was some sort of government spook and one of his enemies had finally caught up with him. Marion had the feeling things were far more complicated than that.

And now her head hurt.

Leaving her office, Marion walked across the floor to the small kitchenette with her empty coffee mug in hand. She refilled the cup and topped it off with a little cream. Then searched for the bottle of aspirin that had a tendency to move from cabinet to cabinet.

Eric came around the corner with his own coffee mug. "Hey. Any luck reaching your contact yet?"

"No," Marion answered, rubbing the bridge of her nose. "You have anything new?"

"Not much," he returned, moving to the exact cabinet that held the aspirin, he handed it over to her. "I called the morgue. They said they ran into some complications with the autopsy on the guitar player, but they should be done by this afternoon."

"Good. We'll head down there in an hour or so, see if we can't hurry things along."

"All right. You okay?"

"I just hate waiting. I need to stay busy."

"Well, hopefully your guy will get back to us soon."

"Yeah, hopefully."

Marion returned to her office with coffee in hand and continued studying the photos and her notes. After twenty minutes, she decided she couldn't wait another forty. She clipped her gun on her belt and walked over to Eric's office. Leaning in the door frame she said, "Let's hit the morgue, I'm tired of waiting."

"Should we grab lunch first?" he asked as he came around the desk. Even though Mann had served in the United States Army, he hadn't seen action, nor had he seen much in the way of homicides while working as a beat cop, then a vice detective in Detroit. He was still pretty green when it came to dead bodies and the best practices when investigating how exactly they had ended up that way.

"It's always better to eat after a visit to the morgue," Marion advised.

"Right."

The two of them took the nondescript, black SUV that was standard among government agencies, out of the parking garage and to the morgue. The Fulton County Medical Examiner's office was on the near south side of town. Mercifully, traffic was lighter than usual for this time of day, and they were able to hit 85 to cut through the middle of town.

Once inside, the partners found Dr. Mitch Kroger, the chief medical examiner, biting into a meatball sub in his office. "Agent Oliver, Agent Mann, what perfect timing. I was just about to call your offices."

"Actually, it's Agent Kern now," Marion said.

"Ah yes, you just got married. Congratulations, Agent Kern."

"Thank you, Doctor. I'm assuming you're done with the autopsy on my guitar player?"

"I am," Dr. Kroger said, with a shake of his head. "Very peculiar body, that one. Best to show you, rather than try to explain it."

Dr. Kroger led the two agents down the hall and into the morgue, munching on his sandwich along the way. With his free hand, he pulled open one of the drawers and slid the table out. Inside was the cold, dead body of the guitar player. "First off," the doctor began. "I'm sure the two of you noticed the black blood. It's also abnormally thick. Black blood appears in the body after it travels through the heart and becomes deoxygenated. The fact that this man has nothing but black blood seems to suggest this process doesn't occur in his body. As if oxygen is unnecessary."

"Do you have an explanation for that?" Marion asked.

"I got nothing," the examiner said. "As for the bullet; it was made of gold."

"Is that uncommon?"

"Not really. You can find them online. They're far less dense than lead, but this is a .45 caliber at point blank range. It should have made a mess out of the back of his head as it exited, but it just stopped, right in the middle of his brain."

"That is odd."

"Yep. Then there's the extra organs."

"Extra organs?" asked Mann.

The examiner picked up a bowl and held it out to them.

Marion was no anatomy expert, so she had no idea what she was looking at. "What are they?"

"No idea. I've never seen anything like them and I can't imagine what purpose they serve. They were located near his back, above the kidneys and may have something to do with these."

The medical examiner grabbed the arm of the body and rolled him so that the back was to the agents on the other side of the table. Marion looked at the two large scars that ran along the shoulder blades of the dead guitarist with a gasp.

"Those scars look to me like appendages have been removed more than any kind of injury," Dr. Kroger said. Marion didn't have to ask him to elaborate. She knew exactly what he was suggesting. Wings.

"Doctor, you know that everything you've shown us here is now considered classified information, right?" Marion asked.

"I figured it might be," Kroger answered.

Agent Mann cleared his throat. "We will send experts of our own to retrieve this body and transport it to a more secure area."

"Got it. I'll email the photos and report over to you and delete all that I have, as per usual."

With that, the two agents left the building and hit the road. They remained quiet for a while before Mann finally broke the silence. "I got to say, I'm freaking out a little here. What the fuck are we dealing with?"

"I'm not sure yet. Now more than ever, I really need to get in touch with my expert."

As if on cue, Marion's cell rang and the call she'd been waiting for showed on the screen. She answered and said, "Mr. Dillard, thank you for returning my call."

The voice on the other end was calm and measured. "My pleasure. And please, call me Adrian. I apologize for not returning your calls earlier. I was in the middle of something...messy."

"I understand. I've just been assigned a case that I think requires your expertise."

"What do we got? Unexplained or scary?"

"A little of both, I'd say."

"Excellent, I'll be on the next flight to Atlanta."

"Great. The FBI will pay the standard consulting fees. Let me know when you arrive, and my partner and I will meet you."

"Sounds like a plan. See you soon."

Marion ended the call and looked at her partner. "He is going to be a big help."

"Who is this guy?"

"Over the last few years, he's emerged as the number one expert on all things strange and unusual. I've worked with him on a couple of other cases I couldn't wrap my head around. Including the Daylight Slaying case. He really knows his stuff."

"I guess I feel a *little* better."

"In the meantime, we'll do some more digging on our own. See if we can figure out just what we've gotten ourselves into."

The afternoon heat undulated off the pavement ahead of them and Marion stared at it, lost in thought. Soon, they would have the answers they desired. Some that she suspected she may know already. She only hoped Agent Mann would be prepared to hear these answers, no matter how crazy they may sound.

# 7

## Judas

Judas couldn't help the skin-crawling feeling he got as he crossed into Washington D.C. It was the same every time he visited, but unavoidable if he wanted to meet his contact and get to the next target. The sooner he was done with this business the better.

There was a small diner on the west side of town that Judas found charming in a nostalgic kind of way, though it was nothing more than a grease pit. Truth was; he enjoyed the greasy food. There was nothing like a huge burger with bacon and cheese, served with fries drowning in ketchup. It had become one of his vices since returning to the states. He had just taken his first bite when the bell over the door rang and the man he'd come to meet stepped inside. He spotted Judas and waved then grabbed an abandoned newspaper off a nearby table and wandered over to sit across from Judas in the booth. "Jesus," the man said, and Judas winced at the name. "I don't see how you can eat that shit."

"Lou," Judas said in greeting. "You're looking...awful. Fuck, I mean really bad, I can't lie. When the hell did you get so old?" It was true. Judas had known the man for years and had always been under the impression that he'd never age. Now, Lou looked ancient. Brittle and unimpressive. Judas liked it.

Lou grinned slightly and ordered only a coffee when the waitress came over. "Judas, my friend, I am old. Really *fucking* old. Close to retirement as a matter of fact. That's why I want to take care of our little business and release you from your duty before you-know-who takes over."

Judas stopped chewing and nodded his understanding.

"Yeah," Lou went on, "that one is still not on board with this little deal you and I have worked out. But, luckily, you're nearing the end."

"Good. How about you cough up the file so I can get out of this fucking town."

Lou slapped the newspaper down on the table and stared at Judas in shock. "You can't be serious! This is a great town. The corruption. The greed. A guy like me thrives in this environment."

"No doubt," Judas commented.

Lou carried on with a gleam in his eye. "It's wonderful. One side claims they fight for the little guy while the other side blatantly strives to make the rich richer, and the truth is, every single one of them is bought and paid for through campaign contributions. And the best part, the cherry on top, the rubes in this country keep voting them into office. They think they live in a democracy. That their leaders will make decisions based on what's in the best interest of the people. But this is a plutocracy and every decision is made based on where the money is flowing and how best to benefit the people and corporations that control it all. It's a wonderful system. I love this fucking town."

Judas smirked. "Yeah, the devil is alive and well in the capital city."

"Goddamn right," Lou said with a chuckle.

"Look, I'm glad you're having such a great time, but this place gives me the screaming shits, so if you don't mind..."

"Ever the fucking professional," Lou said with a shake of his head. "How'd Atlanta go?"

"Got a little messy. I had to take out a couple of bystanders. Could have some heat coming down on me."

"I'll make a few calls. Sweep things under the rug like I always do."

"Good."

"How many bullets do you have left?"

"Three."

"That's good. You may need all three for this guy." Judas was momentarily taken aback. "You mean..."

"That's right; this is the last one. Our deal is done after this. However, I have to warn you, this is going to be the biggest bitch of the bunch."

"Why is that?"

"For one, the guy's hard to pin down. He moves around a lot. Always on alert. Part of this is due to the fact that he's into some criminal activities. This guy's not some kid scraping by on gigs in dive bars, he's head of a biker club, a drug dealer and a murderer."

"Fuck."

"Yeah, this is one bad motherfucker. He's based in Indiana. Indianapolis to be exact, but he has no problem leaving the state and wreaking havoc on the places he visits. A couple days ago he was in Florida, after he left there was a hurricane, a mass shooting, a pop star stabbed on stage, and two people carried off by gators."

"Holy shit!"

"Fucking A!"

"How do you suggest I approach this?" Judas asked.

"Well, he has a daughter that's a waitress at an Applebee's in Cincinnati. You have some time before this needs to be done, get to know her. Use your charms. Bang her brains out. Get her to introduce you to her parents. Then boom, you're all done. Otherwise, you won't be able to track this guy down."

"That's your advice? Bang his daughter's brains out?"

Lou shrugged. "Sure, why the fuck not? Might as well have some fun along the way."

"Alright, I'll give it a shot."

"Atta boy. Here." Lou slid an iPhone across the table. "This should help with your dating life. I may text from time to time as well to check your progress. Now, I have a lunch date at one of the finer establishments in town. I can't stomach the shit they serve here."

"Man, you don't know what you're missing," Judas said as he took another large bite of his burger.

The older man gave him a look of disgust and stood from the booth. "Enjoy. And don't forget. You're nearing the finish line. Soon this will all be over and you'll be a free man. Able to live your own life as you wish."

"Believe me, I won't forget that. In fact, it's all I can think about."

"Hey, I knew you were the right man for the job."

Judas only nodded and mentally willed the old man to leave. Finally, he did, with a half-hearted salute to Judas as he went. Judas watched him go with a feeling of mixed love and loathing that he was never quite able to explain. He supposed it was the way a teenage boy must feel about a father that was far too strict or even abusive, but he couldn't say for sure.

Once he'd finished his meal, he paid and walked out the door and into the stifling heat that he hated more than nearly anything on this wretched rock. Wasting little time, he climbed back behind the wheel of his new car and turned the key in the ignition, then blasted the air conditioning on high. For a moment, he allowed himself to sit back and relish the air that poured from the vents as it cooled the interior of the car. Then he slid the gear shift down into drive and pulled away from the little diner with the file on his next target in the passenger seat next to him.

Cincinnati was not his ideal destination, but it was still an improvement over D.C. or Atlanta. Indy he wasn't so sure about. In all of his travels, he'd never had the opportunity to go there. In the end, he supposed they were all the same. And anywhere was better than where he came from.

# 8

## Garvey

Garvey stared down at the words in the newspaper with a lump in his throat. He thought he'd left Florida in time to avoid causing too much damage, but even after all this time, it was difficult to determine just how long was too long. Passing through states didn't seem to have much of an effect, but if he stayed in one place for any amount of time, he put the lives of others in danger. All because it wasn't his state. Indiana was his state. It's where he was sent. It's where he needed to stay. Retirement couldn't come soon enough.

With a flash of anger, he ripped the paper in half and shoved it into the trash bin on the far side of his bay. What's done is done, he told himself, there was no avoiding it.

"Yeah, keep telling yourself that," he answered his thoughts aloud.

"Would you be pissed about this?" His son's voice came from the doorway.

Garvey turned to find Seth waving his smartphone and, though the screen was lit up, Garvey couldn't see what was displayed there. He could only assume it was the same news he had just read in the paper. The older man gave a heavy sigh and nodded.

"This is all because you visited a different state?" Seth asked.

"Yeah." Garvey sat on his stool and busied himself with work on the bike.

"Then why in the fuck are you leaving this state if you know shit like that is going to happen?"

"Because sometimes you don't have a choice," Garvey answered. "Something you'll learn as you move up."

"All those people died so you could keep selling drugs and running guns?"

"No, they died because if my suppliers are unhappy, they start coming after the families of me and my men. So, if they demand a meeting with me, they get one. No matter where it is."

Seth calmed as if understanding was sinking in. "Are these guys happy now?"

"Nope. They're dead."

---

"What? What happens if he has friends that come looking for us?"

"That's the beauty of keeping a low profile; no one knows about you, or your sister, or your mother."

"And what about the rest of the guys in the club?"

Garvey shrugged. "They knew the dangers when they took the oath to join."

Seth's expression was one of shock and disbelief. "That's pretty fucking cold, Dad. And it totally contradicts what you just said."

Garvey stopped working and let out a sigh. "Sometimes things go wrong and there's nothing you can do about it. It's best you come to the same realization if you wish to continue down the path you're on. Besides, if they send anybody our way, I'll handle it."

Seth let out a defeated breath and let the matter lie.

"Look, thanks for your help around the shop today," Garvey said, veering the conversation away from his trip to Clearwater. "We would have been overwhelmed without you."

"Don't mention it," Seth said. "I'm heading to see Mom. See you tomorrow?"

"We'll be here."

Seth walked out through the bay door just as Buck was walking in. "Have a good one kid," the large biker called as he passed Seth. "Don't go diving without a scuba suit, if you know what I'm saying."

"Buck, I rarely know what you're saying," Seth called with a smile.

Buck laughed and came wandering over to Garvey. "Kid knows his shit. Quick as a motherfucker too. Knocked out the brake job on that Toyota in under fifteen minutes."

"Between you, Huff, and myself, we've poured everything we know into that boy. He should know his shit."

Buck dropped a newspaper on Garvey's workbench that was open on the page that reported the shooting in Florida. "Wanna tell me what's going on there?"

Garvey glanced at the paper, then back up to his old friend.

"I'd rather not."

"C'mon, John, we've been friends for twenty years. In all that time I've never questioned why you keep your name off the books in the business we own together, why you wish to get paid under the table, why you keep your kids and woman distant, even to the point of sleeping in a different location every night. I always just assumed you had warrants out and wanted to avoid bringing any heat down on you and yours. But this shit," he held the paper up in front of Garvey's face. "This isn't the first time it's happened. After all we been through, I think I deserve to know why."

Garvey let out an exasperated breath. He studied his friend's face. "Alright, but if we're going to talk about this, we need to get our buzz on first."

"That's more than fair, let's hit the bar."

Harry's was a favorite hangout for the club. Not quite a shit hole, but close. Harry had even remodeled the place after a small fire brought in a little insurance money. A lot of that money went toward the Colts and Pacers memorabilia that had been used to cover the walls.

Buck ordered a pitcher of beer and whisky shots while Garvey racked a set of billiard balls on a pool table. Once they started drinking, the conversation turned to football and then women. Buck saying for the thousandth time how much he wished he could find a good woman like the one Garvey had.

"She's out there, man," Garvey said, knocking the one ball in the side pocket. "I just don't think you're going to find her in dive bars or street corners."

"Where the fuck am I supposed to look? Church social? 4-H bake-off or some shit like that?"

"I don't know. Maybe I can ask Gwen to set you up with a friend." Garvey had missed the five ball and Buck was lining up his shot but paused at the idea of a blind date. "You think she would do that?"

"I don't see why not."

Buck took his shot. The twelve-ball dropped into the far corner pocket. "She have any pretty friends. I mean, I'm no DiCaprio, I know that, so I'm not all shallow and shit, but I'd like a woman that's at least moderately attractive."

"Sure, I get that," Garvey smiled at his old friend and took a long pull from his beer bottle. With any luck, Buck would forget about his need for more information and be satisfied with the prospect of a blind date instead.

Buck dropped another billiard ball and hiked his jeans up under his large belly. "Alright, see what you can set up for me."

"I'll ask her in the morning."

The waitress brought more shots and the two of them saluted their friendship before they downed the firewater. "Say, you see the new Bruce Willis movie yet?" Buck asked.

"No, I haven't got around to it."

"I tell you what; for my money, he's still the best action star out there. You can keep your Dwayne "The Rock", and the bald dude from all those car movies. Willis is the way to go. Even his Christmas movies kick ass."

Garvey took his shot, then looked at his old friend. "I don't recall Bruce Willis being in any Christmas movies."

"Die Hard and Die Hard 2," Buck shrugged, as if the answer was obvious.

"No, those are not Christmas movies."

"Like hell they're not. The first one takes place at a Christmas party and Christmas music is played throughout."

"No, man, it's an action movie that happens to take place around the holiday. You can't count that shit as a Christmas movie. Look at the fucking body count, for fuck sake. I don't remember seeing automatic gunfire and explosions in It's a Wonderful Life."

"Shit, that movie backs up my argument there. It was only Christmas time in the last fifteen minutes of It's a Wonderful Life, and now it's a holiday classic."

"Again, I think it's the terrorists and sheer amount of dead bodies that disqualifies Die Hard from being in the Christmas movie category."

Buck held out his hand and shook his head, clearly getting frustrated with the conversation. "Agree to disagree, motherfucker." Garvey couldn't help but laugh at his old friend. He poured them each another beer and Buck waved the waitress over to order more shots. Garvey sunk the eight ball in the pocket he'd called beforehand, and Buck racked for a rematch, cursing under his breath all the while. By the time they were done with the second game, which Buck won easily (the biker's pool skills always improved with the amount of alcohol he drank), the two of them were feeling pretty blitzed and Buck asked the question that brought them there in the first place.

"So," Buck slurred as he took another sip of beer, "Lay it out for me man. What exactly *are* you?"

Garvey let out a long sigh, then looked around to make sure he wouldn't be overheard. "Alright, Buck, how much do you know about The Bible?"

# 9

## Marion

The call had come in at ten till five, just as two bikers in Indiana were
deciding to close up shop and head to their favorite bar for billiards,
booze, and deep conversation. A lead that Marion could have never
guessed they'd receive this early in the case. Marion had been
planning on going home for a while before she met Adrian Dillard
at the airport, but Mann leaned into her office and let her know
about the anonymous tip that had come in as she was preparing to
leave.

"Some woman just called the local PD and said she was a regular
at the bar and knew the guitar player well. Bit of a groupie it seems.
Anyway, she just went to a local car dealership with her dad and
she's sure she recognized the guitar that belonged to the victim
displayed in one salesman's office."

"Really?" Marion said.

"Yep, she said it looked like it'd been cleaned up, but she had no
doubt it was the same one. Left-handed Fender Stratocaster, orange
and white."

"Alright, let's go check it out."

The car lot was on the west side of town. Mann had looked into
the history of the place and said it had had a major boom in business
lately and was even in the process of bringing in a fleet of new cars
to sell on its expanding lot. Pulling into a visitor's space, Marion and
Agent Mann exited their SUV into the boiling heat of the evening
air. A car salesman greeted them immediately, breathing down their
necks with all the subtleness of a vulture swooping down upon a
lump of carrion left on the blazing hot pavement.

"Hey, folks. Looking to trade in that ride for something
sportier?" Marion held out her I.D. "FBI. We would like to speak to
Dave, please."

The salesman suddenly seemed nervous. "Certainly. Let me
show you to his office."

Marion nearly felt weak in the knees as they walked onto the
showroom floor and the air conditioning hit them full blast. The
place was nearly frigid, and she was thankful for it. In all her years

living in Atlanta, she could not remember a more miserable summer, and it was still early. The salesman led them to an office where a rather overweight man with thick, black curls on his head, was relaxing back in his chair, a somewhat blissful smile on his face.

"Uh, Dave," the salesman asked, peaking in the door.

"Berry, Christ, I said I didn't want to be disturbed," Dave nearly shouted, his moment of bliss completely shattered.

Marion took over before Berry could respond. "Dave, I'm Agent Kern and this is Agent Mann with the FBI. We'd like to ask you a few questions."

Dave looked at them suspiciously. "Questions? About what?"

Agent Mann stepped closer to the desk while Marion closed the door in Berry's face, effectively excluding him from the conversation. Then Marion moved over to the wall and looked at the plaques and certificates that boasted Dave's achievements. This was their play whenever they questioned someone; Marion trying to seem casual, nonchalant, while Mann stared at their quarry, silent and intimidating.

"There was a murder at a local bar last night," Marion began. "A musician, a bartender, and waitress were all gunned down. My partner and I were brought in on the case because of some...odd details. We got a tip a little while ago that brought us here."

Dave grinned and he seemed unsure of where the conversation was going. "What can I do to help?"

Marion took a step closer to his desk. "Dave, can you tell us where you got that guitar?"

Dave turned and looked at the instrument mounted on the wall behind his desk as if it was the first time he'd seen it. "The guitar? I've had it for years. Thought it would add a certain flair to my office. An accessibility for my customers."

Marion cocked her head as she looked at the man. The sheen of sweat on his forehead. The nervous smile on his lips. The way he fidgeted with something in his pants pocket. It all pointed to the same thing. He was lying.

"That's not what Berry said," Marion bluffed. "He told us you just hung it up there today."

Dave stepped around to the front of the desk and sat on the edge.

"Well, yeah. I brought it from home and mounted it this morning."

Marion crossed her arms. "Funny. Our dead musician had a guitar *just* like it. Matter of fact, it was the only thing missing from the crime scene. No cash or valuables were stolen. Just the guitar."

Dave closed his eyes and took a deep breath, as if he were inhaling something pleasant in the air. A drug that Marion and her partner were not privy to. Mann glanced at her, his expression questioning. Dave didn't respond. His nervousness had disappeared, and the blissful look was returning to his face.

"Dave?" Marion said. No answer. She spoke louder "Dave!"

"Fuck! What?" the salesman snapped. "What the fuck do you want?"

"I want you to tell us where you got the guitar."

Dave was staring at her with anger now, his breathing heavy. "Alright, it was part of a trade-in. This guy came in here this morning for a car. Traded an old dodge and threw the guitar in for good measure."

"We'll need to see the trade-in," Mann said.

"Fine," Dave said. He returned to the other side of his desk and wrote the make, model and color on the back of a business card and held it out to Mann. "Have at it. It's sitting at the rear of the lot."

"We're also going to need all the information you have on this man that made the trade," Marion added. "And the guitar is coming with us. It's evidence in a murder case."

Dave placed his hands on his desk and dropped his head, his breathing even heavier than before. There was a low rumble in the room. For a moment, Marion thought someone in the next office was playing music with the bass dropped low, then she realized it was coming from Dave's chest. Mann looked at her, uncertain, his hand drifting toward his gun.

"Dave?" she said. Then shouted again. "Dave!"

The attack was sudden. Dave was over the desk in a flash, his face had changed into something monstrous and before Agent Mann could react, Dave had latched on to his neck with inhuman, fanged teeth. Mann screamed as blood spurted from his neck and sprayed down the front of his shirt and suit jacket.

Marion pulled her gun and fired three shots, each hitting their target. Dave shook the slugs off as they hit his head like they were nothing more than bothersome fruit flies buzzing around his face. Then he leaped back over the desk, pulled the guitar from the wall and slung it on his back, in movements so fast Marion couldn't get a bead on him. As he jumped over the desk, his body changed into something different. Something that moved on all fours, pounced around the room and blasted through the window of the office and into the blazing heat outside. Marion fired three more shots that hit their mark but did no damage and could only watch as the thing that was once Dave the car salesman disappeared over the next hill.

Marion rushed to her partner's side pulling her cell as she went. She called 911 and removed her jacket to use as a makeshift bandage, putting pressure on the wound in Agent Mann's neck. Marion could feel each surge of blood with every beat of her partner's heart. She pressed down harder on the wound, her mind racing. What had just happened? What *exactly* were they getting into? The car salesman was not human, of that much she was now sure, but what did the guitar have to do with anything? Why was he so protective of it?

"Hang on, Eric," Marion said in his ear. "Help is coming. Help is on the way."

Marion could hear the sirens now, ringing in the distance. She willed them to hurry. To move faster, through the stop lights and around the traffic. There was so much blood. Too much. Something in her head, some voice on the precipice of her subconscious, told her it was too late. Nothing could be done. She may as well relax, because too much of the crimson liquid that was supposed to be on the inside of her partner's body was now on the outside. Pooling on the floor around him.

Around her. On her.

All over. Everywhere.

The blood was everywhere.

From far away, Marion was vaguely aware of the EMTs at her side. One was telling her she'd done good and it was time to step aside, but her panicked mind latched on to the poor grammar the EMT had used. She had done "well", that's what he had meant to say, she had done "well".

The EMT pulled her away from her partner and the two of them went to work on him. Marion moved away, leaned against the wall, and watched them work. Once they were sure they could move him, they placed him on a board and loaded him into the back of the ambulance.

Marion's mind was muddled. As she stood to move, she felt as if the world around her was caught in mangled, jerking movements. It reminded her of the other case she worked that took her beyond the realm of the believable. The killer moved in much the same way due to his disconnection with reality. She had to stop and catch her breath. Force things to return to normal.

The ambulance pulled away and Marion got behind the wheel of the SUV to follow.

The hours ticked by. Marion remained in her blood-covered clothes, sitting in the waiting room of the ER, she forced her mind to focus on something other than the nightmare she was living. Emails needed to be checked and she hadn't forgotten about picking Adrian Dillard up from the airport. Her expert on all things supernatural. There was an overabundance of things to tell him. Questions to ask.

A nurse approached and Marion stood, preparing herself for the worst.

"Are you Mr. Mann's wife?" the nurse asked. She was young and pretty with a southern accent that all young, pretty girls seemed to share in Atlanta.

"It's Agent Mann," Marion answered, "and no, I'm his partner. He isn't married and his parents live in Wisconsin. I've called them and they're catching the first flight, but I'm afraid I'm all he has here."

"Well, his surgery went well. The wound in his neck has been repaired, but the next few hours will be critical with so much blood loss. I'll do my best to keep you updated."

"Thank you," Marion said. "Wait, I have to go."

"Oh?"

"I have to pick someone up from the airport. I'll be back as soon as I can though."

The nurse nodded and walked away. Marion watched her go, unable to move for a moment, as if her legs weren't ready to face any more of this wretched day. It took some convincing, but she finally walked toward the exit. Before she knew it, she was in the SUV and pulling into the pickup lane at Hartsfield-Jackson Atlanta International Airport. The attack on Mann played over and over in her mind during the drive, her focus continually falling on the monstrous face of the car salesman. The way his body changed. The inhuman way he moved.

Marion pulled the car over and she waved to the man waiting there with his suitcase at his feet. His tie was pulled loose and his suit jacket was tucked under his arm. Adrian Dillard moved to the back of the SUV and opened the hatch. As he tossed his suitcase in, he called to the front seat, where Marion waited patiently for him. "How are you?"

Marion didn't answer, but Dillard went on as if she had.

"I got to say, I'm looking forward to working with you again. That Daylight Slayer case was one of the oddest things I've been a part of, and that's saying a lot. Whew! Can't wait to get into that air conditioning." Once the hatch was closed, Adrian came around to the passenger side door and opened it to look in at Marion, disheveled and covered in blood. The expert of the supernatural only smiled. "Alright, diving in headfirst. I like it."

# 10

## Judas

Cincinnati wasn't a bad town. A lot of hills. A lot of trees. And though it was still hot as fuck, it wasn't near as bad as Atlanta. Judas drove north past the smattering of skyscrapers that made up the downtown area (which paled in comparison to downtown Atlanta) and found the Applebee's that Lou had directed him to. The restaurant was like many of the others he'd been in across the country, and he'd been in quite a few in his quest for red meat since he'd been back. Burgers truly were the greatest invention ever. Judas often imagined his own personal heaven being one filled with stacks upon stacks of greasy hamburgers with all the toppings.

It wasn't hard to spot his target. Her red hair was nearly orange and was shaved around the sides of her head, the rest pulled in a ponytail that trailed down her back. She wore glasses with thick black frames and had a smile that lit up the place. On the surface, she seemed short and gangly, and extremely awkward. To the human eye, she was most likely just another pretty face. Just another waitress, a little more punk rock in appearance than others, but nothing special. Judas, however, was able to see beyond that. Most with his particular background would. To him, every curve and feature was exquisite. Beauty in its purest form.

Judas was approached by the hostess, who asked if he would be dining alone this evening.

"Yes, just me," Judas said with a charming smile. "And could you seat me in the redhead's section, please?"

The hostess (who was pretty in her own right, with her deep chocolate skin color and full lips) glanced over her shoulder at the redhead and looked back at Judas as if she were completely dumbfounded by his choice in waitress, but nevertheless wanted to please her customer. She seated Judas in a booth near a window and placed a menu in front of him. He wasted no time finding the fattest burger they offered. The waitress made her way over to his table and gave a brilliant smile.

"Hi, my name's Lizzy. I'll be your server today. Can I get you something to drink to start with?"

Judas studied her a moment and her smile dropped slightly at his hesitation. Mentally, he shook the odd feeling he had away and spoke. "Lizzy? Short for Elizabeth, I take it?"

"Yeah, that's right."

"Elizabeth, I would like the biggest, greasiest burger you serve and a tall, draft beer to wash it down with."

"A man who knows what he wants," Elizabeth said with a nod.

Judas offered his most charming smile. "I'm also a man that always gets what I want."

The waitress' cheeks reddened and her smile faltered as she walked away. Judas knew he had offended her in some way. His usual line of smarmy bullshit wouldn't work here. Elizabeth wasn't the type of girl that could be bedded by a few kind words. A different approach had to be used.

When Elizabeth returned with his beer, Judas held her up before she could walk away. "Wait."

"Is there something wrong," she asked.

"I feel what I said before offended you in some way. I'd just like to apologize."

Elizabeth seemed to relax a little at this and her smile returned, even though it was only faint, like a watercolor brush stroke, a tender pink hue. "It's alright."

"I'm new in town and was just trying to be friendly. I fear I came off as arrogant."

"A little bit," she replied honestly.

This forced a genuine laugh from Judas. "Perhaps we can start over."

"Sure."

"I'm Jude," Judas said, offering his hand.

"Elizabeth," the waitress said shaking his hand. "Jude. That's a peculiar name."

"Well, my parents were huge fans of The Beatles," Judas lied. "It's how they met, actually. Through a fan club."

"Interesting," Elizabeth said in a tone that suggested she didn't find it at all interesting. "I'll be right back with your burger."

The waitress walked away and Judas told himself that their exchange had gone as well as could be expected. Five minutes later, she returned with his burger and her smile was back to its former brilliance, complimenting her dark, brown eyes.

"Thank you," Judas said as she placed the plate in front of him. "It looks incredible."

"You seem like quite the burger connoisseur," Elizabeth observed.

"Well, I went so many years without them. It was only recently that I realized what I was missing. Now, I can't seem to get enough."

"Be careful, too much red meat can kill you."

Judas had to chuckle at this. "I'm not worried."

"Well, I should see to my other tables. Enjoy your meal."

Judas did just that. The burger was juicy and thick. Topped with onion rings, jalapeño peppers, and barbecue sauce. He savored every precious bite and considered, not for the first time, that he may enjoy a good burger more than sex. After the meal, he ordered another beer. And another after that. All the while scrolling through his smartphone as if he were reading and responding to emails, when in fact the only emails he ever received went straight into his spam file. Judas wasn't exactly one for networking. However, now that he'd laid some groundwork with the waitress, he wanted to appear nonchalant.

"Another beer?" Elizabeth asked, and Judas could see she was intrigued by him.

"Please," he said, barely looking up from the screen of his phone.

Moments later, she returned with the beer and stood staring at him.

Judas looked up at her and she seemed to fidget. "So, how long are you in town?"

"A while, I should think. I work for a real estate firm. I'll be looking at property around town."

"Oh. Staying nearby?"

"The Harbor Inn, just up the road."

"Ah, that seems like a nice hotel. They only built it a couple of years ago."

"It is rather agreeable." In truth, Judas had yet to check-in at the hotel. He'd come directly to the restaurant to meet his mark. "I imagine our paths will cross quite a bit."

"Sorry?"

"I'm a man that enjoys a routine. I'm sure I'll be dining here every night."

"Oh. I guess we'll be getting to know each other then."

Judas smiled. "I hope so, Elizabeth.

# 11
## Garvey

Garvey awoke in the morning to the bright sunlight slashing through Buck's living room window. His head was pounding and his stomach ached. Slowly, he stood and shuffled to the kitchen, where he found a bottle of ibuprofen and a bottle of water. Buck's house was a rundown old shack in Miller Park, a neighborhood that specialized in rundown old shacks. Garvey often asked his old friend why he didn't move out of the dump. The garage alone made enough money for him to afford it. Buck's response was always the same: "This is just where I sleep. Rest of my time is spent in the garage, in the bar, or on my bike."

Garvey could see the logic.

After a long trip to the bathroom, Garvey shuffled into the kitchen where he found a note from his old friend, written in his large, loopy script, Heading to the garage. Coffee's fresh. The note said nothing more. Garvey knew Buck was feeling strange about everything he'd learned last night. Unsure. Maybe even scared. Garvey only hoped his friend would pull it together and not let the new information cause a rift between them.

After a cup of coffee and a dry piece of toast, Garvey felt good enough to ride and straddled his bike. The hog blazed to life, breaking the quiet calm of morning, and Garvey rode in the direction of his wife's house.

Garvey walked in the front door to find Gwen where he could usually find her; typing away at her laptop, working on her latest romance novel. She'd yet to have one published, but she kept grinding away. There was the blog she was paid to write for an online women's magazine, which was more than most hopeful writers were able to accomplish, but she had visions of much more.

"Hey," John said, bending to kiss her lips. "How's the book coming along?"

"It's coming," she replied with a shrug. "How are things at the garage?"

"Alright. Seth worked all day yesterday. Said he was going to come by here and see you. Did he?"

"Yes. And I was so relieved to see him. I wish he'd get a phone."

"Well, he's going to have to have one now. At least a burner."

Gwen slammed her laptop shut and stood. "John, I don't want him in the club. It's too dangerous."

"He wants in. Not only that, he wants to be president someday."

"What the fuck, John?" Gwen shouted. "We talked about this. We decided this wasn't the life we wanted him to have."

"No, you decided that. I never agreed to it. Besides, look at the life he's leading now. No steady income, getting shit-faced every night, focusing all of his energy on the next one-night stand. The boy needs guidance. Focus."

"So, running drugs and guns is the way to go?"

Garvey shrugged. "Someone has to take over when I retire."

"Then let Buck do it."

"Buck isn't a leader. He's a great right-hand man, incredibly loyal, but he doesn't have the smarts or decision-making ability to do the things that need to be done."

"You mean like killing people."

Garvey's temper was rising, but he said nothing. Instead, he walked to the kitchen and pulled a bottled water from the fridge. Gwen followed to continue the argument.

"I saw the news, John. All that shit that went down in Florida wasn't coincidence. Why do you make these trips when you know this kind of shit can happen?"

"Because sometimes it's unavoidable. Besides, that's just another reason for Seth to take over. That type of shit *won't* happen if he travels. You're just helping my argument by bringing it up."

Gwen was now trembling with rage. "I don't want *my* son getting into this criminal shit."

Garvey stepped closer to her, speaking in a low, threatening growl. "You married into this criminal shit. This is our life. All of us. Seth learning the trade is the best thing for him. I know you don't see that right now, but if you really think about it, you'll come to the same conclusion. Since you're already pissed, there's something else I need to tell you."

"What?", she snapped.

Garvey let out a steadying breath. "I told Buck everything last night."

Gwen placed her hands on her hips and shook her head in

disbelief. "What the fuck happened after you left here yesterday? Have you lost your fucking mind? Why would you do that?"

"Gwen, it's Buck."

"What the fuck does that have to do with anything? All this secrecy. I'm married and can't live in the same house as my husband. You're like a homeless person. Crashing on someone's couch every night, occasionally staying here, all because you think someone, or something is going to come after you someday and you don't want to put your family in danger. At least that's what you always told me. But in all the years we've been together, no monsters have appeared. Now here you are, throwing your son in the fire and spilling your secrets to your drinking buddy."

Garvey sighed and quietly said, "I know what I'm doing."

"Do you?" Gwen asked.

Garvey drained the water bottle, then crushed it and tossed it into the wastebasket. "I got to go."

Garvey walked past her and slammed out the door. Mounting his ride, he started the bike and pulled away from the house. He knew why Gwen was angry and he couldn't blame her, after all, he had led a life of secrecy all this time and she was right, nothing had happened. Maybe he was being overly cautious. Maybe he was even being paranoid.

What did he expect to happen? The powers that be had all seemed to move on. Things had been quiet for the last century, really. There had been no threats on his life, besides the occasional drug supplier that needed to be put in his place. Maybe they had forgotten about him.

Garvey knew there were others like him around. Maybe it was time to reach out. See if they had been left alone as well. Things were getting out of sorts both with his family and with Buck. He needed to nip it in the bud before it got worse. At least he could take comfort in the fact that Elizabeth was safe.

# 12
## Marion

Adrian Dillard was looking over the case file of the nightclub murder when Marion awoke in the waiting room of the ER. James was sympathetic about her need to stay by her partner's side overnight and she loved him even more for it. As far as husbands went, he was proving to be a great one already. She sat up and rubbed her eyes. Then stood and stretched, her back popping, her knees singing along. Adrian Dillard had put on some weight since last they'd worked together. He was already a big man, six-foot-two with broad shoulders and a barrel chest. Now he had a bit of a beer gut to go along with all of that. He had also grown his beard out dark brown with streaks of gray, full and thick, and hanging down to his chest. The hair on his head, however, was thin. Receding in the front like an army retreating from battle, and a bald spot at his crown. Still, he sported a fade haircut, high and tight.

"Did you sleep at all?" Marion asked.

Adrian looked up from the file. "Yeah, a little. I caught a few Z's on the plane."

"Find anything helpful in there?"

"Several things, actually."

"Well, I want to hear all about them, but I need to hit the little girls' room first."

"Understood," Adrian said with a smirk.

Marion walked down the hall and found the bathrooms. Inside, she voided her bladder and washed her hands, looking up in the mirror to find a crazed, disheveled she-devil looking back at her. "Shit," she said out loud. "People just now saw you like this."

After a lot of work, she was able to clean up her makeup and contort her hair into something more presentable than what the waiting room couch had left her to work with. When she finally got to the point where her face and hair looked halfway presentable, she looked down and realized that her pantsuit was still covered in her partner's blood.

Giving up, she walked out of the bathroom and back to the waiting area just as one of the surgeons was talking to Adrian.

"Oh, here she is, Doc," Adrian said, gesturing to her.

"Agent Kern?" the doctor asked.

"Yes."

"I'm Dr. Molina and I have good news to report. Your partner is going to be just fine, all his vitals are stable and he is recovering quite nicely."

"Oh, thank you so much," Marion said, elated. "Can we see him?"

"Not just yet. He's still under and should get some considerable rest before he receives visitors."

"Right, I understand. Thank you for everything."

The doctor nodded and walked away. Marion turned to Adrian.

"Well, thank you for waiting with me," she said.

"Absolutely," said Adrian. "I'm glad he's going to pull through."

"Me too. I guess that makes you my temporary partner. Come on, I need to go home and clean up, then I'll buy you breakfast and you can tell me what you think."

The two of them left the hospital and, after a quick trip home for a shower (and an awkward meeting between her expert consultant and her husband that seemed to turn into a burgeoning bromance by the time she returned) found the nearest fast-food joint for a bite to eat. Marion was positively famished, and she had no doubt her expert felt the same. "So, tell me what you think," Marion said around a mouthful of sausage biscuit.

Adrian opened the folder and spread the photos and files over the table, pushing his breakfast burrito aside in the process. "Where to begin," the man said, scanning over the mess he'd made.

"How about we start with the guitar," Marion suggested, "since my partner nearly lost his life over it."

"Right. Well, to explain that, first I should explain what we're dealing with."

"Okay."

"The autopsy, with the black blood, the gold bullet, the extra organs, and the odd scars on the back. Pretty sure we're looking at an angel."

Marion sat back in the booth and let out a long sigh. "Fuck."

"Surely you had some idea it was going to be something like this."

"Yeah, I gathered from the scars that he'd had wings at some point. So, why a gold bullet?"

"Much in the way a silver bullet is all that will kill a werewolf, gold bullets are used to dispatch angels or demons. Of course, said gold bullet would have to be forged in the fires of Hell to take out an angel. The holy flames of Heaven for a demon."

"And the guitar?"

"That's the coolest part," Dillard said, sitting forward like a small child excited over opening a new toy. "The guitar acts as an anchor of sorts. You see, this angel, whoever he was, must have been one of the fallen that sided with The Devil in his attempt to take the throne. These angels were banished to earth, forced to remain here for all eternity. When this first happened, the angels were allowed to keep their halos, but these were highly coveted by demons because the angels souls were linked to them. The demons would feed on these souls, almost like a drug. They'd get a rush from them."

"I didn't think angels had souls," Marion said. "Isn't that what separates them from humans?"

"Well, angels were really prototypes for humans, so they did have souls, only they were different. More tangible."

"Hence the halo attachment."

"Right. Only the powers-that-be weren't happy about the angels keeping their halos because it gave them access to all of their powers as well. The solution was to take the halo away from them and anchor the souls to a different object, but this also meant some of the angels' powers could be used through said object. It became a conduit of sorts. The guitar is what this particular angel had his soul attached to."

"And when the angel died?"

"The soul inhabited the guitar completely, making it a valuable commodity among demons." Dillard took a bite of his breakfast burrito and chewed.

"So, are you saying a demon is responsible for killing the angel?" asked Marion.

Dillard swallowed. "Not at all. In fact, the killer trading the guitar to a demon for a car would suggest the man is not a demon. And I doubt he's an angel."

"Back up, Dave the car dealer was a demon?"

"Absolutely."

"And we're looking for a mortal man."

"I didn't say that."

Marion gave Adrian Dillard an exasperated look. "What else is there?"

"Any number of things."

"Adrian," she said, studying the man. "How do you know all of this?"

The man looked uncomfortable. "It's my job to know."

"I get that, but does all of this knowledge come from research or personal experience?"

Dillard shrugged. "A little from column A, a little from column B. I've had my own run-ins with the supernatural."

"Like?"

"You wouldn't believe me if I told you."

"After the two cases we've worked on together, I don't think it'll phase me."

Dillard seemed to consider this a moment, then said, "I'd rather not go into details, but I will tell you I've seen a lot of strange things. Ghosts, ancient deities, nightmare creatures. Angels and demons make for just another day at the office for me."

"So, why would someone be targeting these angels?" Marion asked. "Is it for the souls alone?"

"I doubt it. The killer needed a new car, I'm betting he has something else planned. Probably something big."

"Big?"

"I'm talking biblical."

After breakfast, Marion dropped Dillard back at his hotel so he could get cleaned up and catch a little sleep. Then she drove back home for another shower, still feeling as if she were covered in her partner's blood.

The heat that had sat over Atlanta for the last few weeks seemed to be breaking, at least temporarily, to allow for a heavy storm system to pound the city. Marion was thankful for the reprieve, however short-lived it may be. Inside the house, she was greeted by cool air and an overly excited French bulldog named Joker, an unfortunate name derived from her husband's obsession with Batman. Marion had always hated the comic book and science fiction stuff, frequently teasing her husband. James teased her in return for her love of romantic comedies and sleazy, romance novels.

Marion walked through the bedroom, past her snoring husband (having apparently returned to bed after her last visit) and into the bathroom where she stripped naked and ran the shower. For a long while, she let the warm water cascade over her head, as if she could wash the images of the previous day away and never think of them again. There was movement behind her and she smiled as James' hands moved over her back and down to her waist.

He kissed her lips and then began to trail kisses down her neck.

Then he pulled back and looked at her. "Bad timing for this?"

Marion gave him a seductive smile, then handed him her loofah and body wash. "First do my back, then you can work on the front."

James ran the loofah slowly over her back, taking his time on her plump posterior, then ran his hands up to her breasts, pressing himself against her. Marion knew this was exactly what she needed to take her mind off things, even if it was only for a little while.

"You should really get some sleep," James said after their passion had led them to the bed and a very satisfying finish. Marion was once again dressed and heading for the kitchen to put on a pot of coffee, while James was wandering around in his boxers and showing off his muscular body.

"Duty calls," Marion said. "Not all of us get to stay home and peck away at a keyboard while wearing nothing but undergarments."

James shrugged, "Hey, I didn't choose the life of luxury, the life of luxury chose me."

"Whatever," Marion said, knowing it took James nearly a decade to get his publishing deal. "You just make sure you get at least twenty-five hundred words written in your nerd novel today."

"You my editor now?"

"Just trying to keep you sharp. No writer's block."

"Never happen."

Marion poured herself a travel mug full of coffee, dumped in an ample amount of cinnamon creamer, and kissed her husband on the lips. James pulled her closer and kissed her deeper.

"Don't get me going again," she giggled. "You'll make me late."

"All right. We'll pick this up again later."

"You got it, my muscle-bound blerd."

He laughed. "Why I got to be a 'black nerd'? Why not just a nerd?"

Marion gave a teasing chuckle as she walked out the door.

Adrian Dillard was waiting outside the hotel when Marion pulled up. His dark hair, and beard were wet from a recent shower, and his jeans and Sublime t-shirt gave him the look of a man trying to recapture his fraternity days. Once he was buckled into the passenger seat, Marion pulled away and drove toward the office.

"What's our first move?" Dillard asked.

"Today, we're going to see if we can track down the vehicle the killer got from Dave the Demon and hopefully find Dave as well. Bring him in for attacking a federal agent."

"Arresting a demon may be a little difficult."

"Yeah, I thought about that. I don't suppose there's another way to kill one besides holy, golden bullets?"

"You could remove the head. That seems to work."

Marion glanced at Dillard. "You talk like you've had to do it before."

"Not me personally. I've seen it though."

"Jesus."

In her office, Dillard plopped down on the sofa against the wall and Marion had barely sat down before Director Fuller was on her phone and demanding to see her. She told Dillard she'd return momentarily and walked down the hall to Fuller's office.

"Agent Kern," Fuller said upon seeing her in his doorway. Still getting used to her married name, Marion nearly looked behind her to see if there was another agent joining their meeting. "Please, have a seat."

Marion sat in one of the chairs in front of the desk and waited patiently for Fuller to speak. "It appears Agent Mann is going to survive his attack. He always was a tough son-of-a-bitch."

"Yes, sir," Marion agreed.

Fuller let out a disappointed sigh. "Unfortunately, all of this could have been avoided, if only I'd received word sooner."

"I'm afraid I don't follow, sir."

"I've been ordered to abandon this case. There will be no further investigation into the nightclub shooting."

Marion stood suddenly, angry and confused. "Sir, you can't do this!"

"It's out of my hands, Marion. This has come from high up. D.C. There's not a damn thing I can do about it."

"Sir, I've flown in an expert. I'm closing in on a suspect. And I need to find the bastard that attacked my partner."

Fuller studied her thoughtfully. Then he stood and rounded the desk, speaking to her in a lower voice. "Look, officially, I have to put you on a different case. Unofficially, I can't police what you do with your time. Understood?"

Marion smiled. "Completely."

# 13
## Judas

Judas stepped out of the cold shower into the frigid hotel room. Cincinnati had gone from hot to warm and back to hot again in the week since he'd arrived, so he spent every day holed up in his hotel room with the air conditioner blasting, passing the time reading books and watching movies. The only time he left was, of course, to have dinner at the local Applebee's and chat more with Elizabeth.

Judas did make one other excursion into the outside world. In order to keep up the illusion that he was a man of business rather than a cold-blooded killer, Judas purchased a laptop from the local Best Buy and took it along with him for dinner. Although, cold-blooded wasn't the right way to describe Judas, having great regret for the things he had been forced to do up to this point, it was the way he had to think of himself. A lie he reasserted in order to help deal with his actions.

Judas left the hotel with a spring in his step, whistling a happy tune as he strode to his car. It was dinner time. By far the best part of his day. The only time of day that he wasn't wallowing in guilt and self-loathing. It was the lone part of his day he had come to look forward to.

It was Saturday and the place was packed. Judas waited a full forty-five minutes to be seated in Elizabeth's section and sat in his booth with the laptop opened as usual. Mostly, he created and toyed with fake pie charts to make himself look busy, but from time to time he surfed the web and even discovered he enjoyed social media. Though he had to create profiles with fake names, he'd found several colorful people that he'd taken to messaging.

Elizabeth wandered over and smiled. "Well, if it isn't my favorite customer."

"Good evening, Elizabeth," Judas said. He felt a slight flutter in his stomach and attributed it to hunger pains.

"What kind of burger are we trying tonight?" she asked.

"I don't think I've had the one with the fried egg on it yet."

"I'll get the order in. Beer?"

"Absolutely."

Judas watched Elizabeth go, her ass swaying delightfully in her tight jeans, and felt he was getting close. Over the past week, they'd spoke a lot of their interests and hobbies (Judas of course making all of his up, for he hadn't done much since he got back besides watch movies, eat burgers, and kill people), but Elizabeth had hinted that she had one hobby that she wouldn't reveal to him for it turned most people off. Judas was intrigued to say the least.

Beyond this, though, Judas found that Elizabeth was a fascinating woman. Not only was she beautiful, but she was also intelligent, witty, and charming. She was by far the most remarkable person he'd met since his return.

Elizabeth came back with his beer and placed it on the table in front of him. "Did you miss me last night?"

"I did," Judas replied after taking a sip of beer. "The waitress I was stuck with didn't have half your charm and prompt service."

"*You* are definitely the charming one," she said with reddening cheeks and backed away awkwardly, bumping into another server as she went. Judas couldn't help but smile. With the laptop on the table in front of him, Judas pulled up his fake charts and began to toy with them. A few minutes later, Elizabeth returned with his meal.

"Here you are," she said and placed the plate in front of him. Judas pushed the laptop aside and rubbed his hands together, intentionally overexaggerating. Elizabeth laughed and leaned into the seat across from him on one knee. "How do you eat this stuff every day and not have a heart condition?"

"I work out a couple of hours a day," Judas lied. "A lot of cardio."

"You look like you're in great shape," she said, then smiled bashfully.

"Perhaps the next time you have a day off, in order for me to avoid less than stellar service, you and I could have dinner together."

Elizabeth straightened her glasses and looked away nervously, her cheeks turning an even darker shade of red.

"Alright," she said with a nod. "I should check in on my other tables."

Judas watched her go once again, feeling as elated as a schoolboy must feel when the girl he likes agrees to go to prom with him. She returned once to replace his beer, saying nothing, but smiling at him in her awkward way.

Once he'd finished his meal and was back to toying with his charts, Elizabeth returned with the check and sat in the booth across from him. "Okay, you are good-looking, and charming, and fit," the waitress said, as if picking up a conversation Judas wasn't aware they were having. "I have to ask; what is it you like about *me*."

Judas stared at her evenly. "Well, you're very awkward, nerdy, seemingly uncomfortable in your own skin, and you don't seem to realize just how breathtakingly beautiful you are. I find it very endearing. I've never been so fascinated and smitten with someone in all my life."

Judas was surprised to find that this wasn't a line, but a sincere appraisal of how he felt about her. He meant every word and felt it even more than he could express as he stared into her brown eyes.

She smiled her captivating smile. "That is maybe the nicest thing anyone has ever said to me."

"Well, I meant it."

She nodded. "I know."

For a long moment, they stared into each other's eyes, grinning like idiots and finding it hard to break the connection they'd discovered. Finally, she pulled away. "I should get back to work." She began to walk away, then stopped and turned back to him. "My next day off is Monday."

"Monday it is," Judas said.

"But you have to take me somewhere besides Applebee's."

"You have a deal."

"Okay."

"Okay."

Judas left cash for the meal, along with a generous tip, and walked out of the restaurant in a state of renewed cheer, trying hard not to think about what was coming. Trying, instead, to stay in the moment and think about the future date with the enchanting waitress. Suddenly, Judas was reflecting on just how enchanting she was. It came to her naturally, and he had no doubt that she wasn't even aware of what she was doing, but he was left wondering if his intense attraction to her was nothing more than her angelic genes toying with his...what?

Judas was no demon, nor was he an angel. Judas was something else entirely.

"Did you forget something," came Elizabeth's voice from behind him. He was brought out of his trance and realized he was standing just outside the entrance on the edge of the curb.

"I'm sorry," Judas said, turning to face her. "I guess my mind was wandering."

"Happens to the best of us," she said with a hand on his shoulder. "Have a good night."

Judas watched her walk down the sidewalk, then called after her. "Elizabeth, are you walking home?"

"Yeah, my apartment isn't far."

"May I drive you?"

"Um, I appreciate the offer, but you did have quite a few beers in there." This was followed by a nervous laugh.

"Of course," Judas replied.

"Would you like to walk me home?"

Judas considered the humid air a minute and felt he'd already been in the deplorable heat for far too long, but he did have a job to do. "I'd love to."

The two of them walked a fair distance in silence, Judas wondering just how he should start a conversation with her, while at the same time fully aware that he'd never had such trouble with women before. "So, are you from Cincinnati originally?"

"Um, no. Indiana, born and raised. I've only lived here for the last year or so. What about you?"

Judas had already prepared a back story and lied with the ease of a seasoned veteran. "My parents were Indian, my father made a fair amount of money in real estate. They eventually relocated to South Africa, where they had me. We relocated to London when I was only three and I grew up there. Studied business at Oxford. Now, here I am."

"Wow, South Africa. The U.K."

"Yeah, have you ever been?"

Elizabeth laughed her charming laugh. "Oh no. Believe it or not, where we walk right now is the furthest I've ever strayed from Indiana."

"That is a shame. There is so much to see around the world."

"It sounds like you've seen a lot."

"My business takes me all over." This part was true.

"I'd love to travel sometime. I know it isn't going to happen with the money I'm making from waitressing."

"Is the waitressing temporary?"

"That's the plan. I was accepted to Cincinnati University last fall. Made it through the first year, but it was rough."

"Oh? What is it you're majoring in?"

"Engineering."

"Well, good for you. I'm sure you'll make as good an engineer as you are a waitress."

Elizabeth laughed again and stopped in front of an apartment building, turning to look at him. "This is me," she said. She pushed her glasses up on her nose, a move that Judas found almost unbearably adorable, and kissed his cheek. "Thanks for seeing me home."

Judas felt a warmth move through his entire body and he raised his hand to touch the spot on his cheek that had been touched by her lips. "See you tomorrow?"

"Of course," Judas nodded. "I'll be the guy ordering the huge burger and beer."

Another laugh and she wished him goodnight as she climbed up the stairs. Judas turned and began to walk back the way he'd come. His thoughts turned once again to the mission at hand. More specifically, how much he wished to be done with the whole mess.

# 14
## Garvey

Garvey tossed his ratchet in his toolbox and downed half the bottle of beer that was sitting on the edge of the workbench. His knuckle was bleeding, but the cut was closing quickly and the blood was returning to his body as if someone had just hit the rewind button on his life. Within seconds, the wound was gone and there was no way to tell it had ever been there at all.

Although Garvey was feeling frustrated, the busted knuckle had little to do with it. Gwen had been giving him the silent treatment for the last week. It was so bad, in fact, that Garvey hadn't even bothered to go by and see her in the last two days. Seth had continued to work at the garage and learn more about how the club works, particularly how his father ran it. All this led to a highly disgruntled parental unit. And she wasn't just pissed at Garvey, she was pissed at Seth and Buck as well. Seth for taking the path of his father and Buck for allowing it all to happen.

Then there was Buck. Since Garvey had come clean and told the big man about his true self, things between the two of them had been awkward and weird. They just couldn't seem to talk to each other, and he was even acting stiff and untrusting toward Seth. It was something they were going to have to get past, though Garvey wasn't sure how to approach his old friend. The new information would create a new dynamic in their relationship, if said relationship could be saved at all.

Things were so much easier in the old days. Garvey would wander the world, rarely standing still for any long period of time, meeting new and interesting people, embarking on adventure after adventure, carefree and powerful. Then things changed. Garvey and the others were stripped of their powers and dropped in the most mundane places Earth had to offer. For him it was Indiana.

Garvey tossed the empty beer bottle in the waste basket and twisted the cap off a fresh one. At his age, it took nearly four cases of beer before the buzz started to kick in. A bottle of whiskey would help things along, but that would mean going to the liquor store, and in his current mood, leaving the garage was the last thing he wanted to do. Better to work on the bike, drink his beer, and wallow in self-pity.

"I guess now I know why you don't get a beer gut like this one," Buck said rubbing his large belly from the doorway that led to the storefront. In his other hand, he held two bottles of Jack Daniel's by the neck. "All the beer you drink you should be dead by now. Instead, you look like you jumped right off the cover of one of them romance novels your ol' lady writes."

Garvey studied his old friend, trying to decipher his mood, then smirked. "Chalk it up to high metabolism."

"Yeah right. You pulling an all-nighter or what?"

"I was thinking about it."

"Still on the outs with Gwen?"

"Yeah, she's pretty pissed."

"Well, I guess I could make things a little easier on you by getting past my bullshit hang-ups about your former…occupation."

"I'd appreciate that."

Buck strolled closer to Garvey and the bike he was working on. "Yeah, I've been thinking it over and, I figure you're the same guy I've been rolling with for all these years. There's no need to look at you any different. In fact, I reckon I understand you a little better now. What with the guitar and all."

Garvey looked over at the Martin, sitting in its stand, never far from where he stood. "I'm sure you still have a shitload of questions though, huh?"

"You could say that."

Garvey shrugged. "Fire away."

"What happens if the guitar is taken away from you? Like, what if I just grabbed it and walked out of the building?"

"I'd feel pain. Like, having my entire being ripped out of my body."

"I don't follow."

"Alright, you know the comic book character Doctor Strange."

"Fuck yeah, I love that guy."

"It's kind of like the way he would project himself into the astral plane, only for me it feels like a part of me is being torn away from my physical form. Like ripping a bandage off your hairy arm amplified by a million. My soul is anchored to the guitar. Wherever it goes, I have to go with it."

"Shit."

"Yeah."

"So, how old are you? Really?"

Garvey let out a breath, thinking about the question and not really sure how to answer. He lowballed it. "I don't know. I guess I've been around for a few thousand years."

"Holy fuck!" Buck said with eyes wide and jaw unhinged. "So, what about what it says in The Bible?"

"Look, The Bible didn't get everything right. Hell, not even half of it. There's more out there than God and angels and demons. It's fucking way more complicated."

"Jesus, I feel like someone with my limited mental capacity shouldn't be learning this shit."

Garvey laughed. "If it helps, I don't think there's much to learn anymore."

"What do you mean?"

"I've been stuck here in this state for over a hundred years. I met Gwen and we had Elizabeth and Seth, and all this time I've been overly cautious and paranoid about what may come sniffing around. Wondering what kind of monsters would come to threaten my family and make my life miserable. Over the past few days, I've come to the realization that I'm alone here. No one gives a fuck about me or what I do anymore. I'm just a fucking grain of sand on the beach, like everyone else in the world."

"Wow. That's kind of fucked up."

"Yeah. Worst part is that the past twenty-some years I've been with Gwen, I wanted nothing more than to have a normal life. I wanted my kids to have a normal life. I was so busy wishing for it, I didn't realize I had it all along. And I fucking missed it."

Buck placed a comforting hand on Garvey's shoulder. "It's not too late, pal. Lizzy and Seth are still here. Gwen is still here. Fucking do it. Live that normal life, before they age past you and you're left with nothing but your youthful good looks."

"You're right, man." The two men hugged it out and Garvey pulled away to find Buck had a tear rolling down one cheek. "You fucking pussy."

"Shut the fuck up," Buck grumbled.

The big man wiped his cheeks and Garvey pulled a beer from the mini-fridge and held it out to his friend.

"Don't mind if I do."

"So, what do you say?" Garvey asked. "You want to pull an all-nighter with me? You can help me rebuild this beast."

"I'm down for that."

The two men went to work and before long it was like it had always been. Bikes, booze, and deep conversation. Over the years their debates had ranged from "could a Jedi take Wolverine?" to "What was the best chili recipe to follow?" (Buck's included ample amounts of Jack Daniel's). Eventually, Buck cracked open one of the bottles of Jack and they soon became too incoherent with booze and laughter to work on the motorcycle.

"Hey, you think Petie is still in the shop?" Buck asked. The tattoo parlor across the street was a frequent stop for all the guys in the club and Petie was the preferred artist for both Garvey and Buck.

"Shit, I don't know," Garvey answered.

"Let's go check it out. Get some fresh ink. Oh, we should get matching tats." This last part was spoken with the excitement of a small child.

Garvey laughed. "You sound so gay."

"C'mon, man."

"It's late, Buck. If she *is* over there, she's not going to want to hang around for us till the wee fucking hours of the morning."

"We'll give her a big fucking tip then," Buck suggested, adamant about getting new ink.

Garvey shook his head. "Fine, we'll go see if she's willing, but we're *not* going to keep her from anything. Deal?"

"Deal, man. Let's go."

And they went. On the way out, Garvey grabbed his guitar and slung it on his back, while Buck finished off the first bottle of Jack and brought the other one along. Petie was there, finishing work on a customer, and she agreed to set them up with something small after Buck showed her the one-hundred-dollar bill he'd give her on top of charges for services rendered.

Garvey opened the fresh bottle of Jack and threw back a big swig. It was the last thing he remembered doing.

Garvey came to on the couch in his shop, a puddle of drool staining the tan-colored cushion beneath him. The morning sun shone through the grimy windows, piercing his eyes with its brilliance and detestable cheerfulness. With careful, steady movements, Garvey began the task of pulling himself upright and moving off the couch.

A loud snore alerted him to Buck's presence. The big man was sprawled out on the hard, concrete floor, an empty bottle of Jack clutched under one arm as if it were a stuffed animal, security from the darkness of night. Garvey nudged his friend with the toe of his oil-splattered work boot and Buck was coaxed into wakefulness.

"Oh, Jesus," Buck called out. "My back. Fuck, my back is so stiff."

"Yeah, I think we're too old to be drinking like we did last night."

"I didn't think age matters much to you."

Garvey gave the big man a smirk. "Alright, smart-ass."

"Oh, I feel like I'm gonna barf, but I can't fucking move."

"You better start moving, I just cleaned this bay yesterday. I don't need you fouling it up with the contents of your belly."

"I'm going," Buck said with a grunt. "Give an old man a hand, why don't you?"

"You're not old. Fifty is the new forty. Stone Phillips said that."

"Then it must be true," Buck said just before he dry-heaved.

"Let's move a little quicker maybe," Garvey said, steering his friend toward the bathroom.

It was close, but he made it to the toilet just as he tossed his cookies. Garvey stood outside the door and tried hard not to look, trying harder to block out the sound. Through all of his many years, through all of the grotesque things he'd born witness to, Garvey was still somehow a sympathetic puker.

Buck finished up and came out of the bathroom on his knees. After wiping his mouth on a towel, he looked up at Garvey and said simply, "My arm hurts."

"Heart attack?"

"No, man. Not that kind of hurt."

Garvey's brow furrowed as he tried to recall why Buck's arm would hurt. Carefully, he pulled the sleeve of his own tee-shirt up and found plastic wrap taped to his right bicep. Buck pulled the sleeve back on his left arm to find plastic wrap taped to his arm as well. The two of them pulled the wrap off at the same time to reveal they had indeed got matching tattoos the night before.

"It's fucking beautiful," Buck said, in awe of the fresh ink.

Garvey didn't share the sentiment. If he were to be honest with himself, though the quality was good, the subject itself was horrid and displeasing to his eye. There, on the bicep of each man, was a guitar (much like the one he was burdened to carry around with him) with angel wings, seemingly resting on a bed of clouds. Still, to avoid offending his old friend, Garvey nodded and smiled. "It's badass."

Just as they were studying their new ink, Huff walked in through the door that connected the shop and stopped in his tracks at the sight of the matching tattoos. "What the fuck? You guys got matching tats without me?"

"Shit," Buck said and turned to Garvey for help with an explanation.

Truth was, Huff had been rolling with them for less than five years, and although he believed himself as close to Garvey as Buck was, he actually annoyed the president of the club most of the time. "It's a new idea we've been kicking around. Five-year ink."

"Hey, my five-year anniversary is coming up in November," Huff said hopefully.

"There ya go," Buck added. "You'll be able to get yours then."

"Fuck yes!" Huff shouted.

Garvey and Buck left the shop and walked toward their motorcycles, parked around the side of the building. "Nice save," Buck said.

Garvey laughed. "I swear that guy has smoked himself into a perpetual altered state."

"So, what now? You working today?"

"Yeah, I just need to get cleaned up before I start. Mind if I use your place?"

"Nah, man, go ahead. Still not ready to see Gwen?"

"Not quite yet. I need to get her together with Seth and work all this shit out, but after doing some serious thinking on it, I think it may be time for me to stop acting like an idiot. The paranoia, the sleeping in a different place every night. It's got to stop. I need to be a normal husband and father for a change."

"Well, good for you," Buck said with a pat on Garvey's shoulder.

Garvey looked at his friend sternly. "That also means I have to stop fucking around with the illegal shit. And the club."

There was a sad confusion on the big man's face. "What?"

"I'm stepping down as president. Seth is coming with me. He doesn't know that yet and he sure as hell isn't going to be happy about it, but that's the way it has to be. I'll be a part of this garage alone once I step down."

"Jesus," Buck said, running a hand through his long, graying hair. "This is a lot to spring on a guy with a wicked hangover."

Garvey couldn't help but smile. "Buck."

"Yeah."

"You will be taking over as president of the club. Are you ready for that?"

Buck swallowed hard, but held his chin up a little higher. "Yeah. Yeah, I can handle it."

"Good. Look, I'm not going to just throw you to the wolves. I'll be sure to ease you into things. Any advice, anything you need, I'll do my best to help you."

Buck nodded and embraced Garvey. "Thanks, brother. Thanks for having faith in me."

"Alright. Let's curb the bromance. I'll be back in a few."

Buck pulled away and Garvey was sure he saw tears in the big man's eyes again. Once he was on his bike, Garvey pulled out of the parking lot without another word. In his heart, he knew he was making the right decision, even if he felt terrified in his gut.

# 15

## Marion

Marion sat down at her desk and looked over the stack of evidence she'd compiled over the last few days. The case wasn't the one she'd like to be working on, but she really had little choice in the matter. A string of grisly murders had been committed on the far south side of Atlanta. It appeared there was a serial killer on the loose and local law enforcement had been unable to catch the nut case responsible, thus the F.B.I. was forced to get involved.

The victims were all very similar. College girls, early twenties, blonde, all found raped and missing their fingers on the left hand. Marion was working with a profiler, and a crime scene team to try and connect the dots while gathering every last scrap of physical evidence they could get their hands on. They didn't appear to be getting close. At least it was local.

In the meantime, Marion had managed to keep Adrian Dillard on retainer as a consultant and the expert on all things supernatural was digging deep into old cases, looking for any similar to the Guitar Case, as they'd come to call it. So far, he hadn't turned up much.

Marion had visited Agent Mann in the hospital on the previous day. Her partner was healing well, but he looked pale. Sullen. Weaker than he should be since it'd been a week since the attack. She couldn't help but worry about him.

At home, her honeymoon seemed to still be going with the sex between her and her new husband frequent and steamy. James had stamina and highly pleasing equipment to work with, she only wished the hours out on the job wouldn't interfere. She knew it would eventually slow down and a big reason that it would was going to stem from her exhaustion or the disturbing things she had to deal with or both. Catching killers comes at a high price.

Through all of this, Marion found the case of the murdered guitar player (angel, her mind insisted) was always at the forefront of her thoughts. It was the case she should be devoting her full time to, yet she was restricted by someone with far more authority than Director Fuller. That in itself was a case that needed looking into. Why would someone with that kind of power want to protect a murderer? Just who was this killer and who did he have in his corner?

Marion was almost afraid to find out, but she could speculate based on what she knew. There was a man that had shot and killed an angel, and there was a person in D.C. who wanted this man left alone. Why? The only reason she could think of was; this man was sanctioned by a top government official to take out the guitar-playing angel. Did that mean this person in Washington had some connections to the supernatural?

A knock came at Marion's office door, breaking her train of thought and startling her slightly. Looking up, she found Adrian Dillard leaning in. "Hey, I may have found something. You got a minute?"

"Yeah, come on in. Shut the door."

Dillard shut the door and sat down across from her. He held three file folders in his hand.

"What did you find?" Marion asked, barely able to contain her eagerness.

"I got three cases here that are pretty similar to our guitar player. Phoenix, Arizona. Tacoma, Washington. Dover, Delaware. There are more internationally, but my hacking skills only go so far."

"You're a hacker too?"

"Very much an amateur in that field, I had a buddy that was a wiz at that shit and taught me some things before he went to prison. I *did* know enough to uncover these."

Marion opened the Phoenix file and read over the police report. Another guitar player, this one with a Gibson Les Paul who played on a portable amp at local park for donations. On October third of last year, he finished playing for the day and was on his way home as night was falling. He owned no car and walked to his apartment every night, but on this night, he was followed. Two witnesses say the man that shot him in front of his apartment wore a nice suit and looked as if he were from the middle east.

The Gibson player had no real identity. No dental records, no fingerprints. He died from a single gunshot wound to the back of the head. The slug that was pulled from the wound was made of gold. Autopsy photos showed large scars on his back and strange organs that couldn't be found in the average human body.

Tacoma was another struggling musician. A master at a six-string acoustic. He played a lot of coffee houses and blues clubs, making a decent living from a fairly large fan following. Those that knew the man said he went by initials only (C.C.) and all said the same thing; he was an incredible guitar player and, though he'd received many offers for a record deal, he always turned them down, saying the art is far more enjoyable through live shows.

He was found in his apartment this past February with a gold slug in his brain. There were no witnesses to this crime. No dental records, no fingerprints. Scars on the back. Strange, extra organs.

Dover was a homeless man. His homeless drinking buddies said he always had a banjo strapped to his back and would often entertain them with his skillful finger work on the instrument. Of course, he was incredibly talented and was unwilling to use his gift to gain money or fame. The homeless musician had gone missing for a week and when his friends started looking in his usual sleeping spots, he was found under an overpass, fatally shot in the head.

Gold slug. No dental records or fingerprints. Scars on back. Extra organs.

All three cases had one more thing in common. The instrument was the only thing taken.

Marion sat back in her chair, letting it all soak in.

"What do you think?" Adrian asked.

"There are more, you say?"

"Looks like it. I can't get to them though."

"This guy's a serial killer. Of angels."

"Fallen angels," Dillard corrected.

"Right."

"What's the move?"

"I'm going to take this to Fuller. Maybe we can get back on this."

"You think so."

"I hope so. This guy needs to be stopped."

"Does he?"

Marion looked at her expert with surprise.

Dillard continued. "I'm just saying; there's something biblical going on here. At least that's the feeling I get. Is this something we mortals should be getting involved in?"

"Well, this asshole killed two mortals here in Atlanta, that puts him on my shit list."

"Okay," Dillard said with a shrug. "I'm with you. All the way."

"Good, let's go see Fuller."

Marion and Dillard caught Director Fuller as he was heading back to his office with a fresh cup of coffee. "Director," Marion called out. "Can we speak to you?"

Fuller looked from her to Dillard, a suspicious glint in his eyes. He knew this wasn't about the Atlanta serial killer. At least not the one she was *supposed* to be working on. "My office."

Fuller ushered the two of them into his office and shut the door. "What is it?"

Marion placed the three file folders on Fuller's desk. "We've uncovered three more cases that are clearly related to the Guitar Case. I'd like to request permission to pursue this case further."

Fuller let out a frustrated sigh as he picked up the files and began to read through them. "Very compelling evidence, Agent Oli...sorry, Agent Kern, but I've told you already, you have no clearance to continue on with this case." The director gave her a look that said this was all playacting. That he was putting on a show as if his office was bugged and his superiors were listening. Then he added a sheet of paper to the folder and handed it back with a nod. "Keep working the case you've been assigned."

Marion left the office and glanced inside the folder at the new page. Dillard waited patiently. Finally, Marion looked up from the folder. "Let's get lunch."

"Yeah. I could go for a bite."

Marion didn't speak until they reached the parking garage. "There was a report that came in that may have nailed down the location of our shape-shifting car salesman. We're going to check it out."

"And if we find Dave the Demon?"

"We confront him."

# 16
## Elizabeth

"I am so fucking nervous," Elizabeth said. She let out an exasperated breath that blew the hair away from her face.

Megan Brad was a fellow waitress and had become the closest thing to a friend Elizabeth had been able to find since her move to Cincinnati. They still had their differences, but both disliked most of the other women at the restaurant. Megan was in her apartment now to help with Elizabeth's hair and makeup before her big date with Jude.

Megan chuckled. "Seriously, I have never seen you like this."

"I've never had a guy like this interested in me."

"I got to admit, he is one handsome motherfucker."

"You're not helping."

"I'm just saying. Leave it to me, by the time I'm done with your makeup, you will be at least a little closer to being in his league."

"You are such a bitch," Elizabeth laughed.

It was true. She didn't see herself as beautiful or hot. Maybe pretty on the right day. In the right light. She often wondered why her angelic lineage hadn't conjured up more appealing features than what she had ended up stuck with. Add the clumsy awkwardness on top of that and it was a wonder she'd ever had a date at all. As it stood, she'd only had a handful. And she'd only had sex eight times with three different guys.

Megan on the other hand. "So, are you going to give it up on the first date?"

Elizabeth's mouth opened in shock. "No!" she exclaimed. Then after some consideration, "Would you?"

Megan shrugged. "It really depends on how the date goes. If I find the guy attractive, but don't see a relationship evolving, I will. If the guy seems like a possible keeper, I'll make him wait two more dates. That way he doesn't think I'm a slut."

"But you are a slut."

"Fuck you."

"What if the guy is neither? He isn't attractive or a keeper?"

Megan seemed to think this over a moment. "I guess it depends on how horny I am." They both laughed at this. Then Megan said, "Question is, how do you feel about this guy?"

"I think he's pretty amazing," Elizabeth admitted. She could feel the blush to her cheeks. "He's so charming and funny. Successful. Handsome. Somehow, he's in incredible shape despite downing burgers, fries and beer daily."

"High metabolism I bet."

"I like him a lot."

"Yeah, you've been walking around with a goofy smile on your face since he started coming in. So, my advice to you, make him wait till the third date."

"Right. I will."

"OK. You're done."

Elizabeth studied herself in the mirror. Megan had done a great job. Her hair and makeup were perfect and she did feel a little better about herself. It helped that she knew Jude genuinely liked her. She could see it in the way he looked at her.

There was a knock at the door and Elizabeth felt a nervous flutter through her stomach. "That's him."

Megan held out her hands. "Just play it cool."

"Play it cool. Got it."

"And try not to do anything too...Elizabethy."

Elizabeth smirked at her friend and flipped her the bird.

After one last look in the mirror, Elizabeth straightened her tight, black dress (which was borrowed from Megan) and went to answer the door. Jude looked as dashing as ever in his grey suit and red tie. He took her in and seemed genuinely stunned. "You look incredible."

Another blush. "Thank you. You look very handsome."

Megan cleared her throat from behind her. "Oh, this is my friend, Megan."

"Pleased to meet you," Jude said, though his eyes never left Elizabeth. This made her like him even more. Of the two of them, it had always been Megan, with her dark eyes and hair, and exotic, tan skin that garnered the attention of men.

Megan walked past them and out the door. "Well, I should be going. You two have a great night."

Once she was out in the hall and out of Jude's line of sight, she turned back and mouthed the words "So hot" to Elizabeth. She followed this up by biting her lower lip.

"Goodnight Megan," Elizabeth said to hurry her along.

Megan left them and for a moment, Elizabeth and Jude only stared at each other. Finally, Jude held his arm out for her to take. "Well then. Shall we?"

She took his arm and walked into the hall, locking the door behind her.

Jude took her to a French restaurant in the middle of town. She'd never heard of it and was unable to pronounce the name, but the atmosphere was lovely, and Elizabeth was giddy with excitement about the chance to try such a new experience. Her dates in the past had consisted of a trip to Taco Hut and action movies. She got the feeling Jude was more experienced in impressing a woman than her previous would-be suitors.

The maître d' showed them to their table, where Jude pulled her chair out for her. She sat and nervously pushed a strand of her red hair behind her ear. Jude sat across from her and smiled.

She smiled back. "I don't imagine you're going to find a big, greasy hamburger on this menu."

"No, we may have to stop at a fast-food joint later."

They both laughed, but Elizabeth had no doubt he was serious. The man had a fondness for burgers that was somewhat alarming. She looked over the menu to find it was all in French. "I'm not sure what to order. I can't read this."

"May I order for you?"

"Please."

The waiter came to the table and Jude rattled off several sentences in French. The waiter bowed and left them.

Elizabeth said, "So, you're handsome, charming, and multilingual."

"Well-traveled. When I was in college I backpacked through Europe. It was an enlightening experience."

"Impressive."

"Thank you."

Elizabeth shook her head. "I feel like we're on different social wavelengths here. I'm just a Midwestern girl, born and raised. I've never traveled beyond Kentucky. And that's just because it's right across the bridge from Cincinnati."

"Perhaps that is one of the things I like about you. And perhaps

you just need someone to show you what this world has to offer."
Elizabeth liked the sound of that.

"Are you that someone?"

"Could be. We should probably get through the first date though."

She laughed at this and felt a little more at ease.

"So, what do you like to do, Elizabeth?" Jude asked. "When you aren't working, how do you like to spend your time?"

She exhaled, blowing the hair away from her face. "This is the part that usually scares the date away."

"Oh? Why is that?"

"I may have a strange hobby."

"How strange?"

She held her thumb and forefinger together, leaving only about an inch between them. "Just a little strange."

He chuckled. "Are you going to tell me what it is?"

Elizabeth smiled. "We should probably get through the first date before tackling that subject as well."

"Fair enough," he said softly and smiled in return.

And there it was. She liked him. She liked him a lot.

# 17
## Garvey

John Garvey pulled his motorcycle up into the driveway of the little ranch house he owned but rarely slept in. After tonight, all that would change. As he leaned the bike on its kickstand and adjusted the guitar on his back, the rumble of a truck split through the sleepy neighborhood and Seth pulled into the driveway beside him.

"Since when do we have family meetings?" Seth asked, slamming the door on the old pickup.

"Since now," Garvey responded. Then added playfully, "Now shut the fuck up and get inside with your mother."

"Alright, alright."

Left alone, Garvey took a moment to look up and down the street, considering his life spent playing it safe, always on the lookout, always expecting the unexpected. He listened. The only sound that came back to him was that of a dog barking two streets over and the chirp of crickets as evening fell into place, cradling the cookie-cutter houses in a blanket of darkness.

He felt like a fool.

It had been here all this time. A peaceful life with a good woman. Kids he could have watched grow up instead of seeing only fleetingly. A loving family he let go to waste. It was time to stop waiting.

Garvey entered the house and found that Seth and Gwen were waiting in the living room. Their eyes raised to meet his as he rounded the sofa and took a seat in the recliner.

"What's going on?" Gwen asked.

"I wanted to get you two together to discuss some things. I only wish Elizabeth was here."

"I could call her," Seth suggested.

"I texted her earlier," Gwen offered. "She has a date tonight she seemed very excited about."

"We can get her up to speed later. For now, we need to talk about some changes that are going to occur. Effective immediately."

Garvey's wife and son shared a concerned look with each other and then turned back to him.

"I'm out," Garvey said plainly. "No more club. No more drugs or guns. Just the shop."

The two of them only stared for a moment.

"Does that mean I'm in charge now?" Seth asked excitedly.

"No, Seth. You're out too."

Seth stood. "What? That's such bullshit!"

"It's the way it has to be."

"I just got in the fucking club, now you're telling me I'm out?"

"I'm sorry, Seth."

Seth turned on his mother with rage in his eyes. "This is your doing, isn't it?"

"Seth, it's just too dangerous," Garvey said.

"Fuck!" Seth shouted and kicked over the coffee table. He started for the door, but John stepped in front of him. "Give me your gun."

"What gun?"

"You know damn well what gun I'm talking about. Buck gave you one when you became a pledge. Hand it over."

Seth reached under his shirt and pulled the gun from his waistband, then slapped it into his father's outstretched hand.

John looked at him with concern. "I'm giving up my gun too, son."

"Giving up your gun?" Seth said, incredulous. "What about that fucking guitar strapped to your back? Huh? You can rip a motherfucker to shreds with that fucking thing. Are you giving *that* up too?"

"You know I can't."

"Right." Seth pushed past John to the front door.

Gwen stood. "Seth, don't go. Stay and talk about this."

"Fuck talking. I need a drink."

Then he was gone. Gwen sat and dropped her head into her hands. "Fuck."

"He just needs some time to calm down," Garvey said. "I'll talk some sense into him."

"You didn't think to talk with me alone about all this first?"

"What's to talk about? This is what we've been working toward all our lives. Isn't this what you want?"

"Of course it is. You just kind of sprung it on us."

John ran a hand down his beard. "Yeah, I guess I did."

Gwen wrapped her arms around him and he reciprocated. "Are

you sure about this?"

John considered her question. His mind told him it wasn't time. Caution was still required. But those were old thoughts. Old fears embedded in his psyche over the course of centuries. It was time to let them go. "Yes. It's time."

# 18
## Marion

An abandoned warehouse was hardly an original place to hide out. Marion and Adrian sat across the street from the place in the SUV. Adrian was absentmindedly playing with a Zippo lighter, clicking it open and clanking it shut. After a few minutes, Marion looked at him with annoyance.

"Sorry," he said, sliding the lighter back into his shirt pocket. "Nervous habit."

"We've been sitting here almost an hour, what's to be nervous about?"

"I guess I'm feeling a little restless as well."

"Maybe you could tell me more about those ghosts you mentioned."

Adrian let out a long breath. "They came to me in the middle of the night. Pulled me through my own bed into some strange world. I found myself on a speeding steam locomotive. The very train the nine of them had died on. I knew my son Luke was somewhere on the train, so I started moving forward from car to car and realized all the passengers were dead people. They all moved about as if they were alive. Stuck in some endless loop and doomed to die over and over again as the train derailed.

"Eventually, I came to the front of the train, and that's where I found them. Luke, surrounded by these nine creepy ass ghost kids. The leader of the bunch was named Jeffery, he came forward and told me they were planning on using Luke to channel these special abilities through. Like a conduit. Each had their own gift, see? And they were gathered over a hundred years ago to face off against some ancient evil deity. At least that was the story they were giving me.

"Anyway, I told them to use me instead. If it had to be done, leave Luke out of it and take me. Next thing I know, I wake up back in my bed with these spirits kicking around in my head. I still don't know exactly how it all worked, but they started appearing to me one by one. Training me in their gifts and preparing me for this knockdown, drag-out fight with a god."

"Jesus," Marion said. "What kind of gifts are you talking about?"

Adrian gave her an odd look. As if reconsidering letting her in on all the madness of his past. When he finally spoke, his tone was different. Sombre. "Jeffery could see the dead. Emma could control fire. Then there was shapeshifting, superhuman strength, telekinesis, earth, and water. This doesn't all sound crazy to you?"

"Well, yeah. Doesn't mean I don't believe. The Daylight Slayer alone was enough to open my mind up to such things, now we have demons and angels and a serial killer that's targeting the latter."

Adrian laughed. "Fuck. When you put it that way, I think maybe we both need to be committed."

Marion giggled at this. "So, what happened with these ghost children?"

"Well, without going into too much of the crazy details, they turned out to be on the wrong side of the fight. I was able to get rid of them and I tried to return to a normal life, but I wasn't able to leave the knowledge of these things behind. I started digging into the supernatural and never looked back. Problem was, I became so obsessed that it ruined my marriage. The wife left me and took both the boys with her."

"Adrian, I'm so sorry."

"It happens. I get my time with the boys, of course, but one can't help to look back and wonder. What if things had been different?"

Marion didn't quite know what to say to this. Up to this point, her relationship with Adrian had been purely professional. She knew he'd been divorced but had no idea about the circumstances surrounding it. Luckily, as she was struggling for the right thing to say, Dave the demon appeared. He came around the corner of the warehouse and entered through a side door.

"Is that our guy?" Adrian asked.

"That's him."

"What's our move?"

"*Your* move is to stay in the car."

"What?"

"You're a consultant, not an agent. I can't bring you in and put you in danger. You're a citizen."

"You can't go in alone."

"Not like I can call for backup. We're not even supposed to be here."

"I can be your back up."

"I'll be fine," Marion said opening the door. "I have a gun."

"Yeah, how well did that help you the last time?"

She shut the door on him but knew he had a point and as she walked to the door on the side of the abandoned building, her gun now in her hand, his words stuck in her mind and increased her trepidation.

Marion pulled the door open and silently cursed the squealing hinges. She let the door close and shroud her in total darkness. For a moment, she only listened. No sound came to her, but the hollow hum of an empty warehouse. She reached for the small flashlight attached to her belt and turned it on. The beam from the light revealed an empty dock floor with rows of tall, empty racks off to the right. Marion had the sudden urge to bolt from the place, but the image of her partner's blood spurting all over her clothes reinforced her resolve.

The demon could be anywhere and here she was giving herself away with a flashlight. There came the sound of something metal hitting the floor from the other side of the racks. Marion aimed the flashlight at the floor and used a finger to cover most of the light's beam. Just enough so she could see where she was going and hopefully not give away her position. In her other hand, she held her 9mm pistol at the ready.

Marion picked an aisle randomly and moved quietly along the racks. She picked up more sounds coming from the far side, then saw a dull glow coming from around the corner. Marion killed her own light and put it away, freeing her other hand to help steady her gun. She edged closer to the corner. The light seemed to be coming from a small lamp. Her heart was beating fast in her chest as she prepared to take the corner. Dave the demon kept rummaging away, unaware of her presence just behind him. Finally, she rounded the corner with her gun up, but the demon was on the move before she could get a bead on him.

The wind was knocked out of from her lungs and she was sent sprawling across the floor. The demon was on her. Three shots were fired from her gun into his gut, but they had no effect. She raised her free hand and took hold of his throat, just as he snapped at her with those needle-like teeth. The spittle flew from his mouth and Marion could feel it cover her face. She tried to raise the gun again and he knocked it away. Her grip on his throat did nothing. He was forcing his awful mouth closer to her face.

Marion knew she was about to die.

She had failed her partner. Failed her captain. She thought of her new husband, who in the next few seconds would become a widower. She was stupid to come in alone. Stupid to think she could fight this thing.

From somewhere to her right came the sound of a zippo clicking open. Then the warehouse erupted in light.

## 19

## Judas

The date had gone far better than Judas could have hoped. At least so far. Possibly too well, in fact. There was a quality about Elizabeth that was undeniable. He was drawn to her and still wasn't sure if it was a natural connection between the two of them or some angelic ability she exuded unwittingly. Something that only beings that have been to Heaven or Hell would even pick up on.

The evening was coming to a close and Judas pulled the car up to her door. He got out, rounded the car, and opened the door for her. She walked to the steps that led up to her apartment building and turned to him. He followed, the urge he'd felt all night to kiss her now rising to a roaring crescendo.

"I had a wonderful night," Elizabeth said. "One wouldn't think dinner and a museum would be the ideal date, but you made it work somehow. I'd have to say it was the best date I've ever been on."

The wind blew a strand of her hair out of place. Judas reached out and gently pushed it back behind her ear. An expression of lust came over her at his touch and he knew she wanted the kiss as much as he did. He leaned in and touched his lips to hers and she welcomed him. Parting her lips slightly and running just a hint of tongue into his mouth.

Then she pulled away with a moan. She looked at her hand on his chest as if just realizing she'd placed it there, then pulled it away. "Alright, I'm going to invite you up, but that doesn't mean…you know…anything. I'm just not ready for the date to end."

"I will be a perfect gentleman, I promise."

"Okay. Plus, I think I'm comfortable showing you my strange hobby and unique beliefs."

"I'm of an open mind."

"I believe you. On both counts."

Elizabeth took his hand and led him up the stairs and through the door. The hallway had the same musty smell that all apartment buildings seemed to share. It was a smell that brought unpleasant images to Judas' mind. A different musty hallway in a different state. A bullet sent into the head of another target.

Judas shook the thoughts away as Elizabeth slid her key into the deadbolt lock and let them inside. Judas had only glanced at the apartment when he'd picked her up earlier in the evening. Looking upon it now, he found the place cozy. Not a very large living area, but the plush, maroon-colored furniture was arranged in a way that utilized the space. The living room gave way to a small kitchen and a short hallway held a bathroom and a single bedroom.

Thankfully, the apartment smelled of baked goods rather than the mustiness of the hall. Judas could see a couple of wax warmers placed strategically to give off the scent.

"Coffee?" Elizabeth asked. "Please."

"Have a seat. Make yourself comfortable."

Judas moved to the couch and sat down. The coffee table in front of him held no magazines, but there were two books. A collection of the works of Edgar Allan Poe and another with the works of H.P. Lovecraft. Judas picked the latter up and flipped through it a bit as he talked. "So far, I can see no reason someone should think you strange. You have a love for the macabre when it comes to literature, but I hardly think that's out of the ordinary."

"Well, I try to keep the evidence of just how deep that love goes out of the living room, just in case I'm entertaining. My bedroom is where all the really good stuff is. How do you take your coffee?"

"Sugar and cream, please."

She brought the coffee to him and sat it on the table. "I like how you embrace everything that's bad for your health, like greasy burgers and sugar, but you may pay for these things when you get older."

It occurred to Judas that the only way he'd have a chance to grow older would be by killing the woman's father, and he had a sudden urge to tell her everything and see what came of it. This urge was fleeting and he re-gathered his thoughts. "Well, I believe in living life to its fullest until the doctors tell you to stop."

She laughed at this and sipped her coffee. "I know it's just the first date, but I feel like we have a real thing going on here. Like, a natural connection."

Judas looked into her eyes. "I'd be lying if I said I didn't feel it too. There's something about you I find mesmerizing." And this statement was true. A fact that Judas found concerning. It was something that had grown increasingly concerning since he'd first laid eyes on her.

For a moment, they could only stare into each other's eyes. Judas felt he could be lost in those deep brown eyes of hers. It was Elizabeth that broke the trance. "Okay, it's time I show you."

She stood and held out her hand. Judas took it and followed her toward the closed bedroom door. She looked at him one last time, a sly grin touched her lips, then opened the door. Judas stepped inside and took it all in. Lining one bookcase was a large collection of horror movies, and some of these titles were represented by matching posters around the walls. On the nightstand was a deck of tarot cards next to a mound of marijuana and a pipe. On the bed was another book, this one a weighty tomb on the religion of Wicca. All in all, Judas found nothing about it overly strange. Even with all that he knew and all he'd experienced; he was aware that the Christian God wasn't the only god out there.

"None of this seems all that strange," he said to Elizabeth. "If anything, I find you even more alluring. All this only adds to your individuality."

"I'm so glad you feel that way. Though, the hobby I really worry about scaring you away is here." She gestured to the wall where several sheets of paper hung. On the surface of each, charcoal had been rubbed to cover the entirety of the page. Judas studied them a moment and it came to him what they were.

"Gravestone rubbings," he said.

"Yes. I especially like to go at night. I look for the oldest, most interesting markers to take rubbings from. These are only some of my favorites. I have several more in the file drawers here."

They were intriguing, Judas had to admit. Some were from the late 19th century, while others had peculiar quotes. "Elizabeth, there is nothing here that would scare me away."

Judas turned to find she stood right next to him. He looked down into her brown eyes. A brown so deep they were very nearly black, and he kissed her again. And this time, they kept kissing. He pulled her closer to him, relishing the feel of her body against his, and soon they moved to the bed. Judas felt something for her he'd never experienced before in all his many years and the love they made matched that feeling.

# 20
## Adrian

In the dim light given off by the small office lamp, Adrian saw the demon was on Marion as soon as he rounded the corner. He casually pulled the Zippo lighter from his pocket and flicked it open. A strike of the flint brought a flame to life and Adrian used it to build a powerful attack. The flame shot from his hand and hit the demon full force in his side, spinning him off the FBI agent. Adrian hit him again and the flames engulfed Dave the demon. The creature screeched in pain and Adrian hit him a third time.

Marion was up on her elbows watching all of this with a look of shock on her face. Adrian kept the flames going, a stream of fire belching from his hand as if from the barrel of a flamethrower, until the demon stopped moving and burned against the wall.

"What the fuck?" Marion managed.

"I *did* mention I retained all of the abilities after the nine ghosts were gone. Right?" He helped her to her feet, and she stared down at the blackened body on the floor, covering her nose and mouth with one hand at the stench of burned flesh.

"Is he dead?" Marion asked.

"Probably not. Only sure way to kill these fuckers is to remove the head." He pulled the leg of his jeans up and slid a hunting knife from the sheath strapped to his calf, holding it in the light for Marion to inspect. "Silver blade, serrated. Going through burned flesh, should take no time at all."

"Jesus Christ!"

"Give me some light."

Marion looked around nervously, as if she expected another attack, then shone a light on Dave the demon from both her flashlight and cell phone. The flames had died out, leaving a charred husk.

"This is going to be unpleasant," Adrian said, perhaps stating the obvious. He got to one knee and placed the serrated side of the blade against the demon's neck. The blackened skin gave a cracking sound, like a fork into fried chicken, and the blade sunk easily into the pink flesh beneath. The blood that sprayed from the wound was nearly as black as the burned skin. When he hit bone there was some resistance, but he sawed the blade back and forth to get through to the tender flesh on the other side.

Finally, the head separated from the body and Adrian stood and kicked it across the floor. "Alright. Want to get dinner?"

Back in the SUV, Marion was quiet, and Adrian was afraid she had snapped. He took over driving duties and was heading back toward town. Agent Marion Kern had seen a lot of shit, of that much he knew, but being attacked by a demon and saved by a magic user who then dispatched the demon in the only way one could, it was a full night. Nevertheless, he was hopeful she'd come around.

"We should have moved him," she said suddenly.

Adrian glanced over at her. She still looked a little shaken, but at least she was talking again. "What?"

"The body. We should have taken it somewhere. Hidden it. Right?"

"If anyone comes across him, they'll think he was a homeless guy. Killed by gang initiation or something. There's no evidence we were there. I took care of that." And he had. After Dave the demon was properly dispatched, Adrian had wiped down the surfaces of anything the two of them may have touched and made sure they didn't leave anything behind. He even had the shells from Marion's gun in his pocket.

"I feel like we should have questioned him," Marion said.

"There's no reasoning with a demon in that state. He was obsessed with keeping that guitar and he'd go through anyone who would try to take it from him."

"The guitar," Marion said, as if it had just occurred to her.

"I got it. It's in the back."

They drove on in silence for a moment before Marion spoke again.

"Tell me about the abilities."

Adrian didn't like telling people his secret. It had the potential to place a huge target on his back and bring the attention of some very nasty beings. Nonetheless, he'd used a magic in front of this woman, and he knew she was someone he could trust to keep things quiet.

"When the ghosts left, their abilities stayed with me. There were originally ten children, ten magics. One had survived the accident that had killed them. The missing ability became their weakness.

After the dust settled, I was charged with keeping the abilities. The Keeper of the Ten was a title that went back through the ages. While there are those around the world who can tap into one or even two or three of these abilities at a time, for nearly eight-hundred years there had been no Keeper. Until I came along. One such magic user was the guy in New York City a couple years back. You know, the one who saved all those people during the terrorist attack on the Thanksgiving Day Parade."

"The Goat."

"Yeah, that's what they called him. Wore that freaky goat mask. He used superhuman strength to save a lot of people and take out the bomber. One of the ten magics. There are people out there who can move things with their minds, manipulate fire, see ghosts, pull giant rocks from the ground, read minds, heal illnesses and wounds, change their appearance to look like other people or even nightmarish creatures. Then there's me."

"And you can…?"

"I can do all of those things."

"Holy shit."

"This is not something I broadcast. There are powerful beings out there in the world. I'm a threat to them and their plots. If they found out I was The Keeper, they'd come for me."

"Your secret is safe with me," she said, and despite the new information introduced to her, she seemed to be returning to her old self. "Have you often been involved in such brutal practices?"

"Yeah, unfortunately. I was running with a werewolf hunter for a while up in N.Y.C. Guy was a twisted motherfucker. It wasn't enough to kill these things, he liked to torture them as well."

"Werewolves?" Marion said in disbelief.

"Yeah. Actually, falls under the shape-shifting ability. There are also witches, most of them are talented in one of the elemental magics. The majority of vampires were wiped out a few years back, but there are some still around. They seem to be making a resurgence."

"Holy shit."

"There's much, much more."

"I think I've heard enough." Marion looked as though she were going to be sick. "Funny how none of this came up the last time we worked together."

"Well, that one was new to me. Time travel is something I didn't know much about at the time. Plus, it was such an obscure occurrence, especially considering what created the entire event. One of the craziest things I've ever been a part of."

"Well, that's saying something, I'm sure."

"So, what's our move now?" Adrian asked, eager to change the subject.

"I'll tell Fuller we took Dave down, but leave out the details of how. Since we weren't there in an official capacity, he won't press too hard on how things went down."

"And the guitar?"

Marion pondered this a moment. Adrian wasn't sure if it could be of any use to them at this point. Though it was evidence in a triple homicide, said homicides were being covered up by someone with a lot of influence.

"We'll hang on to it for the time being," Marion finally said. "I'll let Fuller know it's in our possession."

"Okay. So, now we need to hunt down the shooter."

"Yeah. He could be anywhere. We'll check with the car lot in the morning and see if they've figured out which car is missing from their inventory. Whatever tricks Dave pulled, he covered his tracks very well."

Adrian nodded as he pulled into a greasy little diner. "I feel like a burger. You in?"

"I don't think my appetite is going to be back for a while, but a coffee sounds good."

Inside, Adrian ordered the biggest, greasiest burger on the menu. The fact that this craving may be coming from a faint psychic connection with the man they were after was not something he missed.

# 21
## Buck

Morning came to Buck like most mornings did, through an aching haze left behind by another night of whisky and weed. His room was kept dark, thanks to the black, light dampening curtains he had up on the windows, all in an effort to limit the effects of his hangovers and give his pounding head protection from stabbing, morning sunlight.

Snores from beside him alerted him to the presence of a woman in his bed. He got up on one elbow and pushed the blonde hair away from the woman's face. For a moment he had no idea who she was, but the answer came back to him. Jill the waitress from the bar. She was hot. He was proud of himself. At the same time, he also felt as if he may have made an awful mistake. "Never shit where you eat" was a favorite of John Garvey's and here he was on the first day of his presidency banging a waitress at their favorite bar. Oh well. If things got weird, he'd just have Phillis the manager fire her.

Buck rolled out of bed and searched the nightstand for ibuprofen, throwing four in his mouth and washing them down with a half-empty bottle of warm beer. "Fuck," he grumbled. His head began to clear a little as he took a piss, but he knew it would take a morning full of coffee and an afternoon full of water before he was ready to go again tonight.

With coffee brewing, Buck found a pack of bacon in the fridge and whipped up some scrambled eggs to go with it. As he cooked, the blond waitress came stumbling from the bedroom looking exactly how he felt while still managing to be hot as fuck with one of his old Harley shirts swallowing her whole. At the sight of her he thought maybe he'd try to turn her into a regular.

"Morning, darlin'," Buck said. "Coffee? Breakfast?"

"Both please."

Buck poured her a cup and set it in front of her. Then he placed sugar and cream next to the cup and went back to his eggs. His phone chimed on the counter. "Can you check that for me, darlin'?"

"Yeah," Jill pulled the phone to her and squinted at the screen. "Text from Seth. He said he needs to talk to you."

"Shit!" Buck exclaimed. He knew exactly what that was about. He finished the breakfast and, after making a plate for Jill and himself, he picked up the phone and responded. "Come by the shop later."

There was no return text all morning and Buck had to assume the kid was pretty pissed off. He wasn't looking forward to what was sure to be a heated argument with his best friend's hot-headed, asshole kid. As much as he adored Elizabeth, with all of her odd interest and awkwardness, he and Seth had never seen eye to eye on much.

The morning already felt humid. Buck and Jill exited the house to stand in the driveway, where the big biker stopped and looked at the empty concrete in confusion. "Where the fuck is my bike?"

"At the bar, remember." Jill pulled the smartphone from her purse. "We used the Lyft service. We were both pretty fucking lit."

"Right," Buck said, though he didn't remember.

"I'll hit them up again."

After a Lyft ride to the bar, where Buck kissed Jill goodbye and grabbed a handful of ass in the process, his bike was retrieved and he was off to the shop. When he pulled into the parking lot, Seth was already there. His old truck sat in front of one of the bay doors and he leaned against the tailgate, smoking a cigarette. The kid had an uncanny resemblance to James Dean and Buck often envied his way with women. His success rate was staggering. Of course, now Buck knew that John Garvey was an angel, his wife was a knockout, so it stands to reason their kids would be so attractive.

Still, Jill the waitress was a good pull and Buck once again congratulated himself.

Buck cut the engine on his bike and leaned it on the kickstand. Seth was on him before he could even swing his leg over the saddle.

"What the fuck, Buck?" the kid whined. "Why did my dad have this sudden change of heart about the club? You talk him into this shit?"

Buck sighed. "Calm down, junior."

"Don't call me that. You know I hate that."

Buck did know this and it's the very reason he did it. "Kid, you know no one has any sway over your father. Not even your mom." Buck reconsidered this a moment. "Well, maybe your mom. Sometimes."

"I want to know what the fuck happened. Why he all of a sudden had this change of heart?"

"Shouldn't you be talking to him about this?"

"He's in fucking 'what I say goes' mode. Elaborate, Buck. I know he shares everything with you like you're a couple of little teenage girls. Fucking BFFs."

Buck was in the middle of opening the shop for business as Seth talked, but he stopped and looked at the kid. "I know everything."

"Everything what?"

"You know," Buck said, flapping his hand and whistling like a bird.

"What the fuck is that supposed to be?"

Jesus the kid was dense. "I know your dad is an angel."

All of the anger left Seth's face and his expression went slack. "He told you?"

"Yeah. And he also told me that retiring somewhere with your mother has been his ultimate goal all along. Seth, your dad has missed out on a lot of shit over the years because he was worried about the safety of you, your mom, and your sister. He's spent his life scared shitless of what dangers his connection to you three could be brought to your doorstep. And I don't mean drug dealers, I'm talking about nasty biblical motherfuckers that would look to make a name for themselves by taking out a fallen angel."

"Okay, so why the change now?"

"He's come to the realization that he's been worried about nothing. Said the powers-that-be have moved on. So, not only does he feel complete abandonment from that part of his life, he also feels all Cat's in the Cradle over missing out on his family. The guy just wants a normal life at this point. You knew this shit was coming."

"I feel for the guy," Seth said honestly, "but that don't mean he gets to make decisions about *my* life."

"It does when it comes to this club. Face it, you're out kid."

Seth's jaw clenched and his face went red. "Then I'll start my own operation. Fuck this club!"

Buck didn't try to stop the kid. In truth, he thought the little turd had no hope of getting any kind of operation off the ground. There was nothing he could do but let John know what his little fuck of a kid was up to. Buck shook the conversation off and went about his business. With the shop open, he got to work on the line of cars they had on the schedule. Thoughts of Seth's rebellious bullshit flittered out of his mind and soon, he was under a car working on a transmission repair and thinking about Jill's tits.

# 22
## Judas

The morning light shone through the red lace curtains of Elizabeth's bedroom and Judas awoke to the sound of birds chirping outside the window. Looking to his side, he found Elizabeth sleeping soundly, her peaceful face a perfect work of beauty, as if every detail was carved by one of the great renaissance artists. Perfection in pale pastels. He moved behind her and slid an arm around her waist. She moaned and pressed her body against his with a smile on her lips. He kissed the back of her neck and made a trail down her shoulder with his lips.

Elizabeth turned toward him and kissed him lightly on the lips. "I don't want you to smell my morning breath."

He laughed at this and came to the startling realization that he absolutely adored the woman in his arms.

"How about some coffee and pancakes? Then we can come back to bed."

Judas nodded. "I like the sound of that."

Elizabeth climbed out of bed and made her way to the kitchen after a quick trip to the bathroom. A moment of lying in bed and enjoying the scent of Elizabeth that still lingered in the room, then Judas stood and went into the bathroom as well. He was pissing midstream when the shower curtain was slung aside and the man in the bathtub spoke. "What the fuck are you doing?"

Judas jumped and his piss sprayed over the floor. "Fuck! Lou you scared the shit out of me."

"To be fair, that was the desired effect."

"What are you doing here?"

"I wanted an update."

"You couldn't call?"

"I *need* to see how things are moving along for myself, so I thought I'd slide over."

"Slide over?"

"Yeah, I can move about through gates. I still have that much power at my disposal."

"If you can do that, why the fuck do I have to come to D.C. after every job."

Lou shrugged. "Well, I don't like to leave my comfort zone *too* often."

Judas rubbed his temples. The man had always been infuriating. "Can you please go?"

"I'll go in a minute. Are you close to meeting dad yet?"

"We just had our first date."

"And you spent the night?" Lou laughed, clearly amused. "That's good."

"Wait, how did you even know how to find her?"

"I didn't. I know where to find you though. You and I have that kind of connection."

"You have no idea how much I detest you."

Lou considered this, then nodded. "No, I know. I just don't care."

"I'm working on it. Getting closer all the time. There's your update. Now, can you please leave?"

"Fine." Lou stepped back into the bathtub, but stopped and turned back to Judas. His cold eyes were scrutinizing. "Shit. You're falling for this girl, aren't you?"

"Please go."

"You need to remember what's at stake here, old friend. Keep your fucking priorities straight. Don't let yourself be sidetracked by misplaced affection for this woman. It can only end in disaster."

"I know what I'm doing."

Lou lingered a moment longer. "All right. Don't take too long. We have time, but not a ton of it."

"Got it."

Lou slung the curtain closed. When Judas peeked behind it he found only an empty tub. "Asshole."

Judas cleaned up the mess around the toilet, then washed his hands and joined Elizabeth in the kitchen.

"Thought I heard voices back there," she said. "My boss called," he lied.

"Everything okay?"

"Fine. He's a bit of a micro-manager."

"Yuck. I hate that."

The lies were coming easily to Judas. It was something he'd grown increasingly good at since his return, and it was something he never felt bad about. He felt bad now. Elizabeth sat a plate of pancakes on the table and Judas sat in front of it. She then plopped down across from him and they ate, staring into each other's eyes and smiling like love-struck teens. They only made it halfway through the meal before they were up and moving back to the bedroom.

As Judas climbed into bed and took her naked body into his arms, it occurred to him that he in fact had no idea what he was doing.

# 23
## Marion

"What?" Marion was flabbergasted.

"I'm sorry, Marion. You really should have left this alone." Marion's anger flared and she was about to rip Fuller a new one, director or not, but he held up a hand to cut her off. It had been a week since the warehouse incident, and she knew Fuller had swept the whole ordeal under the carpet. There were times that Marion was sure he knew far more about the supernatural cases they came across than he let on. There was never any disbelief or argument about the odd reports she'd file or the wild tales she relayed to him but didn't officially report. Since then, she and Adrian Dillard had continued to dig into the case and the rest of her caseload had gone largely ignored.

"You could use a break," Fuller continued. "I'll have Roth take your caseload. Go, do some traveling. I hear Cincinnati is a nice town."

"Cincinnati?" she asked in confusion.

Fuller picked up a pen and scribbled something on a post-it note.

"Yeah. Head on over there, catch a Reds game, enjoy the nightlife."

Fuller placed his note inside the file folder for the Guitar Case, closed the folder and handed it back to her.

Understanding suddenly dawned on Marion and she smiled slightly as she took the folder, turned, and walked out of the office and into the hallway with Dillard right behind her. They left the office and made their way to the SUV in the parking garage, she opened the folder and read the note inside. "Car spotted in Cincinnati area."

"Not much to go on," Dillard said.

"It'll have to be enough. Ready for a trip to Ohio?"

"As ready as one *can* be," Dillard said with a shrug.

"Alright, I'll get my assistant to arrange a flight." Then she'd have to break the news to her new husband. James understood the inconveniences that came with her job, but he still had a tendency to pout like a toddler when she had to travel. It was something he'd have to get used to and she told him this repeatedly, especially in the months before they got married, but it was easier said than done.

Marion told Adrian Dillard she would text him with the flight information as soon as she got it and called the workday to a close. She dropped him back at his hotel and drove for home, preparing for a big fight. As she did, she thought back to the first time they'd met. She was in the academy in Virginia and he was in the creative writing program at Notre Dame. It was a mutual love of football that had brought them together.

Marion had taken a weekend trip to South Bend, Indiana with friends to catch the game between Army and Notre Dame, having served in the Army before her stint at the Academy, she had become a staunch supporter of the team and was thrilled when her best friend from high school called her up and told her about the extra ticket to the game.

"Call it an early birthday gift," Sydney had said to her over the phone.

Marion had no problem with that. Sydney and Kelly, another friend of theirs, were flying in from Baltimore (their hometown) and had already booked the hotel they'd stay in. Marion arrived early Friday evening and decided she'd wait for her friends in the hotel bar. She'd dropped her bags in her room and needed desperately to relax with a couple of cocktails.

As she strode up to the bar and tried to take the lone open seat, it was pulled away from her by the man in the seat next to it.

"Can't sit here. Seat's taken," the man said. He raised his head and when he turned to look at Marion his jaw went slack and his eyes nearly bulged from his head. "On second thought, have a seat, please."

Marion smiled and looked the man over. He looked like the artsy type, with his trendy clothes and ring-rimmed glasses, at the same time, she found him attractive. Deep brown eyes, a neatly trimmed beard, and skin the color of milk chocolate. The only problem was he was wearing a Notre Dame scarf over his tweed jacket.

"Thanks," Marion said, peeling her jacket off and revealing her Army sweatshirt.

The cute guy shook his head and laughed. "This relationship is already off to a rocky start."

"What makes you think a relationship is in the books?"

"Well, excuse my language, but I'm a pretty charming motherfucker when I want to be."

"Really?" Marion said, finding his last sentence charming in and of itself. Had he planned that or was it completely by accident? Marion suspected it was the latter. "What makes you think I would fall for the drunken, clumsy advances of a Fighting Irish fan?"

"Well, I have something that most don't have."

"What's that?" she asked, fully expecting this stranger next to her to lay claim to having an unusually large cock.

Instead, pointing to his mouth, he said, "This brilliant smile".

And she was hooked. It *was* a brilliant smile. Plus, he *was* charming and intelligent, and had a large vocabulary to fuel both of those qualities.

When her friends showed, Marion gave him her number and the following evening, after Notre Dame gave Army a thorough beat down, the two of them went out for a ton of shit talk and laughs over drinks.

Now, she pulled in the driveway with these happy thoughts in her head and prepared to give him the news. She decided she would follow it up with a roll in the hay. That always seemed to make the medicine go down a little smoother.

The following morning, after a little fight from James that led to a lot of sex after the news of her trip was broken, he kissed Marion and saw her off. She picked Adrian up from his hotel and the two of them returned the SUV to headquarters before having another agent drop them at the airport. There, they waited to board their flight and went over the details of the case. The car lot had finally discovered the missing car from their lot the day after their confrontation with Dave the demon and sent the information over to them.

"Cincinnati is a big town full of black Toyota Camrys," said Dillard. "How are we supposed to find this one?"

"I'll let you know once we get there," said Marion.

"And we don't even know what we're facing. Who the fuck is this guy?"

"That's what I got you for."

"Great."

"We'll get there and get situated. Then we'll do some snooping around and see what comes up. There's a process. Don't worry." This seemed to quell his concerns.

Adrian let out a long sigh and Marion could tell he was on edge, but not necessarily about their lack of any real lead going into Cincinnati. "What is it?"

He spoke in a hushed tone. "You know that Psychic ability I told you about?"

"Yeah."

"Well, it's hard to pick up on things from the mind of a supernatural being. I didn't get much at all from Dave the demon. Slight tremors, but nothing substantial. This guy we're after, I get a gleam here and there."

"So, he's supernatural too?"

"Not quite."

"What does that mean?"

A long pause, then; "I'm not sure. I've only picked up three things. An insatiable love for burgers, a dim hope for a new existence, and a dark and tortured past."

"Well, that doesn't really help us much in the hunt for him."

"No, but it may help in determining motives. Develop a personality, I guess."

"Alright, so is this guy human or not?"

"No, I don't think so. At least, not anymore. He isn't angel or demon either."

"Well, at least we have that going for us. What about these abilities of yours? Do you think he's capable of using one or more?"

"I'm not sure. Though, the gold bullets would suggest he isn't. At least not any of the more powerful ones."

"Do you have a theory at all on what's going on here?"

Adrian seemed to ponder this. "Could be this guy is just a tool. Could be someone dangled the promise of a better life in front of him and sent him on this path that is littered with the bodies of dead fallen angels, not to mention a few innocent bystanders here and there. I don't know, he seems desperate."

"Desperate and armed. That's a bad combination."

# 24
## Garvey

John Garvey was settling into his new life. Sure, he had his moments. A car backfire that sounded like a gunshot. The growl of a large dog that sounded like something more than K-9. All in all, though, things had been quiet.

With Garvey's help, Buck was transitioning smoothly into the role of president of the club. He was taking to it far better than expected and Garvey realized quickly that he should have given his old friend more credit. After all, he'd been the vice president of the club from the beginning. With luck, Garvey figured he'd be out completely within a month.

It was all happening, and beneath the lingering paranoia, John Garvey felt a little giddy.

Of course, the club's suppliers were less than thrilled about the move. They had dealt with Garvey for so long that they were nervous about dealing with anyone else, but they knew Buck and Garvey had given them every assurance that things wouldn't change. Buck had been his understudy for years. They were appeased, but it would take a few months before they really settled back into business as usual.

At home, John and Gwen had rekindled something they hadn't had in a long time. It was almost as if they'd reverted back to the days when they'd first met. The sex between them had always been outstanding, but there was an added passion that had seemingly been forgotten over the years. She often expressed concerns that he'd be less attracted to her once she grew older and he still appeared as if he were no more than thirty. He assured her there was no way that would happen, and he'd meant it. She was the love of his long life and he couldn't conceive of a day where he wouldn't be attracted to her.

It was a strange thing. For the past week, John had got up in the morning, ate breakfast cooked by his wife, kissed her goodbye, and went to work. After a full day at the shop, it was home for dinner with a few beers, then off to bed where he'd make love to his wife and fall asleep. With his wife. In his bed. In his house.

It was the closest thing he'd had to Heaven since, well, Heaven.

Even Elizabeth was settling into a pleasant life in Cincinnati. She had called him one evening with the news that she'd met a wonderful man and that she was falling for him fast. By her accounts, he seemed a perfect gentleman, treated her like a queen, and wasn't scared away by her peculiarities, as she put it. John approved. He wanted nothing more for his daughter than for her to find someone that made her happy, just as any parent would want for their child. She hoped to bring the new boyfriend home soon to meet her parents. John said he couldn't wait.

Seth, on the other hand, was a different story altogether. Since claiming to Buck that he would start his own club and vie for the attention of their suppliers, no one had heard from him. He wasn't answering their calls or responding to texts. John was worried that he'd do something stupid and Gwen was certain he already had. "He rarely goes two days without doing something stupid," she had pointed out.

John knew she was right.

It was with these concerns for his son that he set out after work to check Seth's usual haunts. Several bars, a wings joint, and three tattoo parlors later, no one had seen or heard from Seth in days. Was he even in town? It certainly wouldn't be the first time he'd taken off without telling anyone.

Just what was he up to?

# 25

## Judas

It was shaping up to be a pleasant evening. Judas had left his hotel to find the summer heat had taken a break and the night had just a hint of early fall air. It added to his already high spirits. He keyed the ignition in the black Toyota and slid the gearshift into drive. His destination was a small flower shop down the street, followed by Elizabeth's apartment for their second date.

In the days following their night together, Judas found that all he could do was think of her. The smell of her, the taste of her on his lips, the feel of her body pressed against his. She was truly intoxicating. As a result, he thought little about his reason for getting close to her. Even less about Lou and his warnings to not let his feelings interfere with his mission. All he could think about was the next opportunity to spend more time with her. Outside of ordering food from her, of course.

After purchasing a bouquet of lilies that he placed in the passenger seat of his car, Judas continued on to Elizabeth's apartment with the windows down and the cool breeze blowing through his hair. With a smile on his lips and a song in his heart, he pulled up to Elizabeth's apartment building and climbed the stairs to knock on her door. His light mood came to a crashing halt when another man answered.

"Who the fuck are you?" the man asked. Though, Judas had the feeling he could barely be considered a man. He looked no more than twenty and had the dashing, dangerous good looks of a young James Dean only with red hair.

"I'm, uh, Jude," Judas stammered, nearly offering his real name in his shocked state.

"Yeah? What the fuck do you want?"

Judas suddenly wished he'd brought his gun.

Elizabeth appeared in the room behind the James Dean look-alike. "Seth, stop being a dick head. C'mon in Jude. This is just my rude ass brother, Seth."

Judas felt relief wash over him. "Your brother? So nice to meet you." Judas held out a hand to shake, but Seth only looked at it with an air of disgust.

"I'm sorry," Elizabeth said. She moved past her brother and into the hall. "My brother has always been a bit of douche bag, but lately he's been a little out of hand."

"Hey," Seth said with a hurt expression.

"He's really not a bad guy, just over-protective when it comes to his older sis."

"I understand," Judas said, playing the part of the always sympathetic boyfriend.

Seth sighed and begrudgingly offered his hand. "Alright, I'm sorry. Nice to meet you."

Judas shook his hand. "Likewise."

"Seth, you can make yourself at home," Elizabeth said. "Watch my TV, smoke some of my weed, but stay out of my beer. It's all I have left until payday."

"Relax, it's light beer, I don't drink that fucking shit."

"You say that now. There's a liquor store in the shopping center next door. If you want some – get your own."

"I got it."

"Okay. We'll talk more later, but please consider what I said."

Seth only nodded and closed the door behind them.

Elizabeth took Judas' hand and led him back down the stairs. "Sorry, he's had a fight with my dad and is acting all whiny and pouty. It's his thing."

"Your dad?"

"Yeah, he's decided to leave the family business and cut Seth out completely."

Leave the family business. It was Elizabeth's vague way of saying her father had quit the club. "Is he retiring?"

She shrugged. "Semi-retiring I guess. He always talked about finding a nice cabin hidden out in the woods where he and mom could spend their golden years, but I don't think they're quite ready for that yet."

"How old are they?"

"Mom is forty-five. Dad is…a little younger."

Another vague answer. It was almost like she was teasing him with the secrets she had surely been sworn to keep. Judas decided not to press any further. As he opened the car door for her, he said, "Well, I hope things work out for them."

"Thanks." Judas closed her door and moved to the other side of the car. As he slid behind the wheel, she asked; "What are we doing tonight?"

"Dinner," said Judas. "Then I have something special planned."

"Great. We can make it as late as you want. The moon is full, I'm always wired and unable to sleep during the full moon."

"Really?"

"Oh yes. The full moon offers great magical energy. Tomorrow night I'll even find a secluded place to build a fire and perform a ritual. In the nude of course."

Judas knew there were witches in the world, but they varied in how much magical ability they were capable of, from those who practice the rituals and have little ability, to those who can tap into elemental magic and cast powerful spells. He wondered where Elizabeth fell in this broad spectrum. Witchcraft paired with the blood of an angel could be a very formidable combination. Despite her affection for him, when she discovers he is charged with killing her father, she could do him serious damage. He'd have to investigate further. Assess her true power.

"May I join you in this ritual? I'd be very interested in seeing it."

"Is that because you're interested in learning about it or because you want to see me dance around a fire naked."

Judas pulled the car out into traffic. "Perhaps a little of both."

She laughed at this but agreed to have him sit in during her ritual.

Judas first took her to a French restaurant in town, then to an outdoor movie near the art museum in Johnston Park. The movie was a classic. Bell, Book and Candle with James Stewart, Kim Novak, and Jack Lemmon. A movie about a witch who falls for her neighbor and casts a love spell on him to lure him away from his fiancée. Judas didn't tell her what the movie was before it started, but as they lay on a blanket in the grass, she sighed and leaned into him. "Oh, I love this movie."

Judas slipped his arms around her, taking in her scent. He wasn't sure where this intoxicating aroma came from, but he relished it, even when they parted and it lingered on his clothes and he thought about her for hours. Judas suddenly realized, with startling clarity, he was in real trouble.

# 26

## Marion

"A Super 8 motel?" Adrian said with a note of disgust. "An FBI agent can't spring for a little more? Hell, I could have paid."

"We're trying to keep a low profile," Marion said as she got out of the rental car. "I don't think this guy knows we're looking for him, but he seems resourceful enough to figure it out. Besides, two stars are better than one."

Marion checked in with the middle-eastern woman behind the counter while her husband was busy vacuuming the lobby. The two rooms were next to each other and each held double beds.

"Why do we each need two beds?" Adrian asked. "Two beds are all they offer."

"Weird."

"It's not that weird. Though I'd choose the one furthest from the door."

"Why?"

"There has no doubt been a ton of couples that had sex in these rooms and they will almost always hit the bed nearest to the door. That's where the majority of the bodily fluids are going to be found."

The expert in all things supernatural sighed. "Charming."

Adrian gave a wide birth to the first bed and dropped his bags at the end of the second. Marion chuckled as she walked to the room next door. Inside, she dropped her bags near the far bed as well and carefully added to them the dead angel's guitar. She didn't know exactly what she was hoping to accomplish with it, but something told her to bring it along. Some strange tug at her mind, like the instrument itself was trying to speak to her.

From her briefcase, Marion pulled the file on the case and leafed through what they'd managed to compile so far.

"Pretty fucking thin," Adrian said from the open doorway.

"Yeah. Anorexic."

Adrian smiled, satisfied that she'd picked up on his movie reference. "What's the plan, Marion? We can't just sit here and hope this guy turns up."

"Of course not. We're going to get with the local police. They can put out an BOLO for the car, but it's going to be tricky."

"How so?"

"We're here unofficially, but we need to appear as though it's official. Very few on the police force are willing to cooperate with the FBI, so we'll need to find the right guy. For that I'll need to make some calls."

Marion pulled her smartphone and scrolled through the numbers she'd saved in her contacts. Fuller had actually given her the list of names on the down low. A few cops in the Cincinnati area who would be willing to work with her without too many questions. After calling Lieutenant Dan Frond and getting a nice, juicy "Fuck you!" from the inebriated man on the other end at the mention of her agent status, Marion tried the second number on her short list.

Homicide Detective Jack Billow was far more accommodating and said he'd be glad to meet Marion and her consultant on the case at The Tin Roof, near the baseball stadium at five. Marion ended the call and looked up at Adrian. "Alright, we got a guy."

"Well, that was easy enough."

Marion thought the same. It wasn't until they made it to The Tin Roof that they found things weren't quite so clear cut. The place was a bar and grill as well as a music venue and seemed to accommodate baseball fans as they made their way to the stadium. Marion had no doubt that it made a great deal of money during both baseball season and football season, what with the football arena just down the street. The first thing that struck Marion about the homicide detective as he half stood from a barstool to wave them over, was that the man was positively hammered. He was older, perhaps early fifties, and his face was weathered and worn by years on the job drowned by years of booze. He was bald and his face was covered by a thick layer of white whiskers.

"Sit, please," Detective Billow motioned to the stools beside him. "I knew you were a Fed. Could spot you as soon as you walked in the door."

Marion ignored the comment and sat on the stool beside him. Adrian took the stool beside her and kept quiet. Marion didn't know if he was trying to pick up on something odd with the detective or if he was merely waiting to see how things played out before offering any input.

"Thank you for meeting with us, Detective Billow," Marion said.

The man gave her a half-hearted raise of his whisky glass and a lopsided smile, then downed the drink in a flash. "I'm always willing to help the FBI. My interest lies solely in catching bad guys. Whether or not I get credit is of very little importance."

Though Billow's speech was slurred, Marion knew his statement was authentic. "Detective, we've been led here on a very unusual, highly classified case. We could use the help of a local such as yourself, but it's important that you have your wits about you. We're hunting a very dangerous man."

"Agent Kern, I am not an alcoholic," Billow said with a wry smile. "A highly functioning drunk maybe, but not an alcoholic. I always have my wits about me. Let me buy the two of you a drink and we'll get down to it."

Marion glanced at Adrian Dillard, who only shrugged in return and called to the bartender. "Beer for me, please."

"Great," called Billow. "Beer for the gent."

Marion continued. "Detective, what we need from you is to merely pull some strings to help us track this guy down. A BOLO would go far. We know the make and model of his car. We know-"

"Hang on just a minute. If I'm going to help, I need to know what exactly I'm getting into. Fuck the classified shit. If I'm in, I'm in all the way. Now, come on, pick your poison."

"I'm afraid I'm not much of a drinker," Marion said. She weighed her options. There were a couple of locals left on the list Fuller gave her, but she knew she'd likely run into the same demands from them. She decided to take a chance on Billow. "Perhaps we could find a booth or somewhere more secluded. Away from prying eyes."

"Sure." Billow slid off his stool, stumbled, then stopped to steady himself. Finally, he walked on to the empty booth in the corner. Once seated, Marion placed the file on the table and opened it for Detective Billow to see. As the man perused the information, his light countenance grew more serious and he seemed to sober up a little. He looked through the photos and read the notes, then looked to the agent and her consultant. "Is this shit for real?"

"My partner is lying in a hospital bed in Atlanta with the bite from a demon on his neck," Marion said. "It's real. This...man we're after, he's on some biblical killing spree, gunning down angels and innocent bystanders alike. We've received a tip that he's here, now, in Cincinnati. Most likely gearing up to kill again."

"Is he a nut of some kind?"

"No," Adrian answered. "He's a pro. A hired killer. Though who he works for may be someone we don't want to fuck with. He's got someone in a position of power working hard to cover his tracks. No doubt the same fucker that set him loose on this mission."

"And these angels," Billow said. "They have some sort of attachment to the guitars they carry around?"

Adrian answered again. "They're fallen angels. In the old days, they still had their halos, but some were getting into too much trouble. Interfering in human affairs. So, the halos were taken away. Replaced by the guitars. And the angels were placed in locations that they weren't allowed to stray too far from, or else there'd be repercussions. Before, you could take an angel's halo away. It would strip them of their powers, hell, even their wings would be gone, but they always found ways to get them back. Even if it meant bartering with humans to do so. The guitars, however, have more of an attachment to them. See, they took the place of the halos. Try to take one and it will cause them excruciating pain. They're very protective of their instruments."

Detective Billow took all this in a moment, then looked up from the file to the two of them. "This is fucking crazy."

Marion cleared her throat. "Nevertheless, it's happening. If you don't want to believe anything else about this case, Detective, know that there is a killer on the loose and he's in your city. You said all that mattered to you was catching bad guys. Let's catch one."

Billow's smile returned. "You're good. You know exactly how to appeal to me from my earlier comments. Alright, I'm in. What do you need from me?"

# 27

## Judas

Judas awoke to the sound of birds chirping and sunlight spilling through the curtains of Elizabeth's room. He rolled over and slid a hand over the curve of her waist. She gave a pleasing moan and slid backward to press against him.

"This is nice," she said. "I like waking up in your arms."

Judas kissed her shoulder and then her neck. "I like having you in my arms."

She turned suddenly to look up into his eyes and slid one hand over the stubble on his cheek. "I know it's really soon to be saying this, but when you're sure...Jude, I'm falling in love with you."

Judas stared at her a moment and knew she was telling him the truth. It wasn't confusion for lust or the misguided feelings of a woman who was lonely and longing for companionship. Elizabeth was neither confused nor lonely. When she felt something, she recognized it and knew for certain whether it was real or not. Judas, for his part, knew for certain he felt the same for her.

"I'm falling in love with you, Elizabeth. You're unlike anyone I've ever met."

She kissed him and they made love again. Afterward, she dressed in his shirt and nothing else and moved to the kitchen to make coffee. Judas pulled on his boxers and followed her out.

"So, I've been trying to work up the courage to ask you something," Elizabeth said. "I guess now is as good a time as any, seeing as we just professed our love for each other."

Judas smiled at her charm. "What is it?"

"I have the entire week off and I was thinking of going home. Would you like to meet my parents?"

And there it was. The end of his mission was in sight. Suddenly, he felt great trepidation and fear. Not fear of his target, but fear of losing what he'd only just found. Lou had warned him not to get too close, but there he was. Too fucking close.

"Are you sure you're ready for that?" he asked, hoping she'd back out.

"I'm absolutely ready."

Judas put on his best smile. "Then I am too."

"You can get away from work for a week?"

"That's the nice thing about my job, it travels with me."

"Great."

Judas wished he could share in her enthusiasm. Instead, he worked to bury these feelings deep down and worked to find his way back to the heartless killer he was supposed to be. He had to remember what was at stake. Freedom. And perhaps, it was a slim chance to be sure, Elizabeth would understand his predicament. Understand why he had to kill her father. It was the only chance he had to be with her, for the alternative was an eternity without her.

He was fucked regardless.

As Elizabeth made plans to head to Indianapolis and pack her things, Judas made his way back to the hotel to do the same. Two things he would be certain to pack that he hadn't had on him since arriving in town, were the two guns he'd need to finish the job.

As Judas walked through the lobby of the hotel his phone rang. Lou's name appeared on the screen. "Lou?"

"Judas, I couldn't get away to tell you this in person, so I thought I'd call."

"What's going on?"

"There's an FBI agent snooping around for you. They've traced that car of yours to Cincinnati."

"How do you know?"

"Don't worry about how I know. Just do something about it."

"Well, as it happens, I'm just getting ready to leave town now. I've been invited to meet the parents."

"There's the old Judas I know," Lou said with clear glee in his voice. "You're in the home stretch, old friend."

Judas felt his skin crawl. "Please don't call me that."

"Just get out of town right away."

"I thought you took care of things like this."

"You can't account for rogue agents pursuing cases on their own time. This one clearly has no life. Besides, it was that dumb fuck you got the car from that brought all this down on you. He attacked this woman's partner and she now has a bug up her ass about finding you."

"Spectacular," Judas drolly stated.

"Don't worry about it. Get out of town and leave her looking in the wrong city."

"Right."

"Remember, this one isn't going to be easy. Keep your guard up."

"I got it." Judas ended the call and keyed the lock on his room. His things were still packed. In fact, he never really unpacked. There was no real need to. Judas was neither angel nor demon, but he wasn't human either. He had no need for toothbrushes or showers, though he did occasionally stand under the cold water just to feel it on his skin. After so many years spent toiling in torturous heat, he relished the cold water.

He owned four suits, boxer shorts, undershirts, and two guns. A box of 9mm bullets for one gun, but the .45 carried the three remaining bullets saved for his final target. Judas zipped up the suitcase and made his way back to the lobby where he phoned Elizabeth.

"Hey, babe," she said upon answering and he felt goosebumps rise over his skin at the sound of her sweet voice and her term of endearment.

"Hey, I was just thinking, since we're leaving in the morning, perhaps I could check out and stay with you tonight."

"Yeah, that sounds good."

"Great. Wait, I have an idea. Why don't we just leave tonight?"

"Tonight?"

Judas wanted nothing more than to ditch the car and leave town, but Elizabeth didn't own a car and he wanted to avoid the hassle of finding another one. If they could leave town right away, he thought he could avoid any unwanted attention from local police. "Sure, it's only a couple of hours away. We could get there in time for dinner. Give your folks a real surprise."

"Yeah, OK. I guess that would be fun. I'm pretty much packed."

"Alright. I'm checking out now. I'll see you soon."

"Okay. I love you."

Judas paused. Something strange bubbled up inside him. An unfamiliar flutter in his stomach. An odd sensation at the back of his head, as if a cool breeze climbed up his spine to caress his hairline.

"Jude?" Elizabeth said on the other end.

Judas closed his eyes and when he spoke, he heard the emotion in his voice. Unsteady. Wavering. "Say it again."

"I love you." Jude could see her in his mind's eye. Smiling her perfect smile as she spoke. Her dark brown eyes wet with the emotion she was feeling. The same emotion that changed Judas' voice.

"I love you, Elizabeth."

He ended the call and stared at his phone, where she stared back.

He had set her photo as the background on his phone so that he could see her face anytime he wanted. What was he doing? How was he supposed to go through with this? The moment he pulled the trigger and took her father's life, he would lose her forever. He'd be free, but the woman he loved would hate him for all eternity. It was a new Hell waiting to begin.

# 28
## Garvey

John Garvey pulled his motorcycle into the garage and killed the engine. He was home after a long day of work, and it was something he was already easing into. Inside, Gwen was at the stove making fried chicken and mashed potatoes for dinner. John moved over behind her and slipped his arms around her waist, kissing her neck and then her shoulder. "It smells amazing."

Gwen slid her hands along his arms and lay her head back on his chest. "I love having you home every night."

"I'm digging it too," he said as he kissed her neck.

She moaned and turned to kiss his lips. "How was your day?"

"Mundane and uneventful. So fantastic."

Gwen laughed. "Good. I have some news that's going to make it even better."

"What's that?"

"Elizabeth is coming home for a week."

Garvey was elated. Elizabeth had always been a daddy's girl. Growing up, she was at his side all the time, whenever he was able to be home. They had a special bond that John could admit to himself he was never able to build with Seth. "No shit? I can't wait to see her."

"Oh, and she's bringing a guy home with her."

John felt that old pull at his mind. Excessive caution bordering on paranoia. He carefully removed the guitar from his back and leaned it against the wall, then he grabbed a beer from the fridge and popped it open. "A guy?"

"Yeah. The guy she went out with a couple of weeks ago. Apparently, they really hit it off and she's ready for him to meet the parents."

John pondered this a moment, momentarily giving in to his old ways.

"I know that look, John. Push it aside. Our daughter met a guy that is treating her right. Time to be happy."

John nodded. "I know. I guess it's never going to switch off completely."

"That's good. A father still needs to be protective. Just not overly so."

"Yes. Still, if he does anything to hurt my little girl, I'll put him through a fucking wall."

"That's the way," she said with a laugh. "She also said Seth showed up at her place. Acted like a real dick toward this guy."

"Well, he's as protective of her as I am. Not surprising. Good to know he's still alive."

"Yeah. I wish he'd give up all this nonsense about starting his own club. It would be nice to have everyone home for a change."

"He'll come around."

Before more could be said on the matter, the two of them heard the front door open and Elizabeth's voice calling out. "Mom, Dad, I'm home."

While Gwen rushed excitedly into the living room, John suddenly felt exposed. He moved to the wall and slung the guitar onto his back, then moved to the living room behind Gwen.

Elizabeth was there, smiling and beautiful. Aglow with a happiness John hadn't seen on her face since she was a child. Coming in the door behind her was a tall, broad-shouldered man in a suit, tie loosened. He had dark skin and a great head of jet-black hair that was combed back from his face. Handsome with a dashing smile, he seemed of middle-eastern descent.

John hugged his daughter close to him, keeping an eye on the stranger all the while. Elizabeth pulled away and made introductions. "Mom, Dad, this is my boyfriend, Jude."

Gwen hugged the man and kissed his cheek. "It's so nice to meet you."

John held out his hand and Jude gave it a strong shake. "Nice to meet you, Jude."

"I'm so very glad to meet the both of you," Jude said. "I've heard a lot about you."

"Jude," John said, still sizing up the man. "That's an unusual name."

"His parents were huge fans of The Beatles," Elizabeth said.

"Is that right?" asked John.

"Yes, sir," Jude returned.

John only stared at him a moment. Jude seemed uncomfortable being stared down. Finally, John said, "I was always more of a Stones fan myself." He turned and walked back toward the kitchen. "Want a beer?"

"Yeah, that'd be great."

John opened the fridge and pulled a beer. He turned to find Jude staring at him with an odd expression on his face. "What?"

"Oh, nothing. I was just admiring your guitar."

John handed over the beer. "Do you play?"

"No. Unfortunately, I was never very musically inclined. My strength was always in business."

"What do you do?"

"I work for a real estate firm. It's what brought me to Cincinnati."

"I see." John stared at the man, satisfied with the discomfort he saw in his face.

"Elizabeth says you're a mechanic," Jude went on.

"That's right. I own a shop with a friend."

"Very nice."

The two shared an awkward silence and John couldn't help the twinge at the back of his mind that told him not to trust the guy.

Gwen returned to the kitchen before either of the men could concoct more to say. "Well, we weren't expecting the two of you until tomorrow. Luckily, I always make way too much food for dinner."

"It smells delicious," Elizabeth said.

"And it's ready. Everyone can fix a plate."

John pulled another sip from his beer and eyed Jude closely. The man seemed to feel the gaze on him but went about making his plate as if he didn't.

Gwen slid up in front of John and pulled on his shirt. "John, relax."

John nodded. "Yeah, alright."

It was easier said than done, but John grabbed a plate and decided to give it a shot.

# 29
## Judas

The chicken was delicious. Not as good as a burger, but Judas felt it was damn close. He ate in silence as Elizabeth told her mother and father all about how they met and their first dates. How they texted each other constantly, sometimes staying up to the early morning hours, unable to let each other go.

"Young love," Gwen said with a smile.

"You're like a couple of fucking teenagers," John Garvey observed gruffly.

Judas looked up at the man to find he was giving him the same look of distrust he'd offered throughout the entire evening. Judas knew he had to play this out just right. "So, Mr. Garvey, Elizabeth says you like to rebuild old motorcycles for resale."

Garvey sat back in his chair and sighed. "Yeah, that's right. Would you like to come out to the garage and see what I'm working on?"

"I'd love to."

Garvey stood and slung the guitar on his back and Judas followed him to the garage after receiving a nod of approval from both Elizabeth and her mother. Garvey flicked the overhead light on and moved over to the far side of the two-car garage. Here sat two bikes, one a finished, gleaming masterpiece, the other little more than a frame with parts spread out around it.

"I found this in one of the junkyards over off Tibbs," Garvey said. "Not much of it was salvageable, but I can get new parts fairly cheap through the shop. I may sink a few grand into it, then turn around and sell it for a nice profit."

"Very impressive."

"Thanks."

"I've always envied those who can work with their hands."

"Well, you seem to be more of a thinker. Everyone has their own talents."

Judas stared at the man and knew there were questions he should be asking. Things that could quell John Garvey's suspicions of him. He started with the two obvious ones. "Forgive me for saying so, Mr. Garvey, but you appear as if you're not much older than Elizabeth. It doesn't seem like you'd have a daughter in her twenties."

"I get that a lot. We had Elizabeth when we were both very young, but I'm older than I look. Clean living and all."

Judas nearly chuckled at this. Garvey pulled the guitar off his back and sat it on a stand near the unfinished bike. "You seem very attached to that guitar."

"Yeah. It is special to me."

"May I hold it?" Judas already knew the answer to this question, but the look he got from the man struck a chord of fear within him he'd never experienced before.

"No one touches my guitar," said the man, who wasn't really a man at all.

Judas nodded and said, "Of course. I didn't mean to offend."

The angel sighed and his expression lightened. "No, I'm sorry. It just holds sentimental value."

"I understand." Judas decided a change of subject was in order. "Elizabeth is wonderful. I'm quite taken with her."

"Yeah, she seems to be crazy about you too. Honestly, I've never seen her so happy. You know, Gwen and I didn't think it was possible to have kids. I was told I have slow swimmers." Judas knew this was a lie. They didn't think it was possible for an angel to have a child with a human. "Then it happened. She was late getting her period and we found out she was pregnant. Lizzy, she was always into dark things. Found all of it fascinating. Don't get me wrong, she was a happy kid, she was just especially happy if she was reading about wiccan rituals or watching documentaries about serial killers." This last part made Judas wonder if a documentary about *him* would ever be made. Serial killer of fallen angels and innocent bystanders. Shame filled him for a moment, but he pushed it aside.

"It's one of the things I like about her," said Judas. "She's so unique. Wonderfully strange."

Garvey smiled at this. "Wonderfully strange. That's a great way to put it."

Garvey pulled his flannel shirt off, revealing tattooed, muscular arms. The white tank underneath was adorned with old grease stains that would never be lost completely to a washing machine. He knelt and picked up a socket wrench, apparently continuing from a stopping point when last he worked on the bike. He talked as he tightened a bolt on an engine mount. "Seth, on the other hand – he was the type of kid that was always in trouble. If he wasn't getting kicked out of school for fights, he was getting kicked out for smoking. Or skipping class. Or pulling pranks on the faculty members that went way too far."

As John Garvey talked, Judas quietly moved in behind him, slid the .45 semi-automatic from inside his suit jacket, and held the barrel to the back of Garvey's head. "We all go through our rough patches," he said, and managed to keep his tone light even as he plotted to pull the trigger before the angel realized he heard the safety switched off.

"Well, that's the thing," Garvey continued as he worked on the engine. "It wasn't just a patch. The shit never stopped. To this day, he's been nothing but grief for us. But Elizabeth…"

Garvey let the name hang there as if he knew it would give Judas pause. Whether he realized it or not, and Judas knew he didn't, it worked. If Judas were to blow this man's brains out, what would become of his relationship with the daughter. The answer was obvious. There could be no relationship. She would hate him and he would have to live the rest of his days on Earth without her. He would escape one form of torture only to be forced to endure another.

Still, he had a mission to complete. One that would see him free from an eternity of fire and agony. Judas tightened his grip on the gun and prepared himself while Garvey continued his work on the machine in front of him. Do it, a voice screamed in his head. Then her face swam into his mind. Her dark, brown eyes and warm smile. And that look she gave him that said she'd never been so happy in her life as she was with him. And when he saw that look, he knew the same was true for him.

Judas slipped the gun back into his jacket just as Garvey stood and looked at him. "You alright? You've gone quiet."

"I'm sorry, I didn't realize you were finished with your thought."

"Oh, I guess I did trail off."

The door to the kitchen opened and Elizabeth called out to them. "Dessert is ready. Apple pie."

Garvey patted Judas' shoulder. "After you, Jude."

"Thank you, sir."

Judas walked back inside, his thoughts of freedom from one hell bringing another twisting around his head like a funnel cloud. Inside, the pie was warm and delicious, with a small scoop of vanilla ice cream on top. Jude played the good boyfriend the rest of the evening and then bid Elizabeth's parents a warm farewell.

"Are you sure you don't want to stay with us," Gwen said. "There's plenty of space."

"It's okay, mom. We already have a hotel room."

This said to Judas that, although her father was attempting to lead a more comfortable life than he had up to this point, letting a stranger sleep under his roof was a big leap to make and he wasn't there yet.

As they drove Elizabeth asked, "So, what did you think of them?"

"They were a delight," he answered and found he was telling the truth.

"My mother was certainly taken with you. She loved your accent."

"Yes. I'm not so sure about your father."

"I know he seemed kind of gruff, but to be honest, I've never seen him take to someone so easily."

"Really?" Judas was positively shocked by this.

"Yeah, even Buck, his best friend and business partner. He had to really work hard to get him to loosen up in the beginning."

"Well, I'm glad he liked me."

"I am too." Elizabeth switched gears. "Full moon tonight. Are you ready to witness a ritual?"

"Tonight?"

"Yeah. I have everything I need in the trunk."

"Yes, I'd love to." And this was the truth. Everything about her was vastly interesting to Judas. Plus, it would certainly be something that would take his mind off things. At least for a little while.

"Great," she said. "There's a park in Mooresville with a secluded area where I used to set up in the woods."

"Alright," Judas said, then went quiet for the remainder of the drive back to the hotel. His nerves were on edge and he needed to calm down before Elizabeth realized something was wrong.

Back in the hotel, Elizabeth stripped all her clothes off and jumped into the shower, while Judas sat on the bed and closed his eyes. his breathing still fast and loud to his own ears. He forced himself to take deep breaths and calm down. The moment he'd worked so hard for over these past few years was right there in front of him. A pull of the trigger and he'd have been free. He chickened out. Over a woman. He knew he'd hear it from Lou soon enough.

Elizabeth finished her shower and dressed in a black, lacey gown that looked like something Morticia Addams would have worn.

When he mentioned this to Elizabeth, she only smiled and said, "I'll take that as a compliment."

The two of them left the hotel and Jude handed the keys over to her so that she could drive to the town and the park she knew so well. Down I-70 to an exit ramp with a sign that read Plainfield/Mooresville, Elizabeth took the ramp and turned to the south, where she took back roads that wound around through a neighborhood that seemed older. The houses were fairly nice and sat far back from the road on large pieces of land. Finally, she pulled down a road with a small warehouse on one corner. Beyond this and to the left was their destination.

The park was large and full of shelters and picnic tables. Elizabeth took the narrow road toward the back of the park where the dark shape of a waterslide loomed over a pool that was now closed for the approaching fall season. The road curved around the pool and plunged into a tunnel of trees that led deeper into the park. They came to a set of baseball diamonds and Elizabeth parked the car.

"Back beyond the diamonds," she pointed. "There's a trail that goes over a covered bridge, then deep into the woods."

"Are you sure this is alright?" Judas asked. He couldn't explain the uncomfortable feeling he had about the place. "Aren't there park rangers patrolling?"

"It's fine. I'd always do my ritual here when I was younger."

"Alright. Let's do this."

Elizabeth opened the trunk and shoved a box into Judas' hands. Inside was a collection of candles, candleholders, and several knickknacks, some of which appeared to be old Halloween decorations. Then she picked up a small cauldron, a blanket, and a container of salt. "Follow me."

The covered bridge was nothing like what Judas had expected. In his head he pictured something old and broken down that would look more at home in Irving's fictional town of Sleepy Hollow. Instead, what they came to was a sleek, recently constructed bridge that was pleasing to the eye, but disappointing to one's sense of danger.

On the other side, the trail continued downhill, well-lit by the moon's light as it spilled through the branches of the trees. Eventually, Elizabeth veered off and stepped carefully through the underbrush until they came to a clearing. In the middle of the clearing was a firepit surrounded by rocks. The area was littered with beer bottles. "Clearly my spot isn't as secluded as it once was," Elizabeth said.

"Still, seems quiet at the moment."

"Oh yeah, I'm still going to set up."

Judas watched her as she did. She spread the blanket out and sat the cauldron toward the tip. She then opened a small satchel and spread several rocks around the edges, laying each one carefully in its place. "Each rock holds special powers and will recharge under the light of a full moon," she explained.

After this, she placed each of the candle holders on the blanket around the cauldron, then lit them. Finally, she stood with a container of salt and poured it in a circle around the blanket. "Remember to never break my circle."

"Understood," Judas said. "What purpose does the salt serve?"

"Salt has many great uses. In this case, I'm using it to protect me in the circle from evil influences. Salt has often been used in sacrifices to placate gods. It's also been used in some Christian ceremonies, including baptisms and exorcisms. Then there's the superstition that spilled salt arouses evil spirits. The only antidote to this is to throw a pinch of salt over your left shoulder to drive away the devil. Some link the origin of this practice to the legend that Judas overturned the salt cellar at the last supper. This caused the salt cellar to break, which in and of itself is an old superstition. It signifies a broken friendship." This part was true. Judas was suddenly taken back to that day.

Jesus, surrounded by his twelve apostles. They supped on bread and wine. Jesus told them the wine was his blood, the bread his body. Judas, ever the clumsy one in those days, knocked the salt cellar over as he reached for bread. It broke into several pieces, and for a moment, he stared into the eyes of the man he followed. The man he loved. And there, he saw understanding bloom in Jesus' expression. This, and a sense of heartbreaking sadness.

"Jude, are you alright?" Elizabeth said, bringing him out of his stupor.

"I'm sorry," Judas said, trying to concoct a lie for his cover. In the end, he told a vague version of the truth. "What you said about the salt cellar. It brought back a strange memory."

"A memory of what?"

"I'd rather not talk about it."

She looked disappointed at this but nodded her understanding.

"At least, not right now," he amended. "Please, continue. As if I'm not here."

Elizabeth went on placing the items around the blanket. A skeleton sitting with his knees drawn up to his chest and a candle protruding from his head. The statue of a witch riding a broom, a gnarled tree stump beneath her. A glass whiskey distiller elegantly crafted into the shape of an owl. Another statue, this one of a large ring entwined with a smaller ring, each with a small ball atop. It was abstract, but Judas thought it resembled a man holding a woman close. Or perhaps that's just what his love-fevered mind made him see. He wasn't too proud to admit his thinking had been muddled by this woman with whom he was so enraptured.

"Will you help me build a fire?" she asked.

"Of course."

"If you could just collect some wood while I finish setting up."

Judas moved around the clearing to the trees and began to pile branches and twigs in his arm. Twenty minutes later, he had a nice collection situated in a triangular shape in the fire pit. Elizabeth pulled an old newspaper from her bag and stuffed it around the branches. With as dry as the summer had been, the flames took easily enough and the fire was soon burning bright.

Elizabeth moved back to her blanket and lit each of the remaining candles then knelt in front of the alter. The words she spoke were in Latin and Judas was surprised to find that he'd forgotten much of the Latin he once knew. As she spoke, she stripped her gown off, then stood naked with her arms to the sky. Judas watched this and thought it sounded as if she were pleading with the moon.

There was a noticeable surge in the fire and Judas wondered if Elizabeth truly did hold some elemental power. Real witchcraft. It seemed likely, especially considering her lineage, though she didn't seem aware of any such gift. She carried on with her ritual as if it had never happened. Judas watched her dance around the fire and continued his fall. With every movement, his affection for the woman grew ever stronger. With her ritual complete, she moved to his side of the fire and straddled him where he sat. Their passion erupted and he made love to her there in the woods, the sweat on her naked body glistening by the firelight. As she climaxed, the fire climbed higher.

The two returned to the hotel, where they made love again and fell asleep in each other's arms. It was just after 3 am when Judas heard a strange sound outside their room. It came again. A scratch at the door that ran shivers up his spine. He got out of bed, pulled on a shirt, and moved to the door. Another scratch. Judas went to his suitcase and pulled the 9mm from within. Then he waited for the sound to come again and flung the door open with the gun up.

Lou threw up his hands with a smirk on his face. "Easy, I'm unarmed."

"Fuck, Lou," Judas said and dropped the gun to his side. He stepped out of the room and closed the door gently behind him. "What are you doing here?"

"I wanted an update. Did you meet the girl's father?"

"Yes," Judas said. He knew Lou would be angry with him if he found out he had the opportunity but failed to dispatch his target. "The timing wasn't right."

Lou studied him for a long moment. It was clear he didn't believe what Judas was telling him. "Walk with me," he finally said. Judas walked with the man down the carpeted hallway of the hotel. It felt unnatural in bare feet and sleep clothes that consisted of Batman pajama pants and a Rolling Stones shirt Elizabeth had given him as a gift. The two men walked down the hall a ways and Lou said nothing. If it had been anyone else, Judas would assume they were just gathering their thoughts. Lou, on the other hand, was never one to have trouble finding the right words for whatever point he needed to make.

They neared the door to the stairwell and Lou turned to him. "Judas, I don't think you're grasping the weight of your situation." His tone was a low, threatening growl. "Allow me to refresh your memory."

Then Lou's hand was on Judas' throat. Judas was smashed through the metal door that led to the stairs and slammed against a wall inside. He clutched at Lou's wrist but to no avail. As old as Lou appeared to be, there was still great power at his disposal.

"If you don't *kill* this fuck stick," Lou said, "you're going to end up right back in the pit burning for all eternity. If you want to be with that girl so bad, killing her father is the only way you'll have a chance."

Lou released his grip. Judas sucked air in through his aching windpipe. Then wheezed, "She's not going to understand that."

"Well, then I don't know what to tell you. You and I made a deal. There's no going back. You have two ways out of this. You kill the angel and you're free to live a normal life here on earth, or you don't and you burn. It's that simple."

Judas could say nothing. He knew his options and he didn't need Lou to spell them out for him.

"You want to be with this girl, then spell it out for her. Make her understand. She knows what her father is. She knows sometimes things like this can't be avoided. Let her know it's beyond the control of any mortal on earth. And you know what, champ? That shit is absolutely, one hundred percent, fucking true. This may come as a surprise to you, but I myself am a hopeless romantic. I want to see love win out. And I have seen it come through after some fucked up shit like this. If this thing you have is *real*, she will stand by your side no matter what. Yeah, she'll be upset. And yeah, it's going to take some time for her to get over it, but this is the only chance for you two to make it."

Judas nodded. His breathing had finally returned to normal. "You're right. I know that."

Lou placed a comforting hand on his shoulder. Judas resisted the urge to flinch back from the man's touch. "Good. You're almost mortal now. One last deed and you're home free."

"I know."

"Alright. Good talk, Judas. Let's finish this, huh?"

Another nod and the older man left the younger one in the stairwell. Judas stood upright and straightened his Rolling Stones shirt, tempted to reach up and adjust the necktie he was so used to having around his neck.

Judas *had* to make Elizabeth understand, that much was certain. How to go about it was the part that was foggy to him. All this time, he'd been fighting and killing for a second chance at a normal, mortal existence. All this time, it was there within his grasp. Now, he couldn't fathom having to face that life without her.

Judas opened the door and stepped back into the hall. The middle-of-the-night silence closed in around him. The only sound was the air conditioning blowing in from the vents. Judas came back to the room and let himself in. Inside, he stood and stared at the sleeping form of the woman he was crazy about. How could he tell her he had to murder her father in order for their love to survive? How could he make her understand the suffering that awaited him if he didn't come through on his end of the bargain?

Time was running out.

# 30
## Adrian

The burger was thick and greasy, cheese melted perfectly and topped with lettuce, tomato, pickle, and mustard. Adrian Dillard bit into it and savored the juices as they invaded his mouth. Normally, a burger was a rarity for him. He wasn't exactly a fitness nut, but he was trying to lose the gut cultivated by years of beer drinking and only allowed a couple of cheat days a month. However, whatever thin connection he'd made with the killer, his love of a good burger had invaded Adrian's senses.

"He's not here anymore," Adrian said.

Marion was sitting in the other side of the booth staring at him as he ate with something close to fascination on her face. His proclamation seemed to jar her back to reality. "Who are we talking about?"

"The killer. He skipped town. My guess is our drunken detective was behind that."

"We don't know that for sure."

"He's the only asshole we talked to since we hit town."

"I meant we don't know for sure the killer skipped."

"I know."

Marion glared at him. "Are you saying you can feel him better than you could before?"

"Not really. Still just the burger thing. I have a good hunch about the rest."

"What else are you picking up about this guy?"

"Not a lot," Adrian lied. Truth was; he was picking something up, but he wasn't sure at this point if it was even coming from the killer. There were conflicting feelings. He was fond of someone. Perhaps even in love. But the mission had complicated things. What was going on in this man's head? What had he really gotten himself into? Adrian had a feeling even the killer didn't know. There was something bigger at work. Something even the killer wasn't aware of.

"What are you thinking?"

"What if our killer is just the trigger man? What if there's someone else behind all this?"

"The killer would still have to go down. He is committing the murders. Even if we can't charge him on celestial beings, there were a lot of regular people he murdered as well."

"Yeah, but what if he doesn't have a choice in the matter? Say the alternative is far more devastating."

"For whom exactly?"

"I don't know. For him. For everyone maybe."

"Adrian, I have to do my job no matter what. Even if this guy is out to save the human race, he's got to answer for the crimes he's committed."

"Yeah. I know." And Adrian was aware of this. Nonetheless, he found Marion's response a little disappointing.

"Clearly there *is* someone behind all this, we know that from our being forced off the case, that just means we need to track that person down as well. Hold him or her accountable."

"Spoken like a true federal agent."

"What exactly do you want to hear, Adrian?"

"That you understand there may be something bigger than man's law going on here. That you understand we may be getting in over our heads." Adrian only then realized he had raised his voice. Other diners were looking at the two of them.

"I got it," Marion said through gritted teeth. "I know this is going to get rough, but backing down is not something I do."

"Well the FBI sure as hell does. As one of their agents maybe you should take the hint."

"Let's go ahead and assume you're not going to be able to talk me out of this. Mostly because I used vacation time to come to Cincinnati, where there are no beaches or resorts, and those are two major necessities for major vacation destinations. I came up here to catch a killer and I'm not going back to Atlanta without him."

Adrian let out a defeated sigh. The woman was frustrating, but he knew she would never give in. "Fine. What's next?"

"We need to find out where he's gone."

It occurred to Adrian then that he could not only find out where the killer had gone, but possibly who he was working for as well. "Alright. I have an idea."

"Great."

"We need to get our good detective alone. Do a little interrogation of our own."

"And you think he'll sing?"

"If we put enough fear into him." Adrian gave her a mischievous smile.

# 31
## Billow

Detective Jack Billow agreed to meet her with no real fuss. Agent Kern had told him they'd found the car they were looking for, abandoned on the top floor of a parking garage. There was no doubt they were barking up the wrong tree with the find, but his interest was piqued and he wanted to humor the female FBI agent to see what she was talking about. Billow thought she was pretty hot for a black chick and his mind was entertaining porno movie scenarios as he drove to meet her.

Billow arrived in his unmarked car and crawled out from behind the wheel with some effort. Looking around, he pulled a flask from his back pocket and took a long swig. Kern was there sure enough, but he saw no sign of any cars on the rooftop parking lot. Even her SUV was absent. "I thought you said you found the car."

Marion shrugged. "I lied to get you here alone."

The smarmy detective sneered. "Liked what you saw at the bar the other night, huh?"

"Not quite." Marion slung her arm out and hit Billow in the nose with the palm of her hand. Blackness swept over him.

When Billow awoke, it was full dark. They were in a small room he didn't recognize with a lone light shining on him from a naked lightbulb. He wasn't surprised to find he was tied to a chair, a strip of duct tape over his mouth. It wasn't the first time. Agent Kern was standing over him, her hands behind her back, a blank expression on her face. He shrugged, refusing to show alarm or worry. Just a nonchalant shrug to say what he was thinking. *What the fuck?*

She reached out and yanked the tape off his mouth. Pain erupted throughout his face.

"Ow! Shit!"

"I'm sorry I had to resort to this," Agent Kern said. "I have questions for you, but now that I know you can't be trusted, I had to find more persuasive means."

If there was one thing Billow knew how to do, it was piss people off. He even enjoyed it. "So, this is some kink? Is that what you mean? You gonna drop that black pussy on me while I'm tied in a chair. I got to tell you, that would work. I'll sing like a fucking canary. I never been with a black girl before, but I'm game. It's all pink on the inside, right?" He laughed at the disgusted look on her face.

Agent Kern placed a finger over her lips and shushed him, then tilted her head as if she heard something. There was a shuffling sound from the dark beyond the light around them. Kern continued as if nothing had occurred. "It's come to my attention that our killer has skipped town because he was tipped off by someone. Seeing as you're the only one in town that knew we were here and knew we were looking for him, we've come to the conclusion that you are the one who tipped him off."

Billow laughed. "I have no idea what you're talking about. Now, how about a lap dance. Rub that bubble butt of yours on my crotch. Promise I'll keep my hands to myself." He waved his fingers from the arm of the chair where his wrists were taped and laughed harder. The laughter was cut short as there came more movement from the shadows. Shuffling feet. A low rumble that sounded like a growl.

Agent Kern looked to where the sound came from and held out a calming hand. "Not yet. Let's give him one more chance."

Billow was suddenly nervous, and he could hear it in his own voice as he spoke. "You're fucking with me."

Kern turned her attention back to him and was quiet for a moment. Then she said, "Detective, I specialize in cases that seem beyond the realms of human explanation. Cases that seem supernatural in scope."

"What, like the X-Files?"

"I don't like that comparison, mostly because in almost all my cases, I'm able to find a logical explanation. Sometimes I debunk someone that's trying to make things seem more unnatural than they are, other times the unexplained happens by matter of chance. Freak accidents that occur because some poor soul was in the wrong place at the wrong time."

"So, more like Scooby-Doo," Billow said, trying to rattle her.

She seemed to ponder this a moment. "Yeah, I suppose so. I guess Velma is kind of a kindred spirit. However, sometimes the event that happens *can't* be explained away by natural means. A few years ago, someone murdered five factory workers. Covered the breakroom in their blood and insides, then dragged what was left of the bodies out the back door and piled them up there. We had no idea why, but when we played back the security recording, we saw something unbelievable. A man that was there, but at the same time, he wasn't there. Hard to explain. He would fade in and out of existence, but he was real enough to take a sickle to those poor factory workers. Slit their throats right open, gutted them, and they didn't even put up a fight. Do you know how he managed to do it?"

"No, how?" Billow asked. He now had goosebumps over the entirety of his body.

"He was a time traveler."

Billow smirked. "Bullshit."

"See, he came from the past, long before we started practicing daylight savings time, and by some fucked up chance, he jumped into the very hour that didn't exist anymore. So, when we turned the clock back in the fall, the hour disappeared, and he was trapped in some sort of limbo. Some strange realm that drove him mad. He couldn't escape until the hour came back in the spring, but to him, it was like time stood still. He had an hour to murder these people and pile up their bodies. They never saw it coming."

"Why are you telling me this?"

"Because, sometimes, when you find creatures like this, you can find a way to set them free. Then they owe you. They'll do whatever you need."

The shuffling from the darkness came again and for a moment, a crazed fear washed over Billow. "No. Fuck you, lady. That's just your friend mulling around in there. I'm not an idiot."

"I guess we're about to find out. Last chance, detective. Where did our killer go? Who did you tip off?"

"Eat a dick."

Agent Kern let out a sigh, then backed away as if to avoid any potential mess. "Your turn."

The shuffling feet came forward. Billow turned to the sound with a feeling of dread overwhelming him. Suddenly his heart was pounding. His hands worked in a futile effort to break free from the tape. The thing in the shadows came closer. A hand came into view first, fingers clasped around the handle of a crescent-shaped blade that was typically used for cutting crops. Then the arm faded and reappeared, like a television image with poor reception, and Billow felt a scream building in the back of his throat. The rest of the man came into view and Billow saw an insane rage in his eyes. His hair was wild, his face sallow and pale. A static fade out of existence and the man solidified again.

"Fuck!" Billow managed to bark. He wanted to scream but couldn't seem to find enough air to pull into his lungs. Another static blink out and back in again. The time traveler reached out with his other hand and Billow felt cold fingers slip into his hair and touch his scalp. The feel of the killer's skin on his forced a whimper to escape Billow's throat.

"Detective." Kern's voice seemed to come from far away. "Is there something you'd like to tell me?"

Billow felt the cold blade press against his throat as he stared into the endless blackness of the time traveler's eyes.

"I'd talk if I were you," Kern continued. "He won't kill you right away. He's going to torture you until you start offering answers."

"All right! Lou. I talked to a guy named Lou in D.C. He got a hold of me, gave me some cash. Told me to look out for anyone coming to try and stop his guy."

"His guy's name?"

"He didn't say. Just said he needed safe passage to Indiana."

"How did he know we'd come? How did he know we'd ask you for help?"

"I don't know, man. He just knew. He paid enough money so that I didn't question it too much. That's all I got, now call this motherfucker off. Please!"

The blade pierced skin and Billow felt blood trickle down his neck. Soak into his shirt. He cried out.

"That's enough," Kern said. The time traveler with the crescent blade looked at her with disappointment. The man finally backed away and disappeared into the shadows from which he came. It was only then that Detective Billow realized he'd pissed himself. Agent Kern stepped forward and bent so that she was face to face with Billow. "Forget this happened, detective. Or I'll let him finish."

She opened a pocketknife, cut through the tape that bound his wrists and ankles, and disappeared into the shadows where her creepy friend went. Billow sat in the chair for another hour, unable to move.

# 32
## Marion

Marion climbed behind the wheel of the SUV just as Adrian was changing back to his normal form. She was still astounded by his abilities and nearly screamed in terror herself when the time traveler stepped out of the shadows.

"That was intense," she said. "You looked just like him. How did you do the whole fading in and out thing."

"You saw that too?"

Marion shrugged. "Yeah."

"It was a psychic trick. I was directing toward Billow, I didn't think you'd pick up on it. Admittedly, it is my weakest ability."

"Well, now we know where to look for this guy. Though Indiana isn't exactly narrowing it down."

"Indianapolis. Seems right to me."

"That makes it a little better. Still a big fucking town. The name Lou mean anything to you?"

"Nothing."

Marion pulled out of the parking garage. "Whoever he is, he's got a ton of pull. A politician most likely."

"Probably powerful and wealthy. Do you have any idea where we're going?"

"You're the navigator. Pull that shit up on your phone."

"So, I'm nothing but Chewbacca to your Han."

Marion laughed at this, then a thought occurred to her. "Hey, could you shape-shift into Chewie?"

Adrian shrugged. "I don't see why not. Though, I'm a little drained right now."

"Right. Raincheck then."

"You got it."

Marion said; "So, now we'll be looking for a needle in a haystack in Indy rather than Cincy."

"Yeah, though I'm from Indianapolis. I have a lot of friends there. Maybe I can call around to see what kind of information I can scrape up."

"Well all right. Now we're getting somewhere."

And they were. Still, Adrian didn't like where they were getting.

# 33
## Newt

Newt left the gas station with beef jerky and an energy drink in hand. The truck had a full tank and soon he'd be wired. All this meant it would be smooth sailing the rest of the trip to Chicago. Then, with the delivery made, he'd cruise the local gay bars and try to find some companionship for the night.

Newt made the trip about once a month to deliver a shipment and he was paid well to do it. Not only that, he was the perfect candidate. The old moving truck was refurbished. Garvey had found it in a junkyard and the guys brought it back to the shop, replaced the transmission and most of the engine, then gave it a boring paint job. A drab yellow that wouldn't attract too much attention, but at the same time, would give the illusion of being just another moving van rented from one of the moving companies out there.

On top of this, Newt had an appearance that was unlike the typical club member. All of his tats were on his back, chest, and upper arms, so a nice polo shirt covered them all. Add to this a pair of khaki pants and loafers, then comb his hair neatly and wear his glasses instead of contacts and Newt could pull off the look of a boring guy that lived a boring life that he'd given up and decided to move to Chicago. The final touch to the illusion was his traveling companion; his German Shepard mix Tobi, who rode shotgun and liked to howl along to the classic rock that came through the radio.

Newt climbed in the cab and gave Tobi a scratch behind the ear, then shared some of his jerky with him. The classic rock radio station popped on with the start of the truck and Soundgarden's Black Hole Sun came through the speakers. The fact that the grunge rockers were now considered classic rock made Newt feel old and a little sad. The much-loved music of his teen years was going on thirty years old. It just didn't feel like it. Not to him anyway.

They pulled out of the gas station and onto the main road. Chicago was still an hour away, but it would be smooth sailing for the remainder of the trip. Newt cut down a rural Indiana road, a shortcut he'd found last month that helped him avoid the road construction and subsequent traffic on I-65, and started singing along with the song. Soon, Tobi joined in with howls and barks.

About a mile down the country road, Newt noticed a blue pickup truck in his side mirror. The truck was coming up behind him fast and seemed to be in a hurry. Newt stuck his arm out the window and waved for them to go around. The most important thing in deliveries like these was maintaining the speed limit. You didn't want to get the local authorities involved over speeding.

The truck quickly veered over into the other lane, which was void of oncoming traffic, and proceeded to pass Newt and his moving van. What the truck revealed in the side mirror once it moved made Newt's heart drop. Ten men on motorcycles with helmets covering their faces and automatic rifles slung over their shoulders.

The pickup truck moved in front of Newt and the driver slammed on the breaks. Newt had no choice but to stop the truck. The men on their bikes surrounded him while two more in ski masks exited the cab of the pickup truck. Newt didn't bother going for the pistol in the glove box or the sawed-off shotgun under the seat. He was outnumbered. Tobi barked and Newt did his best to calm him as one of the masked men from the truck walked to the driver's side door and raised the rifle to Newt's face.

In a voice Newt was sure he recognized; the man spoke. "Do what I tell you and you'll walk away from this."

# 34
## Garvey

Buck came into the bar and right away, Garvey knew something was wrong. The big man's brow was furrowed with worry. Garvey had seen the look before and it usually meant Buck was having trouble wrapping his head around something. He took a seat at the bar next to him.

"What is it?" Garvey asked.

He shook his head. "Club shit."

"C'mon, Buck. I said I would guide you for a while. Use my wisdom. What's going on?"

Buck swallowed hard and looked as if he were about to get sick.

"A shipment of guns was hijacked."

Garvey's relaxed mind suddenly shot to life like a man startled out of sleep. "What?!"

"It was on its way to Chicago. To Needles and his guys. Newt was our driver. He said there were six of them, all with full auto rifles. They ran him off the road, tied him up and left him in a ditch, then took off with the truck and the guns."

"Shit."

"John, Newt said he recognized the voice of one of them."

"Good. Did he give you a name?"

"He thinks it was Seth."

Garvey's first instinct was to slug the man beside him, but after further consideration, Seth hitting the shipment made sense. The kid had threatened to form his own club after all, and would know the shipment schedule from being on the inside of this club. Garvey held on to his anger, but it was now focused on his youngest child. His only son.

"How do I approach this, John?"

Garvey looked his old friend in the eyes. "Like you would with any other enemy of the club. Catch them and teach them a lesson."

Buck studied Garvey for a long while. Perhaps trying to determine if he was positive about the advice he was being given. Then he nodded and stood to leave the bar.

Garvey had a few shots and three more beers before he left the bar himself. Enough to get a slight buzz going. As he walked from the bar, his guitar bouncing lightly against his back, thoughts of his son swirled around his mind. Seth had been in trouble most of his life, looking back, Garvey knew his son would walk the path of a criminal. Garvey didn't do much to sway him from that path. In fact, he'd been the perfect role model in that respect. Yet another failure as a father to his two children.

Elizabeth was the total opposite though. She'd always been a good girl. An honor student in school. A beauty pageant contestant as well. Even now, she did nothing worse than smoke a little weed. Perhaps there's nothing you can really do to sway them from their paths. Despite Garvey's centuries on Earth and his angelic existence, life remained a mystery to him. Things like fate and destiny were concepts he was never able to wrap his head around. In his own life, it had always been his own decisions that led him to where he was. It was his support of Lucifer that saw him banished to Earth. It was a deal with a ghost hunter all those years ago that saw his halo stripped away, most of his powers along with it. And more recently, it was his shortcomings as a father that had turned Seth against him. The decisions a man makes have a ripple effect on the path his life takes. An effect that spreads to those around him and helps form their paths as well.

Now, matters were worse. Seth had made a move against the club and there could be no special treatment. He would have to suffer the consequences like any other. It would be difficult to endure, but he would have to learn. No one betrays the club. Telling his mother what was coming would be even more difficult. As Garvey pulled his bike into the driveway at nearly one in the morning, he decided it best he wait until breakfast for that discussion. Inside, Garvey grabbed a beer from the fridge and stood in the doorway to the room he shared with his wife. Gwen was breathing loudly in her sleep. He listened there a moment longer, stress from a business he had retired from settling into the pit of his stomach like a heavy stone, then turned and went back to the fridge for a slice of leftover pizza. He knew tomorrow would be hard. He had no idea just how hard.

# 35
## Judas

Judas awoke with a start. A nightmare swam away from his conscious mind like a fish at the disturbance of water. He tried to grasp the details of it as it slipped away but was unable to do so. He ran a hand through his thick, black hair and it came away slick with sweat. He stood from the bed and looked back to the other side to find Elizabeth was gone. No note. He picked up his phone and found a text there.

"My mother picked me up to go shopping. She's invited us to lunch. Meet at my parents at noon."

Judas cursed under his breath after reading the message. He texted back. "I was hoping to talk to you about something this morning."

He waited. Nothing. Finally, he went to the bathroom to relieve himself, got dressed, and brushed his teeth before the phone chimed with a return text. "So, talk to me at my parents."

Judas didn't bother responding.

He left the hotel room and took the elevator to the lobby for a cup of coffee. He had slept late and it was nearly eleven, so he returned to the room long enough to get his guns, then made his way to the car and hit the road, bound for the house that belonged to the parents of the woman he loved. He was feeling nauseous.

The day was clear and pleasant. The sweltering heat of summer seemed to be leaving them as they entered September, but when Judas mentioned this to Elizabeth she only laughed and said, "It's Indiana, the heat will be back."

He hoped she was wrong.

Judas pulled into the driveway and parked next to John Garvey's motorcycle, being sure to leave room for Mrs. Garvey to pull into her side of the garage. Then he exited the car, took a calming breath, and rang the doorbell. Nothing. He pulled open the screen door and knocked. The door opened and a disheveled John Garvey stood glaring at him, shirtless and covered in tattooed muscle. The guitar was strapped to his back as usual. He seemed to be trying to remember where he knew Judas from.

"Jude," he finally said.

"Yes. I'm supposed to meet Elizabeth here for lunch. She's been shopping with her mother."

"Oh. I wondered where she got off to. I overslept. Yeah, come on in."

Judas stepped through the door and into the dimly lit living room. "Rough night, sir?"

"Yeah, I may have had a bit too much to drink. And stop calling me sir, it's creepy."

"Right. Mr. Garvey then."

"Just John."

"Okay."

They stood staring at each other awkwardly for a moment. "Jude, can I get you anything. Coffee? Gwen left it on so I'm not sure how fresh it is."

"No, thank you."

"Well, I'm having some."

John Garvey turned his back to him and Judas was once again presented with the perfect opportunity to take his shot. Garvey pulled a coffee mug from the cabinet above his head and went about filling it while rambling on about the local high school's football team. Judas found it hard to listen. His mind instead worked on the problem at hand. Should he take the shot now, could he explain everything to Elizabeth and make her understand? Could she ever understand *why* he had to do such a thing?

He doubted it.

Garvey was adding sugar to the cup.

If he waited and explained everything first, she would never allow it. She loved her father and wouldn't let anything hurt him. No matter what kind of spin he put on it, she wouldn't go for it. Why couldn't she be one of the countless girls out there who hated their fathers?

Judas realized he was lost either way. However, if he didn't kill him at all, he would be returned to the depths of Hell for all eternity. He would burn. Should he kill Garvey now so that part of it would be out of the way? There would be no going back. It was the only way to go, he'd just have to pray Elizabeth would eventually understand.

Garvey was adding cream.

It was now or never. Judas made his move. The gun was out of the holster. The barrel raised, pointblank behind John Garvey's ear as he stirred his coffee with a small, black spoon. Judas cocked the hammer and things went wrong.

The angel moved with a speed that was incomprehensible to Judas' very human eyes. The guitar swung around to face forward, and the angel strummed the strings. Pain ripped through Judas' hand and wrist, up to his shoulder. The gun hit the floor with a dull thud. Judas looked down at his arm and found the flesh shredded, blood erupted from the wounds in a warm spray. It covered his face, the floor, the angel and his guitar. An agonizing scream caught in his throat, desperate to escape but unable to.

With his good hand, Judas picked up the gun. Garvey went to strum the guitar once more, but Judas made it around the corner into the living room. The drywall cracked and the kitchen cabinets splintered with the force of the attack. Judas stumbled out of the front door and down the driveway. He dropped the gun into the seat next to him and with his remaining good hand, he keyed the ignition, threw it in reverse and slammed the gas pedal down. As he backed onto the street, the car lurched as if he were rear-ended and the back window exploded. Another attack from Garvey and his guitar. Judas ducked down in the driver's seat and managed to escape more damage.

Around the corner and out of sight, Judas was sure he'd gotten away. As long as the angel didn't hop on his motorcycle and come after him. His arm was a shredded mess. He was losing blood fast and need some sort of medical attention. He was feeling weak.

Twenty minutes later, he was in downtown Indy pulling into an alley for a safe place to hide. He found Lou in his contacts and dialed the number.

"Judas," Lou said upon answering. "You're hurt."

"Yes. Badly."

"I warned you about that fucker. I told you not to take him lightly."

"I don't have time for this. I need medical attention."

"Alright. Calm down. Send me your location. I'll have someone there as soon as possible."

Judas hung up and did as he was told. Then he dropped his head on the steering wheel and worked at calming himself. He had to slow his breathing. Slow his heart rate. The minutes fell away, each feeling more precious than the last. The gray interior of the car had become a shocking red. Judas' vision was dimming. The adrenaline from the fight had drained along with way too much blood. With one last sigh, he gave into the darkness.

# 36
## Garvey

"What the fuck happened here?" Gwen said as she came in and saw the devastation to her kitchen. Elizabeth stood behind her with shopping bags in hand and worry on her face.

"Jude attacked me," Garvey said plainly.

"Bullshit!" Elizabeth shouted.

Garvey was in the middle of sweeping up wood splinters and broken dishes. He stopped and looked at his daughter. "No, Lizzy. He pulled a gun on me. I fought back."

"Did you hurt him?"

"This isn't my blood." Garvey motioned to his sleep pants and the floor.

"Jesus, John," Gwen said. "A little decorum would be great."

Garvey was dumbfounded by this statement. "Gwen, this asshole most likely used Lizzy to get close to me. He's a fucking assassin. This is exactly what I've been afraid of all these years and the minute I let my guard down..."

Elizabeth broke down. Weeping hard. "No, he wouldn't do that. You attacked him."

Garvey spoke in a comforting tone. "Lizzy, why would I do that?"

Elizabeth could say nothing. Garvey would never do anything to hurt her and she knew that.

"I have to find him," she said, suddenly determined. "Mom, can I use your car?"

"Lizzy, he's dangerous. I don't want you around him," John said.

"He's dangerous to you, Dad. Not me."

Gwen looked back and forth between them, then dropped the car keys into Elizabeth's hand. She turned without another word and left the house.

Garvey dropped his hands in exasperation. "Why would you do that?"

"She has to work this out with him."

"And what if he kills her?"

"He's not after *her*."

"He could easily use her as a hostage to get to me."

"Whatever his intentions were when he found her, there's no doubt that he loves her now. You could see it when they were here together. He wouldn't do her harm."

"I'd say killing her father qualifies as doing her harm. This isn't a fucking romance novel, Gwen. Things are going to get bloody. Jude is a dead man. And while we're at it, our son robbed one of the club's shipments last night. Any act against the club has to be repaid in full."

Gwen's mouth dropped open in shock. "Are you saying what I think you're saying? How can you express worry for one child's life then threaten the other in the next breath?"

Garvey could say nothing. She had him there.

She pointed a scolding finger at him. "John, you need to fix all of this."

He nodded and let out an exhausted sigh. "I know."

His phone rang and he looked at the screen. Buck.

"Yeah," he answered.

"We found Seth. Tavern over on West Washington called The Den. It's closed right now, but he and his buddies are holed up inside."

"Alright. Don't make a move until I get there. I'm coming out of retirement."

"Oh thank fucking Christ," Buck said.

Garvey ended the call and kissed Gwen's forehead. "I'll take care of everything."

"Great," Gwen said. Emotion cracked her voice, but she tried to sound facetious as he walked out the door. "I'll just be here cleaning your mess up."

Garvey pulled up to the Roslyn's Bakery on West Washington fifteen minutes later and killed the engine on his bike. The others were inside, Buck stuffing his face with donuts and chasing them with coffee. Huff, Izzy, and Newt sat around the table as well, all three with cups of coffee in front of them. Izzy was dumping a brown liquid that was no doubt whiskey into his from a flask.

"What do we got?" Garvey asked.

Buck swallowed down the food in his mouth and said, "Huff came across them late last night. Followed them there." He motioned to The Den Tavern across the street from the bakery.

"Yeah," Huff added, "they closed the bar down, but never left. Must be tight with the owner or had a party going on or some shit." Garvey stared out the window at the place. It was an old, brown building with a large triangular rooftop. He had been inside a couple of times and enjoyed the farmland motif and cozy feeling.

"What's the move?" Buck asked.

"You and Huff go in through the back door," Garvey said. "I'll take Izzy and Newt in through the front. Kill Seth's buddies. No one hurts Seth."

They all nodded their understanding and the club was on the move. As they crossed the street, Huff and Newt pulled crowbars from their bikes. Garvey readjusted the strap on his guitar, reminding himself to be prepared for something other than humans inside, but reasonably sure that scenario wouldn't happen. Garvey took up position in front of the door with the others and waited for Buck and Huff to get around to the rear door.

The text came across his phone from Buck that they were ready and Garvey nodded to Newt, who jammed the crowbar into the front door and pried it away from the door frame. A kick from Izzy sent the door crashing inward and Garvey led the way in. As his eyes adjusted to the dim barroom ahead of him, Garvey pulled the pistol from his belt. The scene they came to was an unexpected one. The floor was covered with naked bodies, all passed out from booze, drugs, and sex. Garvey couldn't help but chuckle. His son was definitely a wild one.

"What now?" Buck said, entering the bar from the other side.

"I guess we wake them up." Garvey raised his gun to the ceiling and fired three shots, startling the sleeping revelers into consciousness. "Everyone get dressed and get out."

As they dressed, Garvey moved slowly between them toward his son. Their eyes locked on each other, Seth was fuming as he pulled on his jeans and T-shirt. The others moved toward Seth's friends and kept them from leaving as they dressed. Once Garvey was standing in front of Seth, he reached out one hand and bunched the kid's shirt up, then pushed him against the wall and held him there.

The men and women that weren't with Seth's makeshift motorcycle club left The Den in a hurry. Garvey waited patiently until all were gone and the door was closed before he spoke. "Seth," he said to his son in a voice that was almost comforting. "You don't know what you're doing. You don't know the things we've done and the things we're capable of. You're just a little boy trying to play with the big boys."

Seth's hard countenance was faltering. His angry expression had given way to worry. He knew what was coming. Without looking back at his club, Garvey gave the order. "Do it."

The shots rang out. A bullet to the head of each of Seth's friends. Each one crumpled to the floor, lifeless. Then Buck and the others left the bar. And Garvey spoke again as tears spilled down Seth's cheeks. "The fact that you're my son is the only reason you aren't lying there dead with your friends. The next time something like this happens, it won't save you."

Garvey turned and walked from The Den as well, leaving his son to get out and away from the bar. Once outside, he turned to Huff. "Clean up the mess."

Huff nodded and took Izzy and Newt back in to assist.

"Think he got the point?" Buck asked.

Garvey looked out over the heavy traffic on Washington Street and sighed. "I sure as fuck hope so."

# 37
## Marion

Adrian Dillard opened the passenger side door and handed a coffee to Marion. The gas station was off I-74 in a shit little town about thirty minutes outside of Indianapolis. They filled up on gas and caffeine and she was ready to hit the road again. They had decided to stay the night in Ohio and had an early start this morning for the drive to Indy that wouldn't take more than two hours.

"I got a call," Adrian said as he got in. "A friend from town. He said his daughter came home all excited this morning. Told her dad she pulled an all-nighter in a tavern on the west side and in the morning some biker types came in firing guns. Told them all to get out except for a few. Once they were outside, they heard more shots. Like the remaining bar-goers were executed."

"What's this got to do with us?" Marion asked.

"Well, the leader of the biker gang had a guitar strapped to his back."

"An angel?"

"Could be."

"Maybe our killer's next target," Marion speculated.

"Good chance."

Marion started the car and pulled out of the gas station. "Who is this friend of yours?"

"Ed Richmond. Full-time forklift driver, part-time ghost hunter. He often sends any strange shit he comes across my way. His daughter is a wild one. Twenty-one. Party girl. Still lives at home though. I told Ed we'd be by as soon as we hit town to ask her some questions."

"Alright. I hope she's willing to share."

"Sounds like she was pretty shaken up. I'm sure she'll be willing."

Thirty-six minutes later, Marion and Adrian were pulling into the old neighborhood known as Garden City on the west side of Indianapolis. The house that Ed Richmond lived in was tiny and covered in wood siding, the color of which could only be described as fresh shit. The door opened and a squat, fat man with gray hair came out onto the porch. "Dillard, you creepy motherfucker!" he shouted with cheer. He gave Adrian a bear hug as they met and the supernatural expert gave a grunt and laughed. "It's been far too long. Who's this pretty lady?"

"Ed, this is Special Agent Marion Kern of the FBI."

Marion held her hand out and Ed took it. "Nice to meet you, Ed."

"FBI? Shit, is this really that big a deal?"

"We're actually working on a separate case. This incident at the tavern may be related."

"Well, you beat the cops here. They're probably still trying to figure out the entire guest list. Come on in, Roxy is sleeping on the couch."

Marion considered the girl's name. How could someone named Roxy be anything but wild? Inside, the living room was small but tidy, though the dining room was loaded down with equipment used for ghost hunting. Digital voice recorders in three stacks, spirit boxes, electromagnetic field radiation detectors, dowsing rods, full spectrum camcorders, and high-tech thermometers. Ed was clearly part of a large team of hunters.

The girl snoozing on the couch was pretty and blonde, wearing oversized pajama pants and a tank top. Her blanket ran between her legs and up through her arms where she snuggled with it as if it were a teddy bear.

"Roxy," Ed called in a soothing voice. "Rox, wake up."

The girl's eyes fluttered open and she jerked back at the sight of the strangers in the room.

"It's okay," her father said. "This is your dad's old pal Adrian and his friend, Marion. She's with the FBI. They just want to ask you some questions about what happened this morning."

Roxy sat up and placed a hand on her head. "Water."

"Yeah, sure."

Her father disappeared to the kitchen, and Marion asked her first question.

"Roxy, can you tell us about the man with the guitar?"

"Um, he was big."

"Like fat?"

"No, tall and muscular. Tattoos all over his arms."

Ed returned with a glass of water and Roxy took a few sips from it.

"What else can you remember?" asked Marion.

"He had long hair. Dirty blonde. Also, he had a big beard. It was a little darker than the hair. He was over six feet tall. Maybe six-three."

"Had you ever seen him before?"

She shook her head. "No, but he seemed to be interested in Seth."

"Seth?"

"He's a friend."

"How close of a friend?" Adrian asked.

"We drank together a few times. Hooked up once or twice."

"Do you have his number?" Marion inquired. "His address?"

She laughed. "I don't think he has an address. He seems to crash with friends a lot. I can text him though."

"Great. Just let him know there's an FBI agent that wants to talk to him about the biker with the guitar."

"Okay. But he doesn't seem the type to cooperate with the law."

Marion didn't respond to this. She let the girl send the text and waited for a response. Less than twenty seconds later, the phone chimed. Roxy shrugged. "He said to meet him at McDonald's in ten minutes."

Roxy informed them that McDonald's was just around the corner from her house and the two of them were there in four minutes. Five minutes later, a young man with unkempt red hair and a scowl walked in and approached them.

"You the Feds?" he asked.

"She is," Adrian said pointing to Marion. "I'm just a consultant."

"You want the biker, right? I can give you a couple places where you might find him."

"Great," Marion said.

"But you have to buy me breakfast first."

"Seems reasonable to me."

Once Seth had his breakfast sandwich, they took a seat at a booth and Marion waited.

"Got a pen and paper?" Seth asked.

Marion pulled her notepad out and slid it over to him along with a pen. He jotted down two addresses and slid it back over to her. "I hope you send that fucker up the river. For life."

"That'd be a hell of a long sentence for him," Adrian joked.

Seth stopped chewing and studied him with suspicion.

"We're actually not here to arrest him," Marion said. "We think his life is in danger."

Seth threw the sandwich down in disgust. "Aw fuck! If I'd have known that I would have never agreed to meet you. I'd love to see that asshole dead."

"How exactly do you know this guy?" Adrian asked.

Seth looked at them both, considering. "He's my dad," he said finally.

Adrian and Marion exchanged a look.

Marion spoke in a hushed tone now. "Look, Seth, there's a guy here in town that's hunting down people like your father."

"People like my father?"

"You know what she means," Adrian said leaning forward. "Angels."

"Holy shit," Seth sighed. "You know?"

"We know," Marion confirmed. "We've trailed this guy from Atlanta to Cincinnati and now here. He's killed several angels already and his next target is your father."

"Wait, Cincinnati? That's where my sister lives."

Marion leaned forward. "Seth, has there been anyone new in your sister's life recently. A friend or even a co-worker."

"Her boyfriend. Good looking, middle-eastern guy named Jude."

Adrian banged the table excitedly with the palm of his hand. "Fuck, that's him. Sorry."

"I met him at her apartment," Seth went on. "I knew there was something about that fucker I didn't trust."

"He used her to get close to your father," Marion theorized. "We need you to take us to your dad so he doesn't perceive *us* as a threat."

"Okay, first off, I don't think that would work since he threatened to kill me this morning if I ever messed with his precious club again. Second, I don't want to help that dickhead. If he dies he dies. Fuck him."

"You got to look at the bigger picture here, Seth," Marion said. "This guy has killed several innocents that got in the way of his goal. He won't hesitate to kill your sister or your mother if they get in his way. This guy is a serial killer and he's on a killing spree that has moved around the globe. We *have* to stop him."

Seth's expression was one of sickness. He'd gone pale and sat back in his seat shaking his head. "Alright, I'll take you to him. If he's not in one of these two places, Buck will be at the garage, and he may know where to find him."

"Buck?"

"Yeah, his BFF and right-hand man."

"Alright. You can ride with us. We'll bring you back for your car."

Seth nodded and followed the two of them out of the McDonald's. In the SUV, Seth directed them down 10th Street to Girl School Rd. and into the driveway of a ranch house. A pretty, blonde woman was taking a trash bag out to the can in front of the driveway and stopped to look at them with concern.

"That's my mom," Seth said. "Better let me get out first."

Seth stepped out of the car, leaving Marion and Adrian to wait a few seconds before they stepped out as well. Seth broke down what was going on while they stood back from the mother and son a bit. When he was finished, the mother stepped forward and held out a hand. Marion shook it.

"I'm Gwen, John is my husband. The two of you may as well come in. Maybe I can fill in some blanks for you."

As they entered the house, Marion took note of the cozy décor in a rustic theme. Even the furniture looked as if it were handmade with great care. Gwen led them through the living room and around a corner into the kitchen. Inside, the cabinets were shattered, the countertop was cracked.

"I just finished cleaning up the mess on the floor," Gwen said.

"What happened?" Marion asked.

"My daughter and I were out shopping earlier today. Jude was supposed to meet us here for lunch. He arrived before we did apparently and tried to kill John. John defended himself and this is the damage he did."

"With the guitar," Adrian stated rather than asked. He rubbed one hand over the cracked marble countertop. "Fascinating."

Gwen continued. "My daughter rushed out of here to find Jude. He was hurt pretty badly. Lost a lot of blood."

"Have you heard from her since?" Marion asked. "Any idea where she's gone?"

"No. I've heard nothing. I've been texting her and trying to call. No answer."

"Do you know where we can find your husband?"

Gwen shook her head. "John has been hiding from this sort of thing for, well for centuries. If he doesn't want to be found, he won't be found."

"Alright, thanks for your time."

Marion and Adrian left the house with Seth close behind. In the SUV, Seth spoke up. "He could be at the garage, but it's unlikely. Buck will be there though. If anyone can convince him to meet up with you guys, it'll be him."

The garage was small but seemed busy. Seth led the two of them into a bay where a fat man with a scraggly beard was under a car working on an exhaust system. He looked up at Seth and dropped his hands down at his side. "What the fuck do you want?"

"Something's up," Seth said. "This is Special Agent Kern and her associate."

The fat man looked exasperated. "Now you're bringing the Feds right to our door. What the fuck, man?"

Marion held up her hands. "This isn't about your club or whatever you may be mixed up in. We're hunting a serial killer that has made your club president his next target."

"Garvey?"

"He attacked Dad this morning before you guys came to the tavern."

"He didn't say shit about that to us."

"He probably didn't want you guys to get involved," Adrian interjected. "The man we're after is highly dangerous and not completely human."

Buck seemed to turn this last bit of information over in his mind. "Shit. This is some kinda biblical trouble, right?"

"You know about that?" Marion asked.

"He just told me recently. Fucking blew my mind."

"I have no doubt. Do you have any idea where we can find Mr. Garvey?"

"No, when he wants to lay low, he doesn't tell anyone where he's going. I can send him a message, though. I'll tell him about you guys and what's going on. He may want to meet up."

Marion nodded, knowing it was the best they could hope for.

"Here's my card. Give me a call when you find out."

"Will do."

Marion started back toward the car with the others behind her. Inside Adrian asked Seth, "What do you think, kid? Will your dad want to meet up?"

"I think so. He's going to want to know who this guy is before he faces him again. He's going to want anything you can give him."

Marion pulled away from the garage and drove back toward the McDonald's, feeling nervous about the possible meeting with John Garvey. It wasn't every day one came face to face with a real-life angel.

## 38

## Elizabeth

Elizabeth drove her mother's car up to the dingy motel off Pendleton Pike. It took nearly an hour for Jude to respond to her texts, but he finally told her where he was. She didn't see the rental car as she parked but knew Jude would have hidden it somewhere to avoid her dad tracking him down. The irony that both men were currently hiding from each other was not lost on her.

She exited the car and walked around the sidewalk to room 113, looking around at her surroundings as if she could have possibly been followed, though she knew no one would be following her. She knocked on the door. The three knock, pause, two knock code Jude instructed her to use.

The door opened and Elizabeth found herself staring at a bespectacled man in a blood-covered apron. He was wiry and pale with a pencil-thin mustache and stared at her without speaking. When she looked to the bed and saw Jude, her breath caught in her throat. His arm was a bloody mess. Her father had done serious damage and Elizabeth wasn't sure he'd have use of it again from what she could tell. The back-alley doctor that opened the door sure as hell wasn't going to help any.

Jude waved her in and told the creep in the apron to give them a minute. He dropped the apron behind the door and pulled a pack of cigarettes from his breast pocket. Elizabeth shut the door behind him and moved around to the other side of the bed. She took the seat where the so-called doctor sat previously.

"Jude," she said and felt a hot tear roll down her cheek. On her drive over, she felt a mixture of emotions, chief among them anger and worry. Now, at the sight of Jude and his shredded arm, the anger dissipated completely. "Jude, you have to tell me what's going on."

He swallowed and looked away from her. "You're not going to like what I tell you."

"I have to know."

Still, he remained silent. Elizabeth pulled his chin up so that he was forced to look her in the eyes, then she waited.

"My name isn't Jude," he finally said. "It's Judas."

"Like from the bible."

"Exactly the one from the bible."

"I don't understand."

"My betrayal led to the torture and crucifixion of Jesus of Nazareth, the son of God."

Elizabeth shook her head. "How is that possible?"

"Being the daughter of a fallen angel, something like this shouldn't come as a surprise to you."

"So, it's true. You used me to get to my father."

"That's how it started out, but then I fell in love with you. Something I couldn't have predicted."

Elizabeth couldn't tell if he was lying. "Why do you want to kill him?"

"I don't. I was sent to do it."

"By whom?"

Judas let out a steading breath before he spoke. "After my betrayal, I was wracked with guilt. I couldn't bear the pain of what I'd done, so I committed suicide. My sin-filled life was rewarded with an eternity in Hell. There, I was tortured and burned for over two-thousand years, so when Lucifer came along and offered me a deal to get out, I jumped at the chance."

"What was the deal?" asked Elizabeth.

"I'd return to Earth with a case of gold bullets and kill all the remaining fallen angels."

"Fuck," Elizabeth said under her breath. "How many were there?"

"Twelve. And your father is the last one."

"You can't do this to me, Jude...Judas. If you love me, you *won't* do this."

"It's because I love you that I must. Please understand, if I fail in my mission, I will be sent back to Hell to finish out my sentence. If I succeed, I'll be made completely human and allowed to live out my life on Earth. With you."

"Holy shit." Elizabeth took this all in with a storm of thoughts swirling through her head. "Judas, do you really think I'd be able to forgive you for killing my father?"

He shrugged. "It's a chance I *have* to take. You can't begin to fathom the pain that is dealt in that place. To return burdened with the pain of losing you on top of that is not an option. I can't go back."

Elizabeth stood and walked toward the door. "I need some time to process this."

"I understand."

She stopped and looked back at him. He didn't look like a killer. He seemed weak and frail, his right arm a ravaged, bloody mess. She walked back to that side of the bed and held her hands out over his wounds. A blue glow surrounded her hands, bleeding through her fingers. She moved them up and down his arm and Judas grimaced and grunted in pain as the wounds on his arm closed and healed. Judas held his arm up once she had finished, a look of shock on his face. The wounds were closed and partially healed.

"I'm not the best, but it's a start," Elizabeth said.

"I don't know how to thank you," Judas returned.

"You can thank my father. I have that ability because of him."

With that, Elizabeth left the room and returned to her mother's car. She turned the key in the ignition and proceeded to cry.

# 39
Garvey

John Garvey parked his motorcycle in the small lot in front of the hole-in-the-wall bar known as The Dugout, stared up at the old sign with trepidation, and forced himself to swing his leg off the seat. Meeting with an FBI agent wasn't exactly his idea of a wise move, especially considering all he'd done in the past. Hell, what he did that morning. Still, this was about something else. After all this time, he had been targeted. Now, he needed to find out why. And by whom.

"I'll give you ten dollars if you let me kiss your dick," came a voice from behind him.

Garvey turned to the source of this odd proposition and found a scrawny, black man digging through the trash at the base of an overflowing dumpster. "Bad idea," he said in return, concocting a lie. "Genital warts."

The man nodded his understanding and Garvey laughed under his breath. People continuously surprised him, even after a couple of thousand years on Earth.

Inside, the bar was dim and worn down. The bar top looked as if it could stand to be stripped, sanded and re-finished. There were only a handful of patrons in the place, and it wasn't hard to pick out the Fed and her friend. A pantsuit in a joint like this was a dead giveaway. The gun on her belt was the cherry on top. Garvey adjusted the guitar on his back and moved across the room to join them.

He stopped at the edge of the booth and stared at the two of them.

"Mr. Garvey?" The agent said. "Please join us."

"No. We need to move to the back booth. I get the seat facing the door, you two sit across from me."

The Fed looked to her associate. The man with the dark, thinning hair and graying beard gave no indication he cared about seating arrangements one way or the other. Then she looked back at Garvey. "That's fine."

Garvey looked around the bar once again, noting every other person within. Sizing them up and deciding the one that would most likely be a danger to him. The man at the bar in the corduroy jacket probably had nothing to do with this whole mess, but John decided, should things go south, he'd be the first to die.

He slid into the booth and his two companions sat across from him as agreed.

The Fed started. "Mr. Garvey, I'm Agent Kern and this is my consultant, Adrian Dillard. We're glad you decided to meet with us."

"All right, I'm here," John said. "Want to tell me what's going on?"

Agent Kern cleared her throat and explained. "Mr. Garvey, we believe the man your daughter has been dating is an assassin. We've compiled a file on him and tracked him here. We also believe you're his next target."

"I know I'm his next target. Tell me about his previous targets."

Kern opened the folder in front of her and slid it over to him. "The specifics are the same. Gold bullet, scars on the backs of the victims, odd internal organs, and muscle structure. All of it buried by someone in a position of power. Every victim a musician. Every guitar missing from the murder scene. Thanks to my expert in all things supernatural here, I know that all of these victims were angels. I know you're an angel. We were hoping you could fill in some blanks for us. Tell us who he is. What's going on. Furthermore, we want to keep *you* alive."

Garvey looked through the file with a growing sense of dread. Azrael, Raphael, Uriel, even Metatron, they were all here. The list went on and on, but Garvey knew this wasn't all of them. There were names missing.

"Mr. Garvey, what is it?" Kern asked.

Garvey couldn't answer. He was shocked at what he saw.

He was terrified of what it *meant*.

The supernatural expert spoke up for the first time. "I think Mr. Garvey has come to the same conclusion I have, though I didn't want to bring it up until I was sure."

Garvey looked at the man. He seemed familiar. Not in a way that he'd met the man before, but in the way he knew of him. He was no mere mortal, that much was certain. "Who are you really? What's your part in all this?"

Kern looked at Adrian as well, her gaze scrutinizing. "What does he mean?"

Dillard ignored her and addressed Garvey instead. "You know who I am."

Then it dawned on Garvey. Any angel worth his salt would know this man by sight alone, Garvey's eyes were just out of practice. "You're The Caretaker."

"The Caretaker?" Kern asked.

"It's just a title. The Caretaker, The Keeper, many names that all mean the same thing. You already know why I've earned it."

"And what is it you two suspect that I'm not getting here?" Agent Kern inquired.

Dillard looked to Garvey to answer her question. He did. "We suspect that I'm the last one."

"What does that mean?" Kern asked. "What happens if this guy gets to you?"

Garvey shrugged. "I'd rather not think of that until I can confirm it. I'll need to make a few calls." He stood from the booth before either of them could protest and moved to the hall where the bathrooms were located for more privacy. The first number he dialed was answered by a female voice he didn't recognize.

"I'm trying to reach Pete."

"I'm sorry, you have the wrong number."

"He may answer to Michael?"

"Still the wrong number. Sorry."

Garvey ended the call and searched his contacts. He dialed the next number.

"Hello?" the voice was familiar.

"Gabe?" Garvey asked.

"No, this is Steve. Who is this?"

"Steve." Gabe's lover. Garvey had talked to him a couple of times over the phone. The two were married in California two years ago. Gabe never gave in to the paranoia like John. "It's Garvey. Is Gabe around?"

"Garvey. I'm sorry, Gabriel was killed six months ago."

Garvey's heart sank. "How?"

"He was shot and killed by a mugger." Garvey heard the emotion that cracked in the other man's voice. "They never caught the killer. I'm sorry. I didn't think to call you."

Garvey couldn't speak.

"Garvey," Steve said, lowering his voice. "He was killed with a gold bullet. Whoever did it, he knew. And he's still out there. Be careful."

"Yeah," Garvey managed. "I will."

He pressed the end button on his phone. He tried a few more numbers, but all were out of service or taken by someone else. The cold truth of the situation came down on him like a sledgehammer on a railroad spike. He was the last. All this time, with all the preparations he'd taken, he never thought things could go this wrong. Looking out for himself was one thing, the others never took a possible threat to their existence seriously, how could he have stopped this? With as little as they contacted each other, how could he have known? Someone should have warned him. Steve should have known to warn him.

Garvey returned to the booth and slid in across from The Caretaker and the Fed. "It's true. The others are gone."

"Shit," Adrian Dillard said.

"What?" Agent Kern asked. "What does this mean?"

Dillard looked at her with dark eyes. "It means it's absolutely imperative that we keep the last angel alive."

# 40
## Judas

Judas left the car. His arm wasn't quite back to what it was before, but it was close. If not for Elizabeth, he'd have probably lost the use of it altogether. Since leaving the motel and his car behind, he'd returned to the life of a drifter. A different hotel every night. Laying low during the day. He didn't think Elizabeth would give up his location to her father, but he couldn't take any chances.

The diner was a grease pit in the town of Plainfield, just to the west of Indianapolis. He took the booth in the corner and ordered a burger with fries, his appetite just returning after his run-in with John Garvey. The bell above the door rang and Judas was surprised to see Lou step inside. The well-dressed man looked over the filthy joint with disgust clear on his face. When his eyes fell on Judas, he shook his head.

Judas sat back in the seat and blew air through his teeth in frustration.

"So, this is what it's come to," Lou said. "May I sit?"

"Please." As if he needed Judas' permission for anything.

Lou sat and stared across the table at Judas. Finally, he held his hands out and smirked. "Where do I start? You have really fucked things up. And it's worse than you even realize."

"How can it possibly be worse?"

"The Caretaker is here. Snooping around the shit storm you've created of this situation."

"I have no idea what the fuck that means." Judas was losing control of his temper.

"Careful. If tempers flare, I guarantee you'll suffer. You think what Garvey did to you hurt? It'll seem like a fucking titty twister compared to what I'll do to you. Are we clear?"

Judas took a deep breath and forced himself to calm down. "Yes, we're clear."

Lou stared spikes into him a little longer before, miraculously, his expression softened, and he almost looked sorry for the man in front of him. "Look, I'm sorry as hell you're in this position. I know that's hard to believe considering the source, but I truly am. This girl is something special, I can see that. Unfortunately, and this is me being brutally honest with you, you are *not* special. There is nothing special about you. You lived like a coward and you sure as fuck died like one. Then you paid for it just like any other sad sack of shit would have. But *now*, unlike all those other poor souls that will never stop paying for their sins, you have the fucking opportunity of a lifetime."

"You can cut the fucking pep talk," said Judas. "I went for it and got burned. Next time he won't be so lucky."

A grin spread across the older man's face. "That's the old fire I saw in you before. Glad to have you back."

"Thanks. Now, are you going to expand on this caretaker business?"

"Controller of the ten magics."

"Holy shit," Judas said, his eyes wide. "The Keeper."

"Yeah, he tagged along with that FBI agent I mentioned before, and they trailed you to Indy."

"Killing Garvey's going to be hard enough, how am I supposed to get around him."

"You're a clever one, I'm sure you'll figure something out. Maybe use a little misdirection."

Judas considered this. "Right."

"Judas, I'm going to sweeten the pot a little for you. Once Garvey is dead, I'll personally see to it that you and your lady fair are whisked away to somewhere lovely to, hopefully, work out your differences and live happily ever after. The Fed and The Caretaker will never find you."

Judas felt a faint hope blossom in his chest cavity. Of course, he wasn't dumb enough to trust what Lou said entirely, the devil is in the details as they say. Still. "You'd do that?"

"I'm nothing if not a hopeless romantic at heart. I know that's hard to believe, but I've had my fair share of newfound love. Trouble is, it always leads to love lost."

"I've never seen this side of you. I must admit, it's refreshing."

"Well, it's not something I want to get out. I have a reputation to hold onto."

"My lips are sealed."

Lou stood to leave. "Look, I'm trying to keep a lot of plates spinning, but I'll try to keep you informed of any bad shit coming your way. You just focus on getting that arm back to full form. Then, let's end this."

Judas gave a sharp, determined nod and Lou turned and left the diner. For a short time after the old man was gone, Judas felt good about their conversation. He felt Lou would do right by him. By the time he'd finished his burger, however, suspicion was slowly creeping up into his brain and he found himself wondering if a gold bullet would work on Lou.

# 41
## Buck

Buck locked up the garage for the night and, a short ride later, pulled up to the bar for drinks with some of the boys. Though he'd tried to contact Garvey, he hadn't heard from his old friend in two days. Not since he agreed to meet with the FBI agent and her creepy friend. He was starting to get worried about him, but he knew if John Garvey didn't want to be bothered, he wasn't going to be. Buck had decided to take a 'don't speak unless spoken to' approach to it instead. If John wanted the club's help, he'd ask for it.

Buck weaved his way through the crowd and ordered a beer at the bar. As he turned, the blaze of a lighter caught his eye and he could just make out John Garvey sitting in the corner booth, the light in the classic bar lamp over the table was out and left the booth and Garvey shrouded in darkness. Garvey motioned Buck over as he lit the cigarette that hung between his lips.

Buck squeezed into the opposite side of the booth. "I thought you gave those things up for your health. Though, knowing what I know now, that doesn't make much sense."

"Gwen made me give them up," Garvey said with a lopsided grin. "Said it was a disgusting habit. Couldn't let my motorcycle club know how much sway my ol' lady has over me."

"Understandable. So, what's going on?"

"Ancient grudges with religious undercurrents," Garvey said grimly.

"Sounds dangerous. What can we do?"

"Not get involved."

"What?"

"It's far too dangerous. This is not a group of drug dealers I'm up against. Mortals need to steer clear."

Buck didn't like it. The club had always had each other's backs no matter what they faced. Nevertheless, Buck nodded his understanding. "Got it."

Garvey studied him closer. "Do you?"

"Yeah, man. We won't interfere."

"Good. Buy me a beer?"

"Yeah, no problem."

Buck stood and moved back to the bar. He bought two more beers and turned back toward the booth, which was now empty.

"Of course," the big man mumbled to himself. As he drew nearer, he noticed a small note was left behind. Scribbled on the note in black ink were the words, "If I survive this, drinks are on me. Enjoy the beer, JG."

Buck dropped heavily into the booth. After all their years together, John Garvey had always seemed invincible. Any threat they faced, he met with confidence and aggression. The idea that he felt he may not survive this threat was hard for Buck to wrap his head around. He downed both beers as he sat alone in the booth. Then, he stood and joined the others with a round of shots.

# 42

## Garvey

The night had turned cool. The first sign of autumn's impending arrival. Garvey stood in the deep shadow off to the right of the house he owned. He'd parked two streets away and cut through neighbor's yards to get to where he was now. There he waited, unwilling to enter and endanger his wife or take a chance that the hitman or any other threat could appear in search of him. Moving Gwen was next on his agenda, but he had to find the right place. With Jude's injuries, he knew he had time.

Headlights rounded the corner at the end of the street. The car he'd been waiting for. His daughter pulled the rental car into the driveway and, as she opened the door to climb out, Garvey stepped out of the shadows and called her name.

She jumped, startled, and Garvey had to grin at the flash of nostalgia that hit him as he remembered the many pranks pulled when she was a child and afraid of clowns. Halloween was especially heated in their battle of wits. Of course, she was far more easily startled than he, and he was often the victor.

Garvey motioned for her to follow him around the corner of the house and out of sight. When she was standing in front of him she said, "You scared the shit out of me."

"Yeah, I know," he laughed. "Listen, you need to tell me who this guy is. Your boyfriend. I need to know his location too."

"Dad, I don't know where he is. I saw him right after he attacked you, but he's been moving around since then. He hasn't contacted me at all."

"Has he told you anything?"

Elizabeth looked hesitant to share what she knew.

"Lizzy, I'm your father."

"I don't need to be reminded of that. It's just, he's not a bad guy, Dad."

Garvey felt his jaw unhinge and an incredulous anger sweep through his entire body. "Not a bad guy? He's a serial killer, Lizzy. He's killed every fallen angel on the planet, and *now* he's gunning for me. I'm the last one. Do you get that?"

"Dad," she said shaking her head. "His name isn't Jude. It's Judas."

"As in?"

"Yes, that Judas."

Garvey ran a frustrated hand through his long hair. "What the fuck is he up to?"

"He said The Devil put him up to all this. Said he'd release him from his punishment. Let him live a normal life on Earth if he took all of you guys out. You were right, he did use me to get close to you, but we fell in love, and now he's determined to finish the job so he can be with me."

Garvey looked at her, his anger flaring, but at the look of the anguish in her eyes, the fury quickly faded away. "Lizzy, he's been lied to. He doesn't know the full scope of what he's doing."

"What do you mean?"

Garvey studied her a moment. Her deep, brown eyes swimming with tears, then he shook his head. "I need you to reach him. Tell him I want to meet with him before we face each other. Tell him we need to get some things straight. Okay?"

"Okay. What else can I do?"

"Nothing else. Just that. Do yourself a favor, Lizzy, stay out of it. This is something you and everyone else will have to let run its course. Judas and I will settle this. All right?"

She looked unsure but nodded her understanding anyway and pulled her phone to send Judas a text. When she finished, she looked back up at him. "Dad, is there any way both of you come out of this alive?"

Garvey hadn't thought about the situation in that way. He only knew he'd kill the man he knew as Jude to save his life, protect his family, and avoid catastrophe. "No way that I can see, Lizzy."

The pain on her face broke his heart, but he wouldn't give her false hope.

The iPhone in her hand chimed and she looked down at the screen.

"The Top Hat Diner in Plainfield."

"I know the place."

"He said to meet him there at nine tomorrow morning."

Garvey kissed her forehead. "Thank you, Lizzy."

He walked away before she could say anything else. Back through the neighborhood to his bike, Garvey spent the rest of the night on a ride. Country roads between quiet fields of corn that were nearly ready for harvest. It was on rides such as these that he was able to achieve his clearest thinking. Ponder the problems facing him. As much as he wanted to make his daughter happy and avoid either dying or killing the man she loved, he could see no way around it. If all the information he'd gathered was true, their final confrontation would be unavoidable.

Still, Garvey was convinced Judas wasn't told the full story and he had no idea what his actions were working toward. That was what the meeting was all about.

Garvey found the bank of a large pond, parked the bike, and watched the sun rise. There he sat until it was time to head to the diner. Pulling into the parking lot of the old grease pit, Garvey's head ached, and he still had no idea how to keep his daughter from getting hurt.

With one hand on the neck of his guitar, ready for the slightest hint of an attack, Garvey stepped into the diner and found the handsome face of Judas staring at him from the far corner booth. Garvey walked slowly toward the booth and took a seat across from his adversary. Judas kept one hand under the table, where he no doubt had the gun loaded with gold bullets ready for any sign of attack.

"Judas," Garvey said.

"So, you know?"

"I know. I see your arm is healing nicely."

"Your daughter's work. She used her gift to speed up my recovery."

"She failed to mention that."

A smug look came over Judas' face. "Interesting. And what are we meeting for? What's to keep me from pulling this trigger and ending all this right now?"

"Well, for one, you know after our first tussle that you're not that fast. Two, you want to hear what I have to say. It's crucial to your mission."

Judas seemed to relax a little. "Alright. What is it? Are we laying down some ground rules? Are you going to convince me you have a way for me to get out of this?"

Garvey knew he was being facetious on this last part, but there was a slight, hopeful gleam in his eyes, nonetheless. "No, nothing like that. I just wanted to know if you've been made aware of the consequences of your actions."

"Meaning?"

"Do you know what's going to happen after you kill me?"

"My mission would be complete. I'd become mortal to live a normal life. Hopefully with Elizabeth, should she see her way to forgive me."

"Well, all of that would happen sure, and Elizabeth may even forgive you in time. Doubtful, but you never know. However, there are some key details your friend Lou left out." Now Judas looked concerned. He was blinded by hope, of that there was no doubt, but Garvey could tell he was no fool. He added, "The devil is in the details after all."

"What details?"

"The fallen angels that reside on Earth, all of them together, form a barrier of sorts. Well, now that you've killed all but one of us, that barrier has been weakened."

"I don't understand."

"The moment you kill me, you will usher in the end of days. The apocalypse. Hell on Earth. So, yeah, you'll be mortal, but you'll be right back in Hell. See how *he* gets you?"

Judas sat back in his seat and thought about all this. "Fuck!"

"Yeah, changes things up a bit, right? So, why not put your self-serving bullshit aside and think about all the innocent people that would be affected by this."

"Wait, if they're truly innocent, wouldn't I be doing them a favor. After all, they would head to the promised land, while the sinners were left here to suffer. In a way, I'd be looked upon as a hero."

"Jesus, you are delusional."

"*Don't*...don't say that name."

Garvey studied the man before him and suddenly saw him in a new light. He no longer felt anger or hatred toward him, emotions that had been easy for Garvey to jump to all throughout his existence, instead he only felt pity. This tragic, grief-stricken man in front of him had endured pain Garvey couldn't begin to fathom. Was it any wonder he'd do whatever it took to find a better life? Tell himself whatever lie necessary? "You're going to go through with this no matter what I say, aren't you?"

Garvey was surprised to see tears well up in Judas' eyes. "I've struggled with all this, believe me, especially after meeting Elizabeth and falling in love with her, but I can't go back. Any slim chance I have of a normal life with her, even in a world full of Hellish chaos, is a welcome alternative to the torture of the existence I've known since that one fateful day. I won't go back."

Garvey sighed heavily. It was abundantly clear that nothing he could say would change this man's mind, but at least he was now informed. Any decision to abort his insane mission would have to be Judas' alone. Hopefully, a seed was planted. "Alright, Judas. I'll leave you now. Once I'm away from this dump, we're back to being enemies. Take your best shot."

Garvey stood and backed cautiously away from the table. His dexterous fingers were ready to strum if Judas made a move. Once out the door, he hurried to his bike and started the motor. Through the window, Garvey could see Judas hadn't moved from the booth. In fact, he still stared straight ahead as if Garvey was still sitting there. The expression on his face was one of worry. Contemplation. Maybe Garvey *had* gotten through, but probably not.

Garvey twisted the throttle and sped out of the parking lot.

# 43
## Marion

John Garvey had been adamant about Marion and Adrian Dillard staying out of his way. The fight was between Garvey and Judas and it would be Garvey and Judas who settled it. "I'm an FBI agent, Mr. Garvey, staying out of this is not an option," she had said.

"Agent Kern," Garvey had answered, his voice strong and commanding even through the speaker on the iPhone in Marion's hand, as if he were her superior, "I am an immortal being and, though I'm not entirely sure *what* Judas is, I'm pretty sure he isn't mortal. Any mortal who should get in the middle of this will be harmed."

"I'll take your warning under advisement," Marion had said. Director Fuller had always said her stubbornness would either propel her career or get her killed. So far it had done the former, but she kept waiting for the latter to catch up with her.

Now, back in the hotel room with Adrian Dillard, Marion felt confident in the decision to stick around. After all, she had Dillard. The man apparently held a highly respected title among the supernatural. The Caretaker. Keeper of the Ten Magics and the only being capable of tapping into all ten.

Their purpose had changed. Catching a killer was no longer in the cards. They had to kill Judas before he could get to John Garvey. Still, their killer was a slippery bastard. Garvey had met with him in a diner as if to make sure they each had the rules straight before starting a game of capture the flag. It seemed ridiculous to her. Garvey had him there in front of him and didn't kill him.

"I know what you're thinking," Adrian Dillard said from the doorway to the bathroom. "Why didn't Garvey kill Judas while he had the chance?"

"I'd rather you didn't use your abilities to go picking through my thoughts."

"I didn't need to, it's written all over your face."

"Well, do you have an answer?"

"It's the daughter. Garvey wouldn't do anything to hurt her. This way they each let the chips fall where they may, and she'll have to deal with the results."

"So, what? These two are going to have a Wild West showdown?"

"I think if Garvey can find a way to avoid it, he will."

"And Judas?"

Dillard shook his head and paced across the room. "I think Judas is desperate enough to do whatever it takes to put one of those gold bullets in Garvey's skull. I think he's going to push and push until the angel has no choice but to face him."

"Adrian, what's it going to take to kill Judas?"

"Well, he's no demon. No angel either. He's a tortured soul, sent back to earth in an effort to save himself. Nonetheless, I expect we could dispatch him much the same way we did Dave the Demon."

Marion shivered at the memory of Adrian sawing through the demon's burned flesh. "Well, we have to find him first."

"Yeah, that's the tricky part. He's no doubt ditched the Toyota."

"You can bet on it. In most cases, the perp will boost a replacement car."

"Yeah, but that doesn't seem like his style."

"Not at all," Marion agreed. "He'd be more likely to purchase a new vehicle."

"Or..." Dillard said, revelation clearly written on his face. "This guy was one of the apostles. He followed Jesus everywhere, he sure as hell didn't do it in a car."

"On foot?"

"Right."

"You think one of Jesus' apostles is walking Indianapolis in search of the one angel that's going to keep mankind from facing Judgment Day?"

"Yeah."

It sounded preposterous when spoken out loud. But it was the reality of their situation. Marion's iPhone rang in her hand and made her jump. She didn't recognize the number but slid the green answer button across the screen anyway. "This is Agent Kern."

"Hey, it's Buck. Remember me?"

She switched the call to speaker. "John Garvey's friend. Of course. Do you have something?"

"Well, I've had the guys out looking for this ass clown. Sort of an all-points bulletin biker style."

"Okay."

"One of the guys caught sight of him at a hotel on the northwest side called Old 6 Tee 7. Place has been there forever. Room 202."

"Great. Thank you, Buck," Marion said as she jotted the name of the place down. Then after some consideration, "Listen, Buck, you know you need to leave this one alone? Let the professionals handle it?"

"Lady, I'm far more professional than my appearance alludes to."

Marion had to smirk at this. "I'm sure you are, but there are immortals involved here. If you get in the way, you could get hurt."

"Yeah, I got the same bullshit from Garvey. Doesn't mean we're going to listen."

"Buck," Marion started, but the big biker cut her off.

"Tell you what, last one there buys a round at the bar later."

Buck hung up. Marion cursed out loud.

Adrian looked at her with worry.

"Garvey's gang found Judas. We need to move and get to him before they do."

In a snap, they were out the door and in the SUV. Pendleton Pike was on the other side of town. Marion took I-70 to cut through downtown Indianapolis and was exiting onto Pendleton Pike less than thirty minutes later.

# 44
## Elizabeth

The sun was setting and the evening it brought on its heels had the chill of early fall. Elizabeth moved up the stairs of the hotel to room 202 and knocked on the door. She could hear Judas fumbling inside, then the door opened, and he ushered her in.

"Elizabeth, what are you doing here?" He was slightly out of breath. Sweat apparent on his brow.

"What were you doing? Is there another woman here?"

"*What*? Of course not. But you shouldn't be here either. It's entirely too dangerous."

"I overheard Buck on the phone with one of the other guys. That's how I found out where you were. They're on their way."

Judas smiled slightly. "And you felt the need to come and warn me?"

Elizabeth said nothing. Judas moved closer to her, turned her face up to his, and kissed her lips. "Elizabeth, I'm sorry for all this. I hope you know that."

"I understand the difficulty of your situation. I get how you have no choice but to go through with all this. But you do realize that you'll be putting *me* in a difficult situation should you succeed. I can't promise I'll be in your life if you kill my father."

"Elizabeth, I don't just want you in my life, I want to *build* a new life around you. Whatever happens, you're the only woman in this world for me. Which makes it vastly more difficult to go through with this. The alternative is unbearable."

Elizabeth wrapped her arms around him and laid her head on his chest, taking some small amount of comfort from being in his arms. "I just hope you know what you're doing."

"Me too." They came apart and Judas looked into her eyes. "You *must* go now. I don't want your father's men to see you here."

There was something more to it than that. She could see it in his eyes. But she didn't press the matter. Instead, she nodded and kissed him again. Then she turned to leave.

"Elizabeth. I love you."

The tears came. She couldn't bear to turn back to him. "I know. I love you too, Judas."

Then she was out of the stuffy little room. The cool air felt good on her burning eyes. Down the stairs and into her mother's car, Elizabeth pulled away from the hotel with her mind desperately working to find an alternate solution to all this. She needed to speak to her father, but these days, he was even harder to track down than Judas.

# 45
## Buck

Buck pulled his motorcycle into the hotel parking lot that Elizabeth had left only twenty minutes before. Behind him rode Huff, Izzy, Newt, and four new pledges that Buck still hadn't gotten the names down for. He had always been awful at remembering names. They all parked near the office and killed the engines on their bikes. Room 202 was across the parking lot and up the stairs. Buck could see the television flashing just through the curtains.

"Think he heard the bikes?" Izzy asked.

Buck studied the window. No sign of Judas peeking out at the sound of their hogs. Then he shrugged. "No, I think we're fine."

"What's the plan?" Huff inquired.

"We go up the stairs, kick the door in and shoot the fucker."

The others only stared at him, uncertain.

"What?"

It was Izzy who spoke up. "Isn't this guy supposed to be pretty badass?"

"It's a fucking hotel room, Izz. There's a door and a window. I don't know what else to tell you. There's eight of us and one of him. He's outnumbered and out gunned."

Izzy threw his hands up. "Alright, man. You're the fucking prez."

"Fucking A right! Let's go."

Buck strode across the street keeping an eye on the window and the flashing TV all the way. He expected Judas to pop his head around the corner of the curtain at any second, but it never happened. Up the stairs and over to door 202, Buck moved to the other side and pulled his pistol from his belt. He cocked it. The others followed suit. Huff stood in front of the door and waited for Buck to give him the signal. Buck gave a nod and Huff kicked the door in. Buck was first inside. Gun held high. The bed was still made and empty. Through the room, to the bathroom. The door was open a crack and the light was on. Buck slung it open and found nothing. He relaxed and looked back at the others. "He's not here."

"Fuck!" Izzy exclaimed.

Buck was about to instruct them to leave, his next idea being a stakeout to see if their target returned, but something caught his eye before the words could pass through his lips. Beneath the bed was a red flashing light.

"Shit!" Buck cried. "Out! Get out!"

The others ran out the door and as Buck came out of the room, he saw the FBI agent and her creepy associate walking across the parking lot. Buck screamed. "BOMB!"

Then the night erupted around him.

# 46
## Marion

Special Agent Marion Kern and her consultant, Adrian Dillard, arrived at Hotel 6 Tee 7 in time to see one of the bikers kick in Judas' door and Buck lead the way inside.

"Shit!" Marion exclaimed. "They beat us here."

Adrian didn't reply. Marion parked the SUV on the other side of the cluster of motorcycles and the two of them were out of the vehicle and crossing the parking lot fast. Marion pulled her gun. She expected to hear shots from room 202 at any second. Instead, the bikers came rushing back out of the room. Buck came last. He shouted one word to them before reality took on a blazing new light.

"BOMB!"

In the flash that came, Marion saw Buck and his cohorts engulfed in its destructive brilliance. The force of the blast lifted her off her feet and sent her hurtling back toward the SUV. Pain ripped through her body as she hit the hard pavement and tumbled to a stop. Her ears were ringing. Head pounding. Knees and forearms bleeding. As the purple flashes cleared from her vision, she saw a door open on the other side of the U-shaped hotel. A man emerged and came down the stairs toward her. Judas held up his hand and waved an object at her. A detonator.

"I was hoping to get all of you with that blast," Judas said. There was no joy or triumph in his tone. He spoke with a calm, businesslike rationality. "Buck was smarter than I gave him credit for. Figured out my trap before you two could enter the room."

Marion couldn't speak. Her lungs were still trying to readjust to the air. She rolled onto her hands and knees, the agonizing pain from this action glaringly apparent, and began to search for her gun. It was in her hand before the explosion, she was sure of it. Adrian. Where was Adrian? Was he in worse shape than her right now? Did he even survive the explosion?

"I'm truly sorry you had to get in the middle of all this," Judas said. He tossed the detonator aside and pulled a 9mm pistol from a shoulder holster beneath his suit jacket. He pointed the gun at Marion and pulled the trigger.

# 47
## Judas

Judas remained calm and collected. The bombing hadn't gone precisely as he'd hoped, but he'd wiped out the majority of possible hindrances to his plan. The other two could be cleared up easily enough with lead slugs to the head.

He exited room 223 and coolly took the stairs down to the parking lot. He showed the FBI agent the detonator and spoke to her in his flat, serious manner. He didn't enjoy killing people. It was a necessity to attain the things he wanted – he needed. It was imperative to distance himself from the situation.

Judas spoke to the woman again as he pulled the 9mm from its holster, but he wondered if she could hear him at all. No doubt the explosion had left her ears ringing something awful. Judas pointed the gun at her head and pulled the trigger.

In an instant, the ground erupted in front of him and a slab of solid rock appeared in front of the FBI agent, shielding her from his shots. Through his stupor, Judas caught movement from his left. Adrian Dillard, the man Lou had warned him about, the man Judas should have had the foresight to eliminate first. The man that was on his feet, stumbling forward with one hand out.

Judas raised the gun to aim at Dillard but was suddenly pushed back by some unseen force. Judas was sent hurdling away from the parking lot and smashed through the window of another hotel room where he fell to the floor. He stood and brushed the glass from his suit. In the bathroom doorway, an old woman with earplugs in and a sleep mask on her head, stood flabbergasted, toothbrush in hand, water running.

"Sorry for the intrusion," Judas said. He had a feeling this one didn't hear him either. He climbed back through the broken window and scanned the parking lot for Dillard and the Agent. They were gone. As was their SUV.

# 48
## Garvey

John Garvey awoke to sunlight streaming through the tattered curtains. His eyes fluttered open and, once they'd adjusted to the light, he took in his surroundings. He'd slept in a different place every night for the last few days. All of them in tiny, dilapidated houses. The owners or squatters that lived in them were all on drugs of one kind or another. Or in some cases multiple drugs at one time. They were his people though.

Through the years of running drugs, John Garvey had become the junkie messiah of sorts. A savior to the hopeless and downtrodden. They looked to him for drugs in times of financial strain and he had obliged, always willing to work out a deal. The "do me a favor and someday I'll ask a favor of you" kind of arrangement that now saw him sleeping on a couch here, a recliner there. This morning, it was a floor. He thought these days were in the past.

It was a dangerous area of town. There were dangerous people around. In the end, he knew a junkie would turn on him for a score without hesitation. That's why he kept moving. And, unless they wielded a gold weapon forged in the fires of Hell, he had nothing to worry about should he be attacked by a junkie directly.

It had been a few days since he'd talked to any of the guys. Not quite as long since talking to Gwen, but close. He texted Gwen, then Buck, using a burner phone he'd dispose of later that night. Gwen responded with a "Good Morning" and informed him that things had been quiet. Elizabeth hadn't heard from Judas lately and the club had been going about their usual business. "Judas is just as off the map as you are," she ended.

A funny thought occurred to John at that moment. What if his enemy was hiding out amongst the very junkies that John was hiding out with. A ridiculous notion of course, but John scanned the room and then the area outside the window nonetheless. Then he picked up his guitar and slung it over his back. Time to move.

Paranoia was a constant companion throughout his many years. Like an ever-present friend that fed obscure and preposterous urban myths into his brain. Leaving a fork in your food while it's in the fridge can give you salmonella. If you made a funny face and someone slapped your back, your face would stick that way forever. Always check your Halloween candy for razor blades. And of course, the man that's trying to kill you and rolled into town only a week ago, knows all about your junkie hideout system and is using it as well.

Absurd.

John stepped through a living room littered with old clothes and old food. Cockroaches scattered at his approach. Big Scott was passed out on a flat air mattress, snoring loudly with a needle hanging limp from his left arm. John left through a front door that no longer shut tightly, the last police raid leaving the doorframe shattered.

Garvey had stashed his motorcycle. He was trying to remain inconspicuous, and the bike was a dead giveaway. Long sleeves covered his tats and a hood over his head helped a little, but the guitar stood out like a sore thumb. Nothing he could do about that. He walked through the shabby neighborhood and stuck to the allies that ran between the houses. Into the dollar store on the corner, he purchased a few snacks and toaster waffles, which he'd let thaw and eat without toasting. It was urban survivalism. Live off the land, even if that land is littered with broken beer bottles, fast food bags and dirty syringes.

John checked his phone again. Still nothing from Buck. It was unlike him. He texted Huff, then Izzy as well. If he got no response, he'd try calling. He wondered if he should give the Fed a call. Maybe he could use them. Find Judas before Judas found him. A showdown was inevitable, but John would rather take his would-be killer by surprise if possible. He knew Judas wouldn't be hiding for long. He was waiting. Healing fully. Concocting a plan. Then he'd make a move.

A cool wind blew through the trees and several yellow leaves drifted down to the cracked and cratered pavement ahead of him. Fall was fast approaching. It was his favorite season. It wasn't something he shared openly, as a president of a biker gang shouldn't put such things out there, but... he enjoyed everything about fall. The leaves, the pumpkins, the cool weather, and of course Halloween. Gwen knew all of this about him and each year, she'd go all out. Decorating the house and baking pies. Carving pumpkins and picking out costumes for them to wear for Halloween parties. She even managed to make the guitar an accessory in many of them.

Of course, he wouldn't always go. His paranoia would kick in and plans would be canceled. Before Judas had shown, Gwen had them going as Johnny and June. Something he was looking forward to. Hopefully, this situation would come to a close before Halloween.

Still no replies from the guys and Garvey's old paranoia was kicking in again. He called Buck's number and got no answer. He called the others and there was no answer there either. Finally, he broke down and called the Fed. Still nothing.

"Fuck." Garvey said out loud. Something wasn't right. He could feel it. Now he was aware he'd felt it all morning, it had just continued to grow. What was his next move? If he were in Judas' shoes, where would he go next?

The answer was obvious. If something had happened to the club, if Judas had got to them somehow, he would look for someone that would know how to find his target. He would never harm Elizabeth to get information out of her. At least, Garvey didn't think he would. And he knew Seth was on the outs with his old man. Questioning him would be a waste of time and energy. That only left…

Gwen.

Garvey quickly dialed her number. The phone rang. Then rang some more. Finally, it was picked up by her voicemail. John Garvey began to run. Legs pumping. Arms moving back and forth like pistons. His bike was stashed in the garage of a friend three blocks away. He had to get to it. He had to get to Gwen.

# 49
## Gwen

Gwen Garvey had finished texting her husband and refilled her coffee mug. She added cinnamon-flavored creamer and stirred, then moved to return to her laptop and get back to work on her latest smut-filled novel. As she crossed out of the kitchen into the living room, she caught movement in her peripheral. Before her brain could register what she was seeing, she was struck in the face. Pain erupted through her head and neck. She was knocked sprawling to the floor, her favorite coffee mug shattered and the smell of cinnamon coffee permeated the air.

The man that stepped over her wore an expensive suit, his skin of a caramel color, his hair black and pushed back from his forehead in a wave. With a cold calmness that was nearly as unnerving as the fist to the face, Judas rubbed his knuckles and said, "Gwen, where's John?"

Gwen got to her knees and looked into the dark eyes that stared down at her. "Fuck you," she managed.

Judas took up the front of her blouse in both hands and pulled her to her feet. "Don't make this any worse than it already is. Tell me where he is."

Gwen spat a bloody wad of spit into Judas' face. Then she was pulled off her feet and thrown into the China cabinet. Agony raced through her body as the glass broke and the China and figurines inside crashed down around her.

Judas pulled a chair around from the dining room table and took a seat while Gwen bled on the floor. "I really wish you wouldn't make me do this, Gwen. I love your daughter *very* much. It's bad enough I'm forced to kill her father, I've gone and killed all of *his* friends. And *now*, I have to beat the whereabouts of John Garvey out of you. Her mother. With every move I make, I lose favor with her."

"Then why do it," Gwen mumbled.

There was a noticeable shift in Judas' countenance. He looked pained. Troubled. As if repressed memories came rushing back to him. "You've no idea the pain one must endure there. Perpetual suffering. For over two thousand years I experienced the torture. And when a deal was offered to me, an opportunity to return to the living and leave all that pain behind. I jumped at the chance."

"You deserve to suffer," Gwen said through gritted teeth. "There's a word my husband uses for people like you. Snitch. He says next to terrorists and rapists, they're the worst scum of the Earth. You deserve everything they can dish out."

A right cross hit her cheek and a flare of pain spread through the left side of her face and down her neck. Judas pulled her to her feet and put a hand around her throat. Gwen saw her opportunity and drove her knee forward and into her attacker's balls.

Judas released her and doubled over in pain. Gwen crumpled to the floor, working hard to take air in through her burning throat. She wanted to get up. Kick the fucker in the face and make a break for the front door. But her mind couldn't will her beaten body to cooperate. Judas recovered before she could. He pulled her across the floor by her hair to the kitchen.

Gwen screamed out. She prayed one of the neighbors would hear her and call the police. Judas pulled a large butcher's knife from the cradle on the counter. Frantically, Gwen searched for anything within reach that she could use as a weapon. What she found was an empty wine bottle in the trash. She thanked her own procrastination in not changing the trash bag right away and the bottle sat atop a full bin of garbage.

Before Judas could turn on her with the knife, she used all of her strength to bring the bottle across his right knee. His legs buckled and he dropped to the floor. Gwen swung the bottle again and it hit Judas' head with a dull thud.

Judas was on his back. Gwen got to her feet and raised the bottle over her head with both hands. She wanted to cave his head in now. She felt almost feral in her rage. This man had fooled her daughter and attacked her and her family. She would not go down without a fight.

Judas kicked her in the stomach before she could deliver the blow to his head. She was sent reeling backward, knocked to the floor once again with all of the wind kicked from her lungs. She could hear Judas clambering to his feet. The sound of his hand hitting the counter for support. The clank of the blade as it hit the countertop as well. She looked back to see him stumbling toward her. Then he straddled her waist. He pulled both of her hands up over her head and held them there. In his other hand, he held the knife in front of her face as if he were selling it in an infomercial.

"Where is your husband, Gwen?" Judas asked calmly. He looked unsteady. Even woozy.

Gwen smiled through her bloody, swollen lips. "Eat a dick, you backstabbing cunt."

Judas brought the knife down slowly. The point of it bit into the flesh above her right breast. Gwen screamed.

"Where is John Garvey?" Judas growled. He was finally losing his composure.

"Fuck you!" Gwen screamed.

Gwen listened for any sign of sirens getting closer outside. Nothing. Judas pushed the blade deeper and Gwen broke down and cried. She tried to remain strong. Tried to fight back. Now, he had the advantage. She couldn't move.

"Gwen," Judas said. Trying to regain his calm demeanor. "Tell me. I don't want to hurt you any more than I already have. Tell me where he is."

Unable to endure more pain at the hands of this killer, Gwen calmed herself and spoke. She told Judas exactly what he wanted to know.

# 50

## Garvey

The air felt almost frigid in Garvey's face as he rode. Soon, it would be time for the club to store the bikes until next spring. That fact was far from his mind though. Something was wrong. He could feel it.

Weaving between traffic, the motorcycle ran hot and felt like a blazing rocket between his legs. He took the exit ramp from 465 onto 10th Street and sped west until he came to the housing edition. The bike's V-Twin engine roared through the sleepy neighborhood, winding down the streets until he came to the house he'd purchased for his wife all those years ago.

Garvey killed the engine and dropped the bike on its kickstand. At the front door, he went inside with his guitar slung forward and ready for any attack. He stepped into the living room quietly and the first thing he saw was the smashed China cabinet. His heart was racing. For a moment, he only listened. Waiting for any sign that Judas may still be there. When no sound came, he took a chance and spoke quietly. "Gwen?"

"John," came a weak reply from behind the recliner.

John rushed round to the other side and found her. She was badly beaten and bleeding from a wound in her shoulder. "Oh fuck! Fuck! Fuck!"

"John, I told him," she said through the tears that came when she saw him. "I couldn't help it. I told him where you were staying."

Behind his panic, this surprised John. Mostly because he didn't think Gwen knew where he was staying. "It's alright, baby. It's okay. I'm going to get you to a hospital. You're going to be alright. Can you walk?"

"I think so."

John helped Gwen to her feet and then got her into the passenger seat of her car. The keys. He ran back inside and looked everywhere for them, finally finding them on the hook by the door that was attached to a sign that read "keys" in yellow letters. "The one fucking time," Garvey mumbled to himself.

With the keys in hand, Garvey tossed his guitar in the backseat and drove his wife to the nearest emergency room.

Methodist Hospital was Indianapolis' go-to for everything in the city. Along with a helipad, that often saw Indy Car drivers delivered via chopper, the hospital was equipped for virtually any medical emergency or condition.

John Garvey hadn't left his wife's bedside since they'd brought her in nearly an hour ago. She was sedated. Sleeping. Garvey was left to his own thoughts which revolved around plotting revenge on the man who had done this to her. Judas had gone too far. Coming after him was one thing, but to hurt Gwen. Garvey hadn't thought it a possibility given Judas' feelings for Elizabeth. The man was far more desperate than Garvey thought.

The door opened and a doctor came in followed by a police officer. Garvey stood.

"Mr. Garvey, your wife is going to be fine. She has a couple of cracked ribs, her left cheekbone is fractured, and a mild concussion to go along with the stab wound, it'll take time, but she will recuperate."

Garvey breathed a sigh of relief. "That's great to hear."

"Mr. Garvey, Officer West here would like to ask you some questions."

"Of course." As far as Garvey was aware, he'd managed to stay off the radar with authorities in all the time he'd been involved in illegal activities. Still, he couldn't help but feel slightly nervous.

"Sir, do you want to tell me what happened to your wife?" the officer started.

"There was an intruder," Garvey said. "I wasn't home at the time. I had gone in to work but was coming home for lunch."

"Is that so?" the officer replied with an expression of disgust. "Cause those look like freshly busted knuckles there on your right hand."

"Are you suggesting I did this to her?"

"We have to rule out the most likely possible suspect."

"The scabs on my knuckles are not from beating my wife, they're from punching my son."

The officer's eyebrows went up in surprise.

"He's not a kid," Garvey said. "He's a grown man and a pain in the ass. He had it coming."

"Classy," the officer said sarcastically.

Garvey was angry and in Officer West's face before he could

control himself. "You want to check that fucking attitude after the week I've had."

"I ain't no boy and I ain't your wife," West returned. "Tangle with me and you'll end up with that goddamn guitar busted over your head."

Garvey nearly threw the first punch but was stopped by a familiar voice.

"Officer, I'm Agent Kern with the FBI and this man is under our protection."

Garvey turned to Kern. She was dressed for FBI success in her charcoal grey pantsuit, but it appeared as if she'd been in a scuffle recently herself. There was a bruise under her right eye and a cut across her forehead.

West studied her credentials a moment, then turned and walked away without another word.

"What are you doing here?" Kern asked. As always, Dillard stood behind her, silently observing. The guy gave Garvey the creeps.

"Judas attacked Gwen. I found her all beaten to hell, brought her here. I thought that's what brought you two here."

"No, I was just discharged, and I recognized your unique bitterness in one of the raised voices I heard from down the hall."

"What happened to you?"

"We were at the hotel last night. Arrived just as the bomb went off."

Garvey was confused. "Bomb?"

Kern and Dillard shared a strange look. Then Kern said. "You haven't heard?"

"Heard what?"

"It was a trap, John. Judas lured all of us to a hotel room. There was a bomb inside."

"All of you?"

Kern paused before she continued. "Buck got a call from an informant that led him to the hotel room. He called us and we tried to stop him, but he and the other members of your club got there before we did. There was a bomb in the room. Judas detonated it as Buck and the others tried to escape. John, they're all dead. Judas wiped out your club."

John Garvey felt a sunken, empty weight in his chest. He stumbled backward and fell hard on his ass. Kern dropped beside him. "John,

I'm so sorry."

"Gwen. He beat her this morning to get information on where I was."

"Jesus. He *has* to be stopped."

"Yeah, and I'm the only one that can do it." It was true. Garvey knew it from the start, yet he chose to run and hide, assuming Judas would eventually hunt him down and they'd have their standoff. He never dreamed things would go like this. Judas, as it turned out, was a ruthless, aggressive killer. Somewhere along the line, Garvey had lost that edge, at least when it came to the supernatural. A drug dealer tries to touch his guitar and he drops him in a heartbeat. An assassin from Hell comes calling and he runs and hides. Now his friends and family had been made to pay for it. In his attempt to avoid his greatest fear all these years, he rushed headlong into it.

Agent Kern leaned closer. "John, Mr. Dillard here possesses incredible powers. He can help you stop Judas."

"No," Dillard said. John and Kern both looked at him in confusion. "He's got to do this. Judas came for John Garvey. It's going to be a fucking Wild West showdown. We've already seen what happens when others get involved. Marion, this isn't our fight."

"He's right," Garvey said. The sadness and guilt were leaving his body. What replaced it was a seething rage with a thirst for payback. "This will only end with one of us dead. And I will make that fucker pay for what he's done."

Before Agent Kern could respond, the trio was interrupted by the arrival of Elizabeth and Seth. Garvey got to his feet. Elizabeth wrapped her arms around her father's neck with tears streaming down her cheeks. "Daddy, how is she?"

"She's going to be fine, Lizzy. She's pretty bruised and has a few broken bones, but she'll be alright." Garvey pulled away from his daughter and looked to his son. Seth only looked away, awkward after the tension between the two of them.

"I heard about the guys too," Elizabeth went on. "How can he do these things to the people I love?"

"Lizzy, Judas is a product of his environment. I'm not trying to make excuses for him, but the guy's spent 2000 years in the pits of Hell. Whatever was left of him that was human was brought out by you. He has a mission to complete, and nothing is going to stop him but death."

"And you're the one that has to kill him."

"Yes."

She seemed to ponder this a moment, then nodded her understanding and the tears came harder, but she said nothing more. "Seth, take your sister to the waiting room. There's free coffee in there. I'll be in after I finish with Agent Kern."

The boy put a comforting arm around his sister and led her away. Garvey watched them go thinking about how close they'd always been. Throughout their lives, Seth was the wild one and Lizzy was the only one that he'd really listen to. John Garvey knew he'd never have his son's trust in the way Elizabeth did. It saddened him, but it was the way of things and he couldn't change it.

Garvey turned back to Kern and Dillard. "Alright, I'll text you the address where I'm staying. If you want to see this through to the end, be there tonight. I have no doubt Judas will show up. He's ready to be finished with all this. That's why he made these moves."

"And you'll be there to meet him?" Kern asked.

"Yeah. This has got to end tonight."

"Alright. We'll be there. And we won't interfere."

Garvey nodded and walked away. In the waiting room, he sat with his daughter and again noticed how his son went out of his way to avoid him. Seth left the room without a word.

"Daddy, I'm so sorry," Elizabeth sobbed. "I brought him here. I brought all this on us."

"No, Lizzy. Don't do that. You met someone special and you wanted him to meet your parents. That's the way normal people behave. It's relationships. It's fucking life. You just happen to have a fallen angel for a father. It's easy to forget."

"It really is," she agreed. Her crying had stopped. "I guess I kind of dropped into this routine. Work, home, sleep, school, repeat. I just forgot where I came from."

"You're guilty of nothing but wanting a normal life. Just like the rest of us." John spoke these words with more conviction than he felt. A voice at the back of his mind insisted his daughter *was* at fault for all of this mess.

The two of them were quiet for a while. Then Elizabeth spoke again. "There's something that's been bothering me about the bomb."

"What's that?"

"Judas seemed to get a hold of it in a hurry. I thought around these parts, your club was the only one that dealt in that kind of stuff. I can't see Buck or one of the others selling to Judas. Knowing who he is and what he's after."

"Well, only Buck knew the whole story behind Judas' attack. Still, the other guys wouldn't have made a sale without running it by me or Buck first. Unless..." Unless. John Garvey turned and looked at his son as he came into the waiting room. Seth again averted his eyes. John suddenly knew the truth. He stood and walked casually over to where Seth had taken a seat. There, he stood in front of the man that he once held in his arms as a baby. The man that he'd had light saber duels with as a child. The man he'd thrown a football with as a teenager. The man that he knew for certain had sold the bomb to Judas.

"What is it, Seth?" Garvey said. His tone was taunting. "Feeling guilty about something?"

Seth looked uneasy in his chair. "What? No, Dad. I have nothing to feel guilty about."

"Oh? You sure about that?"

"Yeah."

"Nothing you want to tell me."

"Dad, what the fuck? Where is this coming from?"

Garvey shot forward and pulled Seth to his feet by the collar of his shirt. Then forced him into the wall across from the chair so hard the complimentary pot of coffee tumbled from the adjacent table and onto the floor. "Was this a power move, Seth? Payback for the bar the other morning? You snake some goods from one of our suppliers then turn around and sell it to one of our enemies. All of a sudden, everyone in my club is dead and you have no competition for this little fucking get-along-gang you're trying to get off the ground."

Seth said nothing but struggled to get away from his father's grip. Elizabeth was beside them now, begging them to stop. In his rage, John paid her no attention. Instead, he punched Seth in the mouth and dropped him. "Is this what you wanted? The men that have been there for you for your entire life are dead. Your mother is beaten to a pulp and hospitalized. Everything going as planned?"

"No," Seth shouted back. "It was supposed to be you!"

John was struck by the brutal honesty of the statement. He stopped and stared at his son in shock.

"He told me the bomb was for you," Seth continued. His lip was busted and bleeding. "I jumped at the chance to blow you to hell. It wasn't supposed to be this way."

John slowly shook his head. "Why do you hate me so much? Because I tried to steer you away from this shit? Tried to keep you out of trouble?"

"You tried to control me. I wanted that club. You promised me the club, then you pulled it out from beneath me. I'm an adult, but you still think you can make my decisions for me because you're my father."

Garvey stepped closer to him and spoke in a low threatening tone. "Now you don't have to worry about all that. The club is dead. And you are no longer my son. The next time we cross paths, it will be as enemies."

Seth sat stationary. His breathing was heavy. His eyes were gleaming with tears. John turned his back on his son. He silently prayed Seth wouldn't speak. One snide remark or off-color insult would be all it took for John to lose what little patience he had left. He was afraid he'd been driven to kill his own son. Though he'd technically just threatened to do just that, there had been too much violence in the past twelve hours already. And there was more coming. This was John Garvey's way of giving Seth a head start. And he only received that courtesy because he was John's son.

Seth said nothing. He walked from the waiting room and was gone.

"Daddy, he made a mistake," Elizabeth pleaded. "You can't punish him like that."

"His whole life has been mistakes," John snapped. "One fucking mistake after another. Now he's responsible for getting my friends killed. My brothers!"

"He didn't mean it. I know he didn't. Eventually, you'll have to forgive."

Garvey turned to her. "No, I won't. That's not me. I hold fucking grudges. You're the forgiving one, Lizzy. Let me ask you this, if Judas succeeds, then what? He killed the men that have been family to you all your life. He beat the living shit out of your mother. What happens when he kills your father and, in the process, plunges this fucking planet into eternal Hell on Earth? Will you forgive him?"

"Stop it. You don't need to speak to me like that."

"No, I want to know how much is enough. How far does this cock sucker have to go before it's *too* fucking far?"

Tears toppled down Elizabeth's cheeks.

Garvey only then realized there was a nurse standing in the doorway. He glared at her. His eyes conveyed how he felt about her intrusion on the tense moment between father and daughter.

"I'm s-sorry," the nurse stuttered. "I just wanted to let you know your wife can have visitors now. If the two of you would like to come back."

The nurse left and Elizabeth started toward the door, turning when John Garvey didn't move.

"Aren't you going to see her?" Elizabeth asked.

Garvey swallowed the lump that had suddenly formed in his throat. "I've been with her all morning. I can't go back in."

"Dad."

"I can't face her again until I kill the man that did this to her."

Elizabeth reluctantly nodded her understanding but couldn't look him in the eye.

"Lizzy."

"Yeah?"

"Help your mother. The way you helped your boyfriend." Elizabeth nodded. "You know I will."

Garvey adjusted the guitar on his back and left the hospital.

## 51

## Judas

Time moved at a slow crawl.

Judas now knew where his target was staying, and it was time all this came to an end.

After a cold shower, Judas stood naked at the edge of the bed in his latest hotel room. On the mattress, he'd placed his guns. The revolver, which housed three gold bullets forged in the fires of Hell, and the 9mm semi-auto that held a clip full of lead that was ready to bring a swift end to any humans that got involved.

Though the agent and her magic-user had survived the bombing, Judas was sure she'd been hurt enough to keep her out of the fight. Dillard was a different story though. He was barely scathed in the explosion and was dangerous should he show up. Of course, Judas was thinking too much. Even if the two of them were still on the case, they had no idea where John Garvey was hiding.

Judas knew.

Gwen Garvey broke far quicker than he thought she would. Judas was sure he'd have been inflicting pain on her for hours before she gave up the information he wanted. Part of him thought she'd never give it up. Another part felt she didn't even know herself. But she caved early. Hurting Gwen Garvey the way he did was going to be another challenge he and Elizabeth would have to overcome if they were going to be together.

Surely Elizabeth would understand. She knew full well the situation he was in now. She knew what had to be done in order for him to escape an eternity in Hell. And he had no doubt that she knew something like this was always going to happen. All throughout her childhood and into her twenties, her father had always made it clear that he was a fallen angel. He always told his family that other beings of a supernatural existence could threaten their way of life. John Garvey had prepared his family for this eventuality. Now that it was here, none seemed prepared. Ironic.

John Garvey's daughter had fallen in love with the man that was sent to kill him. His wife gave up his whereabouts. And his son, the most traitorous of the three, had sold the explosives that had wiped out the men Garvey had called his brothers. Now, in the calm before the proverbial storm, Judas sat back and looked at all the damage he'd done to this family and he was filled with a familiar sense of self-loathing.

It was what he felt at his betrayal of Christ.

It was what he felt as he slipped a noose around his neck.

Turning back was not an option. It never was. From the start, Judas slaughtered his targets without a second thought. Always relentless. Always keeping the ultimate goal in sight. Despite the guilt that was setting in, Judas would see this through. Of all the awful things he'd done throughout his life, this would not be the worst. In that, he took at least some measure of solace.

Judas dressed in his suit, the very one he'd worn upon returning to Earth. The suit he'd killed all of the previous fallen angels in. He carefully knotted the tie and pulled it snugly against his throat. Then he picked up the 9mm and slid it into the holster on his belt. Finally, he picked up the revolver and opened the chamber to view the gold bullets loaded within.

"Moment of truth, right?" Came a voice from the dark bathroom doorway. Judas was not surprised at Lou's appearance this time.

"It occurs to me that you've shown up far more with this target than the others," Judas pointed out.

"There are several reasons for that."

"Enlighten me."

"Well, this is the final target for one. Moral support is crucial, never more so as when a task of such importance is so near to being done. Also, Garvey is the toughest mark you've faced. Encouragement is needed when facing such a powerful opponent. Then, you went and fell in love with his daughter. I was bound to be the voice of reason in your ear. The rational one that continuously reminds you of what's at stake should you fail. Finally, Judas, I need you to see how important your journey is. An evil being is set to take over Hell. By completing this mission, you restore me to power and set things right."

"Lou, you are the Devil. A being of malevolent evil. Does it really matter which evil being controls Hell?"

Lou looked offended. "That's a common misconception about me, Judas. And it's one that hurts. God demands sinners be punished, and I am the one who makes sure that punishment is dealt. In a way,

I'm doing God's work."

"And if what Garvey told me is true and The End of Days comes when he's dead and gone?"

"There's no guarantee that will happen." Lou placed a comforting hand on Judas' shoulder. "But if it does, all that means is that *you* are doing God's work as well."

Judas tried to decipher the hidden meaning behind all Lou's words. The same saying occurred to him again, the very one John Garvey had used during their palaver in the diner; the devil's in the details. But this time, Judas could find none. Maybe this *was* The End of Days. Maybe Judas' actions were always meant to set it off. How would he be remembered then? Not as the betrayer of Jesus but the bringer of Hell on Earth to sinners? Deliverer of the pure to the light of Heaven?

"And where would I end up?" Judas asked. "You promised me freedom and a mortal life. Where does that leave me if The End comes?"

"It would mean salvation, Judas. It would mean that when Gabriel blows his horn, you will be reborn a hero of God. I imagine you'd be given anything you'd want as a reward."

"Anything?"

"Anything at all."

Judas could see a life in a cabin nestled in the woods. A simple life undisturbed by the endless drama that raged between the forces of Heaven and Hell. A place where he could live out his mortal life with Elizabeth by his side.

"Did you forget?" said Judas. "I killed Gabrial."

Lou waved this off. "Then someone else will blow the damn horn. Judas, It's time to go."

"Yes. John Garvey is about to meet his fate."

# 52
## Garvey

The days were growing shorter. The sun was low in the sky by the time six came around. John Garvey was back at the shack that passed as a home for some. A makeshift crack den for others. He stood at the window, stroking his beard, lost in thought. The guitar strapped to his back gave him some sense of comfort.

It wouldn't be long.

He pulled himself away from his view of the street and went to the squat, old refrigerator in the kitchen. From inside he pulled a bottle of beer, twisted the cap off, and took a long pull from it, drinking eagerly like a babe from a tit. He needed to relax, but there was so much on the line. If he failed. If he died...

He pushed the thoughts aside and returned to his place by the window. The street was still empty. The light in the sky fading. Why had it taken so long for something like this to happen? In all the years he'd been stuck on Earth, why now? All his years of planning and preparing for this eventuality and it comes when he finally lets his guard down. Now, all those he loved have paid the price for his mistakes. Gwen is beaten. Elizabeth is broken. Buck and the rest of his brothers were dead. And then there was Seth. In his attempt at living a normal life, John had pushed his son away and, in the end, his son had turned on him.

John Garvey had nothing left. Nothing but a thirst for revenge that boiled in the pit of his belly.

The beer was gone and he walked back to the fridge for another. There wasn't enough in the house to get him drunk, but cold beer was hard to beat regardless. It too soothed him, much like the weight of the guitar on his back. He moved back to the window and stared out to see a man standing in the middle of the street. Judas had come. The phone in Garvey's pocket rang. He pulled it and looked at the number. Then his nemesis in the street, who was holding a phone to his ear. Garvey answered. "Judas."

"I'm outside, John," Judas said. The man Elizabeth had introduced him to was gone. This version of Judas was emotionless. A man that knew what had to be done whether he wanted to do it or not.

"I see you."

"No more hiding, John. Come and face me."

"Oh, I'm not hiding," said John, his voice the cold edge of a knife. "I'll be right down."

He hung up and slid the phone back into his pocket. Then he pulled the gun from his belt and placed it on the window sill. Across the room and out the door, he took the stairs down the side of the building to the street. John Garvey walked into battle with nothing but the guitar strapped to his back.

Outside, the staircase was a rickety set of steps that descended the side of the house. Garvey took them slowly, his eyes on Judas as he went. Judas, for his part, only stood in the middle of the street. He was dressed in his finely tailored suit, the revolver with gold bullets in the chamber hung limp in his right hand. It was a showdown. Old West style. With weapons of supernatural origin.

A black SUV pulled to a stop off to Garvey's right. Agent Kern and Adrian Dillard emerged from inside, and Garvey was surprised to see his own daughter get out of the back seat. "Elizabeth, stay back."

"Dad." It was all she could say. She knew this was the only way it could be finished.

Kern and Dillard also stopped in front of the vehicle. They knew how this had to go down as well. Finally. The Old West showdown now had its spectators, watching with tension in their expressions, helpless to do anything to stop the bloodbath that was about to begin.

Garvey walked a few more paces until he was in the middle of the street, facing Judas. He slung the guitar forward and prepared to strum an attack. Judas visibly tightened his grip on the revolver. The two stared each other down. Garvey half expected a tumbleweed to blow through between them.

The seconds stretched out, neither fighter prepared to make the first move. Garvey thought Judas would make it eventually. In his desire to be done with Hell and his punishment for his sins. Sins known the world over by followers of Christ. Judas was a man whose name had been associated with betrayal and cowardice. Now, here he was. His only chance at redemption. Perhaps even salvation. But at an awful cost.

Garvey then knew, with sudden certainty, that Judas was allowing him the opportunity to make the first move. He *knew* Judas wasn't evil. He *knew* this killer of fallen angels was no more than a puppet. Judas knew this too, but he had come to accept it in exchange for the new life promised him. But now, for the sake of humanity, Judas was giving Garvey the first shot. A chance to avoid an early onset of The End of Days.

Garvey took it.

His fingers danced across the strings. The attack rippled through the air and hit Judas in the left shoulder. His suit ripped. His flesh beneath was shredded. But the attack was off target. At this distance, the aim of Garvey's guitar was inaccurate and Garvey himself was rusty in battle.

Judas raised the gun and squeezed off a shot. The gold slug slammed into the crescent moon inlaid on the neck of Garvey's guitar. Miraculously, the neck remained intact and the strings didn't break, though with a strum of the strings it was clear the guitar was now out of tune.

Garvey attacked again. Relentlessly fingering the strings like the player in a heavy metal band hitting his marks on a guitar solo. The invisible blades created by the music tore into Judas. His face was slashed, his abdomen pummeled. Soon, the expensive three-piece suit was a tattered reminder of what it once was and the blood rushing from the cuts on Judas' body made it no more than a tailor-made tourniquet.

Yet still, Judas was able to raise the revolver and fire another shot. The pain that blossomed in Garvey's head was something he'd not experienced in ages. The gold bullet hit his eye at an angle, obliterating the orb and ricocheting off the bone that surrounded his eye socket. John Garvey stumbled and fell to one knee. Judas had him now. Garvey was struggling to recover. His remaining eye was shut tight against the stinging pain in his head and he couldn't pry it open. Garvey waited for the finishing blow to come, but it didn't. He calmed himself, rubbed his good eye, and finally forced it open. Judas was a few paces closer now. Walking toward Garvey slowly. He wanted to be sure. He wanted the barrel of the gun against John Garvey's head. Garvey struggled with his guitar. He needed to get off another attack.

Then the unexpected happened. Judas dropped to his knees with an expression of utter shock on his face. Garvey could only look at him in confusion. Then he realized, Judas was no longer paying any attention to him. Judas was looking past him. The shock on his bloody face turned to horror. Agony.

John Garvey turned to follow Judas' line of sight and finally saw what had stopped their duel. Elizabeth stood wavering on the sidewalk. Blood was spreading from her stomach, soaking into her gray sweater and jeans. Garvey knew what had happened. The bullet that took his eye and ricocheted off his skull had then buried itself in her abdomen. Elizabeth fell.

Garvey got to his feet and rushed to his daughter's side. Panic ablaze in his mind. "No. No no no!" Garvey took her into his arms. Her head lulled. Her eyes rolled back in their sockets. She was trying to speak. Her mouth was moving, but nothing came out.

"Elizabeth, please. Hang on," Garvey pleaded.

Things were happening around him. Judas was on the other side of Elizabeth now. Tears rushing down his ruined face, his hand running repeatedly through her hair. Agent Kern was on her phone calling for an ambulance. Adrian Dillard stood over the dying girl, a glow emanating from his hands. He was attempting to use the very same healing ability that Elizabeth possessed.

Garvey was only vaguely aware of all this. His focus instead was on his daughter. Judas' tears were worthless. Agent Kern's call was pointless. Dillard's efforts were too late. Elizabeth Garvey was dead. John's daughter was gone.

Rain began to smack the street around them. The two men that faced off against each other now wept in that rain over the dead girl they'd both loved so dearly. The FBI agent and her associate were helpless to do anything but watch the sad scene.

Garvey's tears slowed and he reached across Elizabeth's body to take Judas' right hand. The gun was still gripped there. Garvey lifted the killer's hand and place his forehead against the barrel of the killer's gun. "Pull the trigger, Judas."

"What?"

"You've killed my brothers. Beaten my wife. Turned my son against me. Now you've taken the life of my daughter. The life I cherished above all others. I no longer care what happens to the people on this rock. I no longer want to live. Pull the trigger and start your new life."

Judas licked his lips and then swallowed the lump in his throat. With his thumb, he cocked the hammer back on the gun and prepared to fire his final bullet into the fallen angel's brain.

Then, he looked into John Garvey's eyes and saw a truth there that he'd not noticed until now. Garvey could see the revelation as it dawned on his would-be assassin. "It was *you*. All this time."

"End it," Garvey continued, ignoring Judas' words. "I beg you. End it now. Your salvation is at hand."

The former apostle shook his head. "Not without her."

Judas pulled the gun away from Garvey's forehead and placed the barrel against his temple. The revolver's thunderous report echoed through the quiet neighborhood. Judas' limp body tumbled to the street.

Garvey pressed his face against the forehead of his lifeless daughter and cried. He mourned the loss of his Elizabeth. He mourned his continued existence without her.

# 53
## Marion

The plane touched down in Atlanta three days later. Agent Marion Kern had returned alone with Adrian Dillard's statement in her briefcase. Her time away was unofficial of course, but she wanted Dillard's view for her own records. This case would be filed with the Daylight Slayer and others that were far too unbelievable to be filed with regular cases. Time-traveling madmen and real-life characters from the bible had no place in official FBI files.

Marion was exhausted. In the end, her involvement in the events of the past few days was very limited. What she had witnessed in the street that day was the dealings of beings that have more of an effect on the world than any Fed from Atlanta. Judas, in a move that would make Shakespeare proud, had decided he couldn't live without the woman he loved. In taking his own life, he saved the world from the apocalypse. It was difficult for her to wrap her head around that fact.

All she wanted now was to get home, shower, and lie in her own bed with her husband's big arms wrapped around her. She was an FBI agent. Highly trained in firearms and hand-to-hand combat. Yet she found warmth and a sense of safety in her man's arms. Perhaps it was Judas' lost love that made her long for hers. Whatever the reason, she had a desperate need to be with him.

As she rushed out of the airport and waved down a taxi, she thought of John Garvey. A fallen angel. A walking tragedy. A man who seemed wired into sadness. She could sense it when she first met him, and of course, now it was worse. She could only imagine the loss this man had known. He had lived lifetimes on Earth. How many women had he loved? How many children had he watched grow and die while his age never changed? How awful his existence must be.

But the one thing that bothered her is the one thing she would never know. Who was John Garvey? Judas was well known because of his exploits from the bible. What angelic name did John Garvey go by?

# 54
## Garvey

Garvey walked into the diner and let the smell of fried greasy foods fill his nostrils. It was welcome to say the least. It had been a while since he had a nice big burger from a dive like this. He needed it. The last week had been a rough one. Gwen was inconsolable. The loss of their daughter had sent her spiraling into depression and John wasn't so sure she would be able to come out of it. The one good thing that had come out of the tragedy was the mending of his relationship with Seth. After losing Elizabeth, he felt it was best he and his son get back on good terms. Not only for their sake, but for Gwen's as well.

Now, John was grabbing a bite while Seth sat with his mother. She was back home after her hospital stay, but a stay at another sort of hospital may be in her future. John knew it. So did she.

In the booth at the far end of the diner, someone rattled a newspaper loudly catching John's attention. He recognized the man in the booth and felt a fiery hatred swell in his mind. Nevertheless, John walked to the booth and stood in silence as the man read his paper.

"What are you waiting for?" the man said without looking up. "Take a seat."

John Garvey slid into the booth and waited. Finally, the man folded the paper and set it aside. "Sorry, have to keep up on current events in my line of work. So, Jesus, how have you been? You don't mind if I call you by your real name, do you?"

"Only if I get to call you by yours, Lucifer."

Lucifer looked around them to make sure no one had overheard. "Just keep it down. If that gets out, I'll have every fucker in here wanting to sell their soul for something."

"Isn't that your aforementioned line of work?" asked Garvey.

"Not so much anymore. Things are...changing."

"Is that what all this was about? You sending Judas after all of the fallen? After me? Trying to kick-start Armageddon?"

Lucifer sat back in his seat and let out a long, defeated breath. "Yes. Honestly."

"What has happened that would force you to do something so

reckless?"

Lucifer studied him a moment, then in true politician form, avoided the question. "Did anyone know the truth about you? Or were you just John the fallen angel to everyone? Did your family even know?"

"No. No one was made aware of my true identity."

"What about Judas? Do you think he figured it out?"

"In the end, yes. He looked into my eyes and recognized the man he once called friend. The man he'd betrayed."

"That doesn't sound very forgiving. You were always about that shit."

"Times change."

"You *certainly* have."

"You're avoiding the question. What brought all this on?"

Lucifer let out another heavy sigh. "I've lost the throne, Jesus. I'm no longer in control of Hell. That's why the deals I can make are limited these days. The one I made with Judas took a hell of a lot of string-pulling on my part. Then he went and fucked it up."

"He killed my daughter. Give me one reason I shouldn't shred you to pieces right here?"

Lucifer chuckled. "Because this is all Uriel's fault. I'm talking about one fateful night in 1883 when a certain ghost hunter came to one of your angels for help. And he agreed to help him if he busted down a certain demon's door and got his halo back for him. Do you remember that?"

How could Garvey not remember that night? It was that very night and Uriel's decisions that led to all of the fallen angels having their halos stripped from them and replaced with instruments. It also led to them being dropped in confined areas. Unable to leave without serious consequences on the human race. The people they were doomed to feel compassion for. And when Garvey, (also known as Jesus Christ, the son of God) dared to defend the angels and oppose the punishment, he was forced to join them. "Yeah, I remember."

"Well, the angel got his halo back that night, but Ghost Hunter Z cut a deal with Seether for it. He came through on his part of the deal when he killed Asmodeus and allowed Seether to begin his rise to power. Now he's pushed me out."

"Fuck. What does all this have to do with you taking all the fallen angels out?"

"If I brought Hell to Earth, I would have had a chance to wrestle control back. Jesus, if Seether's plans come to fruition, you'll be praying for The End of Days."

Garvey had no trouble believing Lou's words. Seether was, in actuality, the original Antichrist. A creature born from the death of the evil one in his human form. When the second of the three Antichrists died, Seether absorbed the soul before it could become another being in the afterlife, making him even more powerful.

"There's got to be another way to get rid of him," Garvey said. "One that doesn't require Hell on Earth."

"You could join me. Together, we may be able to defeat him."

Garvey laughed. "If I'm going to do this, I'm doing it *my* way. And, if at all possible, I'm going to get rid of *you* as well."

"Oh, come on, J.C. Don't let the loss of a few of these meat sacks hamper your decisions. We are above them."

Garvey pulled his guitar up and gave it a quick strum. A large cut appeared up Lou's neck, splitting open his head. He gripped the table to help withstand the pain. "There are none below *you*, Lou. I'm holding you responsible for my daughter's death. There's no more running. No more defending myself. From now on, I'm on the offensive. I'm going after Seether to fix Uriel's mistake. To seek my own salvation. Anyone who stands in my way will be slaughtered without a second thought. Spread the word." Garvey stood to leave.

"You'd need a vast army to take this on," Lou said.

"No, just the right team of people." With that, Garvey left.

***

John Garvey clicked the send button on the email and waited for a reply from Adrian Dillard. The man would be integral to his plan and if anyone could track down the type of people he was looking for, it would be Dillard.

The house was quiet. Gwen was finally sleeping, and Seth was back in his old room, sprawled on his old bed with his feet dangling off the end. Garvey walked through the kitchen and into the garage. Inside, he went to work on the motorcycle that was there. It was nothing more than a skeletal frame at the moment, but Garvey could see the potential. It was a gift he supposed.

He picked up the socket wrench he'd left on the floor when last he worked on it and began to loosen a motor mount that had become a useless hunk of rust. As he worked, he thought about what he had to do. Life was going to be different. His retirement with Gwen would have to be put off. To rise to this challenge, he would have to leave the state at some point and lives would be put at risk, but in the end, far more would be saved. If he should succeed.

Garvey noticed the dim corner of the garage where he worked was suddenly growing brighter. A sound came with the light that was exceedingly pleasant, like snow falling on frozen ground. Brighter and brighter the light came, and a familiar shadow appeared on the wall in front of him. And a familiar voice spoke in his ear. "Daddy?"

Garvey stood and turned to face the figure emerging from the light. His chest grew warm. His eyes filled with tears. His smile was bigger than it had been in ages. When he spoke, emotion flooded into his voice. "Welcome home, Elizabeth."

The Beginning

# A WORD FROM THE AUTHOR

Salvation was inspired by the Citizen Cope song of the same name. The rest came about through pondering how best to tie the story together with previous novels in the newly minted Salvation Saga, as well as the tales to come. I couldn't have made it this far without the support of my family and friends. My number one fan Sandy (RIP), and all the good people at Poe Boy Publishing and Provoco. Finally, thank you, dear reader, for taking the trip into my little corner of the literary realm.

Garvey, Elizabeth, and Adrian Dillard will return in Absolution: Salvation book 2, and this time they will be joined by a few new friends.

D

# ALSO AVAILABLE FROM D.A. SCHNEIDER

Salvation Saga Books-

The Ghost Hunter Z Trilogy:
* Ghost Hunter Z
* The Nightmare Tree
* Staff of Set

The 9 Ghosts of Samen's Bane
The Goat
Crow on the Cradle (Kindle Vella exclusive)

The Franklin Stewart Series
* The Mourning Mansion
* The Legend of Lilith's Hollow

Other books:

The Wes O'Brien detective series
* Irish Black
* Freezer Burn
The Holly Reynolds Mysteries
* Death of a Scholar